Rami Yudovin
Wind in the Hands

I0538569

Illustration by Rami Yudovin

ISBN 978-965-555-731-2

Rami Yudovin, Israeli author of scientific and theological works on bible researches and ancient history, represents the novel parable about the good and evil, about a duty and a freedom of choice.

He put some question in his book: Can a person be under the shadow of God's grace, being outside the church? Does he recognizes the freedom of choice or should follow his calling? Should human reflect, ponder and doubt himself, friends, and even Providence? Is he able see a difference: whether he is a performer of divine Predestination or just is used by forces taking kind of Angels of Light.

For readers also might be interesting another point: How and where prophecies are born? How they affect people. Who has the right and privilege to unravel them? Whether has a person his choice, if he has been led by evil so that to create divine deeds?

Despite the visible storyline is quite simple, the novel is exciting fiction. In the book there are no names of places and heroes. They all have symbolic character. The Stranger, having come across the ancient prophetic text about upcoming arrival of the Enemy, experiences the feeling similar to the wind. He tries to understand the meaning of it. He hears a voice ordering him to follow into the City. Stranger realizes that should execute special mission and he needs people with unusual abilities for that. He finds the Soldier, a person with a special intuition to distinguish danger, and the Seer, a telepathist and a hypnotist. However the Seer considers that the Stranger poses a threat to the residents of the City and decides to stop him…

Wind in the Hands

All characters appearing in this work are fictitious. Any resemblance to real persons, living or dead, is purely coincidental.

Part One
Getting to Know Each Other

Chapter 1. The Stranger

THE STRANGER

The Stranger preferred solitude as his way of life and had lived so for several months. He liked to climb up the mountains where he was standing on the top observing through the mist the fuss of the city, which seemed small and weak from above. It is different in a metropolis where the man seems small. The Stranger lay down on his cape, raised his eyes up towards the eternal heaven and addressed the Invisible. He felt that the old world was going away, very special time was coming and significant change was pending.

The Stranger had believed in the Creator from the time he was young, unconsciously and never doubting His existence assuming that belief in God was a natural state. But he might be feeling more at ease with this than others as it was more than just belief. He had a sense of the Presence. You believe in something invisible and intangible, but when you can see and feel it, you are speaking about knowledge and not just belief.

He was searching the signs of the Creator by reading sacred books thoroughly, learning philosophy, history, and science. His search was ambiguous and disappointing. There is a streamlined system and its laws that harm people. The System, or fate as it is referred to by some people (although this word does not reflect the most complex aggregate of all factors), is so strong that the Stranger felt powerless and unable to resist it.

But it all changed one day…

Late in the evening he was still reading a manuscript of a doubtful origin. That ancient manuscript seemed to contain confused original and invented, pictures drawn by diseased imagination and true prophesies. The manuscript narrated about future events, promised catastrophes, wars, and arrival of a person named the Enemy.

Unexpectedly the Stranger felt something strange in his head and shoulders, something like a wind and breath showing to a different extent. At first he was surprised and even touched his head, but soon calmed down and got used to the feeling and a while later the breath gradually subsided.

As he failed to find an accurate word to describe the feeling, he called it the Wind. At that time he saw himself as a man possessing power and very special knowledge.

The Stranger could foretell future but still could not fully manage that talent. He had difficulties to tune to that channel accessible to some and that required a huge mental strain.

Being a beholder he could see the true essence of many things around him but considered himself a passer by and did not interfere with events, often saying: "Live and enjoy, do not harm creatures. Help as much as you can. Learn from experience and acquire new experience. Live by spiritual law and hope that in the other world you will see an open door to the abode you have built in this world."

He believed that knowledge and understanding of the essence of things meant freedom that prevented from errors and was required for inner development. Although sometimes he seemed that he could do more, like open secret doors or influence consciousness. The Stranger knew how dangerous it was to summon humankind to change. From ancient times onwards, prophets had been killed with the greatest violence. Although they never called to the overthrow of power, wars, or riots, and just pointed out to human vices and infidelity, they had always been resisted by authorities and false priests. However strange that might sound, the most successful attempts against the chosen ones were made by religious authorities who seemed to be kindred. Prophets paid with the same coin by summoning the people to distrust priests, pointing out to their expressed and secret sins. The Stranger thought that the so-called shepherds and other helmsmen did not know the way to the Light but felt desire for power, respect, and money.

But there were other shepherds who were indifferent to secular values, suffered for their beliefs and were ready to face death. It was not only their stubbornness and unwillingness to submit to authorities, but the belief that was blessed with the ancient tradition. The Stranger was apprehensive of them even more than of those avaricious shepherds as they were always willing to shed blood of both their friends and their enemies, and the price to achieve the goal was not important. He called these priests Hood servants.

A coverlet is a barrier on the way to the Heaven. An attempt to tear it off or at least make a hole in this veil often costs the chosen ones' life. The Stranger could see how the Hood adapts the most progressive ideas and distorts them. The diamond of knowledge is the gift for all people that is inside us. It does not shine but remains valuable and is waiting for the hands of an experienced jeweler to clean and grind the stone, turning it into a brilliant. A sun ray will appear, and the stone will explode into many sparks, and its light can never be taken for the shine of a minor piece of broken glass.

The Stranger knew that all who fight illusions do not toil in vain. He was ready to risk own life and even die consciously, following in the footsteps of his spiritual advisor, the Prince, who had lived several centuries before in the dark years.

However, he thought it unreasonable to act as he wished without a special sign. Mere desire is not enough. A man is chosen as a native privilege. The Heaven nominates and not by mere chance, but its criteria remain a secret to all. What if the Stranger is one of those? Will it be possible to live normal life with all of its anxieties and joys? You can survive, especially if you follow worldly rules: achieve your goal by any means and live within the restrictions of the criminal code. Still, there is an internal code apart from the criminal one. By consistently violating the internal code, we destroy ourselves. We acquire little and lose more. We win in a battle but lose in the war.

The Stranger was confident that means were no less important than the goal, and selection of means was sometimes the goal. He was confident just in one thing: if you were fleeing your destiny, you would not feel happy but just anxious because you failed to use and buried your talent. Of course, you can fill your life with work, love to a woman, get buried in your cares deep enough to have no time or power to climb the mountain and look at the stars.

He was more often asking, "Who covered the Earth with the Coverlet? Who is on the way towards spiritual development of humankind? Who is in organized opposition to the chosen ones?"

Once, when he climbed up the mountain, looked into the sky, smiled at slowly floating clouds, he suddenly and unexpectedly heard a distinct and firm Voice in his head saying, "Time has come! Get up and go to the City!"

He did not know what was to be done in that case. He had no action plan and thought that he needed associates. Having returned to his small rented flat, he ate some dried figs, and sat down on the floor cross-legged. He concentrated, trying not to think, and asked a question about the search direction. Listening to his feelings, he took a map from his bookcase, closed his eyes, and started to feel it with his hands. A minute later his finger stopped all by itself, and the Stranger opened his eyes.

"Is it so?" he was both surprised and anxious. "Let's check once again."

The result was the same, and his finger stopped at the same spot. He recollected a computer game, where a hero had overcome many barriers, left the tunnel, a collapse occurred directly behind his back, and he had to move forward to ominous monsters.

"It is high time," he thought, looking in the mirror. "And nothing has changed but the heart is worried. I have been waiting for this time to come, and now everything is as it has always been before!"

The point, where his finger happened to be by will of fate (or game of luck), was the place for disarmament of mobile rebel gangs. There were checkpoints, mobile patrol units, and military observers in the area.

He was quizzically watching the map when there was a memory flash, bringing out the last year's newspaper article, which described how an army pathfinder found a mobile-triggered powerful bomb in the road ditch. The explosive was in a hard case camouflaged as a stone slab. Its form and color made it identical to many stones scattered near a death weapon. Its finding prevented a powerful explosion, cynically triggered at a school bus, touring historical places.

The Stranger understood whom he needed and was getting ready to embark on his journey. Leaving his home, he glanced at shabby walls of the building, his window with a heavy curtain, indifferently shrugged his shoulders, and strolled to the bus stop.

Chapter 2. The Soldier

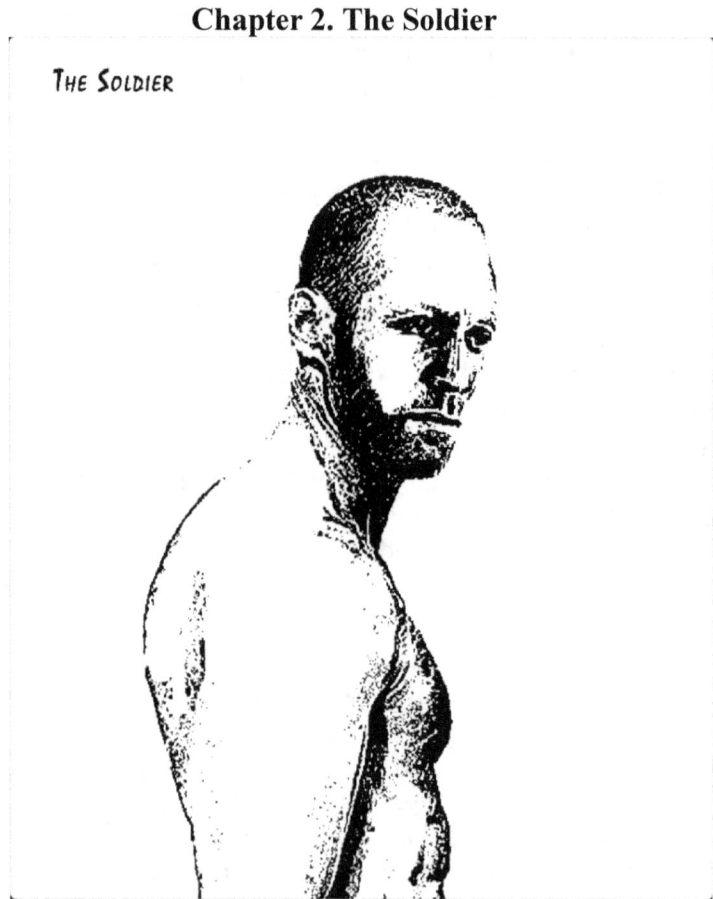

THE SOLDIER

Since early morning the Soldier had taken his position and was sure that he would see unwelcome 'guests' soon. He had been in the ambush for three hours when he suddenly felt that an object was nearing. He blinked, making his tense eyes comfortable, and closed his eyelids for several seconds. His finger smoothly touched the trigger. Less than ten minutes later, a traveler appeared from behind the hill. He did not have a gun or a bag but was wearing a tight sleeveless T-shirt. "Nothing on him," the Soldier thought. "But he is neither a farmer, nor a worker. He has a fighter gait: he is looking around and peering. No doubt, he is a warrior but I cannot shoot, he is not the main aim. I need to wait not to frighten off others. Still, they will show up soon, nearly close, and the first one here is a dummy, their scout, a straw. A cheap trick."

Much time elapsed but 'guests' did not appear. Strange, could there be mistaken? He doubted if his decision was correct: maybe he should have liquidated the terrorist. The Soldier lived by simple principles as any other warrior would: if I did not destroy my enemy, they would destroy me, my dear ones, children, women, and innocent people. He never said 'killed'. 'Liquidated', 'destroyed', sometimes 'wiped off'; these words seemed to confirm the need of physical extermination of enemies.

The value in a war is not only cunning or valor. It is also ruthlessness to your enemy. You differentiate between your people and others, friends and enemies. People who do not know each other join their efforts and are willing to sacrifice themselves to save their comrades whom in the peacetime they would hardly lend money to. The Soldier thought that the war revealed the best qualities in humans, meaning self-sacrifice, which conflicted with the strongest instinct of survival. Still, we should not forget the pressure of society, which sometimes pushes people to sacrifice their life to benefit humankind. Others spew their accumulated aggression and hatred. Sadistic inclinations and cruelty, hidden deep down, are easily vented in a battle. Some people break in extreme situations, and others grow stronger.

The Soldier could tell a real danger from the assumed one. His feelings never failed him, although he had contributed much effort and had bitter experience when he was trying to tell that difference. Despite the nature of his work, he believed in God in his own way. Before each business trip or after a battle, he visited the sanctuary, listened to religious singing, and always donated to church. That helped the Soldier to find an inner balance for at least a short time. Unlike his colleagues he did not get drunk, did not take drugs, trying to relieve stress. But still he felt that burden deep down in his soul which even grew heavier. And yesterday, while in church, he promised to quit his job, retire, and move somewhere to live in the quiet.

A mobile phone vibrated. The Soldier took it out from the coat sleeve fast and read an encoded message saying "Leave immediately. Cleaning pending." The area will be searched and cleaned. The specified area will be cordoned off and searched for all suspicious persons. "Thank you for warning", but it was not dark yet, and it was hard to move unnoticed. You could encounter rebels or, still worse, fire of the cleaners, shooting from all directions at all who look suspicious or just didn't like.

A cleaning operation implies the use of the so-called 'fifty' device which scans the area and responds to living objects. Camouflage is of no avail in this case. If cleaners see him holding a gun, they will never investigate and just start fire without warning. Nobody will risk and act slowly: an armed person is a danger. It is a reflex with an index finger, bending and unbending on the trigger.

Cleaners are contract soldiers who carry out the dirtiest work. Battle is their elements where they can slop their aggression and instead of being punished, receive gratitude. Usually they cover their face with a scarf or a mask not to be seen. There were many complaints against cleaners but legal proceedings were never started as it was hard to find witnesses to testify against their comrades or 'masks'. A legal action was taken only when the suffering party presented a video or in case of a favorable public opinion.

The Soldier was against cleaning operations as they resulted in the death of innocent people. Thus, cleaners who took a drill for a gun in the dark killed a young electrician, a father of three kids. After he had learnt about that, the Soldier challenged the reason of war, which entailed suffering of the civilian population. Can kind deeds be evil, although unintentionally or by mistake? Why are professional soldiers, who would never kill an electrician, unmistakably see fighters, and destroy them, mobilized for liquidation so rarely? The Soldier was the master of surgical strikes and was confident that his work did not require an excuse as he was wiping killers off the Earth. When he saw innocent victims of fighters, beautiful women and strong men torn to pieces by explosions, or slaughtered babies, he stopped to doubt and was ready to shoot all those who were connected with rebels: militants with guns and explosives or ideologists inciting killing. The Soldier considered himself a hunter for wolves that were ruthless to sheep…

Chapter 3. Meeting

The Soldier hid his shoulder arm. It was much safer to go unarmed in that case not to raise any suspicion. He took out earlier prepared clothes from his bag, changed and then looked like a pilgrim on a tour around famous sights. Warriors lower their arms when they see such weirdoes, joke and insult them but never shoot.

Slowly and carefully, and slightly clumsily the Soldier was going down the steep mountain. Having walked about three hundred steps along the path towards the nearest settlement, he saw a man approaching him. He carefully looked around trying to understand where to run in case of shooting but did not feel danger. He inhaled and exhaled slowly and listened to his feelings again: "Definitely no danger. Who dares walk here? People warned of a cleaning operation do not leave their settlement."

When they met, the travelers glanced at each other. The Soldier seemed to feel that the yearning, which was with him all the time, was evaporating without any church singing. He wanted to speak with the stranger who spoke first.

"Be in peace. I am glad I've found you. It was not easy."

He was wearing simple comfortable clothes, had a beard and long hair but did not look like a rebel and spoke without any perceptible accent typical to local residents.

"Who are you?" the Soldier asked the man who was penetrating him with his kind and slightly ironical eyes.

"I am your friend."

The Soldier felt the traveler's geniality.

Have you seen a couple of people with bags or sacks nearby?

"Yes, I have seen them and spoken with them and warned them of a deadly peril."

"Do you know them?" the Soldier grew suspicious.

"No more than you," a Stranger answered calmly.

"Then why have you helped them?" the Soldier ground his teeth. "They are killers, enemies. How do you know?" he checked himself. "Who are you?"

"They have not killed anyone, but you killed a lot."

"They are killers," the Soldier reiterated stubbornly, but suddenly under the changed glance of his companion, he felt limp and slightly dizzy.

"You don't know how killers are made. You can see only a small fragment of a large mosaic and not the big picture. You are digging in earth looking for worms for your hook, but not catching large fish with a net. You have a talent but you are wasting it."

"What sort of a talent do I have," the Soldier was staring at this latter-day preacher open-eyed.

"Your intuition, good grasp of the situation and all that without any background. But your capabilities are within the narrow world of first person shooters, and that's why you are in worm digging," the companion looked away.

"These shooters rescued many lives," the Soldier was appearing calm but his voice betrayed poorly concealed rage.

"While you rescued some people, you brought death to others. This is not the best solution."

"I have rescued my people by destroying the enemy who has been dreaming of killing us all," the Soldier believed he was saying the universal truth.

"There are no my or other races, peoples and tribes in the world of peace and justice."

"What country do you mean? I do not care about other customs. I haven't heard about this country in the news. Where is it?"

"There is no such country on the Earth, but its laws have reached us. If you want to get there, you will have to live here following its rules."

"I see. You mean life after death. Do you seriously believe that? Who cares for us there..."

"Yes, I do. Let me tell you a funny story:

Two twin would-be babies are talking inside a pregnant woman. One of them is a believer, while the other is a non-believer. The non-believer baby asks,

'Do you believe in life after birth?'

'Yes, I do. We are here to get ready to live after birth,' answers the believer baby.

'But it is impossible! There is no life after birth! Can you imagine that other life?'

'I don't know the details, but I believe that we will have more light and we will be able to walk and eat with our own mouths.'

'That's absolute crap! You cannot walk on your legs or eat with your mouth! That's so absurd! We have an umbilical cord, which feeds us. Listen to me, life after birth cannot exist because our life is our umbilical cord and we will die without it.'

'I am sure it is possible. Just everything will be slightly different.'

'But no one has returned! Our life just ends with birth. And generally life is enormous suffering in the dark.'

'Oh, no! I am not sure what this life is going to be but we will see our mother in any case and she will take of us.'

'You are speaking about mother? Do you believe in mother? And where is she then?'

'She is all around us; we are inside her and can move and live owing to her. We cannot exist without her.'

'That's nonsense! I have never seen the mother and it means that she just doesn't exist.'

'But you have the inner knowledge of the mother. You know this word, can imagine her, although vaguely. Just remember, when everything is quiet all around, you can hear her singing and feel how she is stroking our world. I believe that our real life will just start after birth'."

The Soldier grinned and shook his head.

"Not bad. But I am not a follower of the death religion. To reach your country, I will have to die first, that is what the die-hard rebels' philosophy is about. But what do you want from me? I will never believe you have come to preach about eternal life to a lost sheep."

"In the sheep's skin," corrected the companion, nodding at his short-sleeved T-shirt, and kept silent for some time staring in his eyes, "I need your help. I am not a follower of the death religion. We are going to either have this country here on the Earth, or have nothing."

The Soldier endured his stare but felt extremely weak in his legs.

"Are you a prophet?" he asked quietly.

"No, I am not a prophet. They call me 'the Stranger'. In order to understand me, you will have to get rid of any false perceptions," the Stranger explained as softly as he could. "Tell me, who is more dangerous: an assassin's paymaster or a killer?"

"The person who organizes assassination: an intermediary between the customer and the contractor. He appears to be innocent, sleeps calmly, and risks nothing," the Soldier grinned.

"You know best, but if one kills the assassin's paymaster you will have no job for killer and facilitator," the Stranger looked at him inquiringly.

"I quite agree," the Soldier sighed.

"So, you see, evil thoughts are more dangerous without any weapons as they direct the killer's hand. A kind person will not sneer, rape, or kill. If a lost person changes his views, starts to value life, shows tolerance to the men who are as blind as himself, we will have love and knowledge on the Earth that will destroy the evil. A war against evil will bring peace and well-being to the Earth," the Stranger smiled.

The Soldier became thoughtful. It seemed that the man was not saying anything special and his arguments were naïve and banal, but for some reason they penetrated his soul and infused him with hope to get out from absorbing nets of anguish. However giving it a little thought, he asked himself a question: "What if this man is just a hypnotist? What is his purpose? Why should he take risk? A provocation?"

"Why have you come here? Do you understand where you are now?"

"I know it is not a quiet place, but we will be able to escape," the Stranger replied.

"The guy is apparently out of himself," the Soldier had not had such a surprise for long.

"What do you think, partner? Does it make sense to hide until complete darkness and quietly crawl to our settlement, or do we have to go now? Pretend we are two cranks who have mistakenly made it to a closed area. If we are lucky and are not shot, we will play exalted nitwits," he proposed openly showing his sarcasm.

"It's no problem for me to pretend an exalted nitwit, so the second option is OK," the Stranger smiled again.

"You even don't have to play," the Soldier was looking at him attentively. "You are smiling all the time."

"I always smile when I'm happy," the Stranger answered.

They were walking in silence for some time. Suddenly the Soldier halted.

"What has happened?" asked his new companion.

"Do not speak our tongue," the Soldier whispered. "Locals can see us, but do not let them know who we are. It means they will spend time to think the situation over, then consult, inform the settlement, and meanwhile we will have time to leave. Pretend tourists."

They were lucky not to see the surprised faces of local people, otherwise they would laugh out, seeing the rounded eyes and open mouths of local peasants, because the Stranger spoke the language, and excellently, of sacred texts which was not spoken daily anymore. Priests read the ancient manuscript, written in this language, only at the local community meeting.

The Soldier imitated him and spoke gibberish ruthlessly distorting words. Suddenly he noticed out of the corner of his eye that a teenager separated from the group of villagers standing nearby and rushed to the settlement.

"Beware!" he told his companion roughly. "Some fifteen minutes and militants are here. Let's run as fast as we can. I have a shelter not far from here, if we can make there, we'll survive. Come on!"

The Stranger shrugged his shoulders and said discontented:

"We'll walk there."

The Soldier was running fast scolding himself for not quitting smoking on time: he was short of breath.

"What has happened to you? Faster!" he shouted turning around, gesturing wildly and mentally swearing: "I must run there and run back to fetch this loony. This Stranger, although crazy, is not alien and is real. I can see through people."

The Soldier was not turning round; he seemed to hear the sound of an approaching car with armed militants. Having reached the aim in ten minutes, he inhaled deeply, moved a heavy stone aside, and took out an automatic rifle wrapped in oily rags and four doubled magazines with rounds. He was nauseated and his head pulsed from fast running.

"Keep calm, keep calm, they are far away, you still have time", the Soldier took several deep breaths. Clicking the bolt, he inserted a magazine, loaded the rifle, moved the safety latch in the 'fire shot' position, lifted the rifle to the chest level, and moved towards his new companion fast.

The Stranger started to move faster, but seeing the weapon, halted. The Soldier saw an approaching car and waved him sharply to move aside. He hid behind a stone slab and sighted a moving aim.

The Stranger understood everything, looked in the sky and begged,

"Oh, God, I don't want to spill blood. I'm not here for that reason. What shall I do?"

He started to think feverishly, what is to be done. He was standing embedded, with fear slowly engulfing him.

"I don't believe. I don't believe it. Go way," he whispered.

"Run! Lie down! Fall down!" the Soldier was shouting from his shelter, but the Stranger was standing in the way, closing the line of sight.

"I can't shoot. I might wound him accidentally. The bullets are loaded, you hit the leg and it comes out of the belly. If militants jump out of their cars and scatter, I don't know how it is going to end. What if they have shells and grenade launchers? I don't have time to climb up. I have nothing to do but wait till they come and get out and start to talk. First talk and then kill. But he had better be out of the way. Why hasn't he run away? Why? He is evidently out of his mind."

Suddenly shooting started nearby with machine-gun bursts. Hearing the sound, the Soldier could define a gun grade and smiled thoughtfully, "Our people. Just on time. Cleaner fighters."

The car stopped about hundred meters from the Stranger and turned towards the settlement.

"Thank you," he whispered. "The path has been paved and blessed."

The Soldier exhaled, clicked the lever and engaged a safety latch.

"You haven't left me. I have not been mistaken," the Stranger said overtaking him.

"You even can't understand how lucky you are. Hurry up, cleaners are here. By the way, they have saved you. Why haven't you run?"

"I'm not prey to run away. The God has saved me; cleaner fighters do not know me. The God has saved you, too. Our time has not come yet."

"It will come, and much faster than you think if we do not hurry: cleaner fighters are nearby."

"Aren't they our people?" the Stranger grinned.

"Our people are at home. I'm armed and it's a signal for them to start shooting," the Soldier calmed down and even stopped being angry. "Crazy man, nothing to be done."

"And if other units are here, will cleaner fighters still start fire seeing armed people?"

"First, joint actions are coordinated, second, you can tell your allies by weapons and uniform, well, mainly by helmets," the Soldier explained.

"Helmets?" the Stranger asked again. "Is it possible to tell a helmet of a Salvation Army fighter from a rebel helmet?"

"It is possible, but hard to do, especially for someone like you," the Soldier laid a trap.

"Why?" and the Stranger got trapped.

"Because militants do not wear helmets," the Soldier threw up his hands in a theatrical gesture.

The Stranger smiled approvingly wagging his head.

"Then, let's hurry. Listen, I guess you can take your helmet out of the shelter, can't you? You looked cool in sandals, rugged jeans, Love Save the World T-shirt, and the Salvage Army helmet with a punishing sword," he added seriously.

The Soldier sighed and tried to smile. His face muscles seemed to be unable to allow a smile, although he had good sense of humor. Approaching his shelter, he turned around, removed the magazine from the rifle, unloaded it, picked a cartridge and placed it in a case, wrapped his weapon in a cloth, placed in an opening of the shelter, closed it with a stone, and then nodded to the Stranger and they moved on. In an hour, they approached the roadblock.

"We have come, they know me here. But they think that I'm helping local people, and they will not be excited to see us, but will not shoot either. That's not bad."

"I can see that you are liked by all, our people and others," said the Stranger with mocking respect.

"I don't need love of these nitwits. I once was in a situation at that roadblock. Two Soldiers drank and decided to have their pictures taken for their girlfriends, and with arms for better effect. They drank more and decided to have their picture taken in a battle. One of them made a severe face and started to shoot, but when you are making a picture from the side you cannot see fire properly. So the half-witted photographer stood in front of the line of fire and shouted, 'Shoot, friend, and say cheers.' Well, his friend did not think twice and shot."

The Stranger looked at the Soldier questioningly,

"Is the photographer alive?"

"He is, such fools, however surprising that might sound, are tough. It seems they quite like such idiots up there. Not only we have found them funny."

The five fighters were scattered at the roadblock. A sniper at the tower was looking through the scope sight at villagers, passing through the roadblock, and swearing at them bored giving orders over the intercom in the local tongue and making peasants look around bewildered. Fighters were roaring with laughter.

The Soldier and the Stranger approached the borderline. An officer waved his hand sharply calling them to be checked. They moved towards him, but at the safety line, they heard an order via the intercom,

"Stand still! T-shirts up!"

"Hey, you loon up there! You'll give yourself away!" the Soldier shouted and said to the Stranger, "Animals! They can see that we are not strangers and still humiliate us."

"Local villagers also feel bitter, but can't you see how gladly they raise their shirts," the Stranger noted.

"Some of them may be militants with weapons and explosives and they generally like to undress…"

"And will surely demonstrate their death belt, hoping no one will notice it."

"If you do not check, there will be many militants. It's a psychological game."

"Our world is a game, you always play to win, deceive, cheat, but not only players suffer."

"Can we go?" the Soldier shouted. "Or do we have to take off our trousers?"

"Good idea," the fighter came down from the tower. "Go, take off your trousers. We'll look and might see something, I have magnifying optics."

Guffaw could be heard all around.

"I will let you watch, you brat. You won't find it funny! You will have nothing to watch with," the Soldier snapped and moved towards the wit.

Three fighters immediately aimed at the Soldier, bolts clanked, and safety latches clicked.

"You cross the second line, you lie down and never get up," the officer said and added scornfully, "attack at a roadblock, so I have the right."

The Stranger caught the Soldier's hand that was ready to vehemently attack them all hand-to-hand.

"Stay calm. I will speak with them," he said softly. "Brethren, do not humiliate us. You don't know the reasons we are here. We have almost been killed by rebels, and do you want to kill us too? Search our papers if you don't believe your experience. We are peace makers. If I'm not a good peace maker, my friend is a real pacifist," he nodded at the Soldier.

"Such pacifists do more harm than terrorists," said one of the fighters spitting at them.

"I won't argue your point, but you are not politicians or judges. Do you really believe we have explosive in our pants? I won't protest, we have explosives in our pants, but its action excites ladies."

The fighters at the roadblock laughed approvingly. The officer waved his hand and they passed through the fence to the bus stop.

"I would never think you can joke like that. So strange. I cannot see through you. And I have seen many kinds of people," the Soldier looked at the Stranger and asked him sharply, "what do you want from me? Who are you?"

"We must understand something. I have heard something. We need associates, we find them and discuss everything," and the Stranger looked his companion directly in the eyes.

"Who do we need?" the Soldier asked suspiciously looking aside.

"The Seer."

"Himself?"

"Yes," his new companion shrugged his shoulders indifferently.

"The Seer will not let us in. Who are we and who is he? Rulers, ministers, generals, and wealthy people from all over the world are dreaming of talking with him. This person does not care for us or respect anyone."

"He will admit us," the Stranger was confident. "Let's exchange mobile phone numbers. Think and let me know if you are coming with me to him or not."

The Soldier fell thoughtful for some time,

"Ok, write down…"

Chapter 4. The Seer

The Seer had lately rarely spoken in public, although he thought it important to show his rare talent he was lucky (or unlucky, opinion differed) to have. In his childhood he knew that he could feel what people were thinking, could see something others could not see or determine (although that required special conditions) the past and the future, mentally influence the behavior of people and not only of those susceptible to hypnosis.

Travelling around the world, he met people with paranormal abilities, learnt from them, and perfected his skills to earn using his talent. He performed in shows, consulted businessmen, and helped politicians. He was rumored to make bets via his nominees but was not known to win.

He did not consider himself a healer but could suppress pain and alleviate disease symptoms. He helped with different nervous disorders, mobilized the organism to have an energized immune system find and repair failures.

Before solving a complex issue, the Seer was in absolute solitude, ate almost nothing, and concentrated on his task, like a vibrating string, all nerves, and ready to fight without the smallest doubt in his success.

He usually had mass hypnosis sessions making people embarrassed. He seemed to enjoy when he made respectful citizens, politicians, military men, or businessmen helpless and especially those who looked down at him helpless. Such people irritated him most of all.

Once during his anniversary performance the Seer asked a man sitting in the first prestigious seats and wearing an expensive suit to go up the stage. This man was eyeing externally non-representative Seer with scorn and grinned: the Seer was short, made fussy and

nervous gestures, was always frowning, lame and wore old-fashion spectacles. A man, sitting in the first row, was unlucky to say unceremoniously, "Now, let's see your tricks."

The Seer's eyes burning through flared with anger: most of all he could not stand when people took him for a manipulator, a trickster and did not believe in his abilities. He would never forgive that.

The manager standing near the stage perfectly knew what the Seer could do when he was enraged and literally took his head with his hands. That expensive-looking man was a district prosecutor who was known as a cruel, proud, and influential man. Without doubt, the Seer recognized him. Like a boa constrictor, he looked at the Prosecutor with an unblinking and paralyzing stare and crushed his will. At first, the hypnotist made up the image of a small dog. Fixing it in his head, he conveyed the dog image to the Prosecutor as if placing it image with a mouse click to the head and said firmly and clearly, "You are a dog."

The Prosecutor's eyes became meaningless and glazed. A respectful man went limp, became drawn, went down on his knees, stood on all fours and started to sniff something. His wife opened her mouth amazed and stared at the stage with horrified eyes. The Seer took a pen out of his pocket, threw it down, and ordered,

"Take it and bring it to me."

Even when he was young and was in the service or military courses, the Prosecutor did not fulfill commanders' orders so high-spiritedly as that one. On all fours, leaning on his knees and palms, he ran up to the pen lying on the floor, carefully fetched it with his teeth and brought to the Seer in the same manner.

"Good dog. Good dog," he took the pen out of the Prosecutor's mouth, wiped it fastidiously with his handkerchief and tenderly tousled a new dog at the back of his neck. The Prosecutor had never been happier in all his life as at that time. His eyes were shining and he even tried to lick the Seer's hand, but the Seer removed it just on time.

The Prosecutor's wife rushed to the stage.

"Stop this immediately!" she cried out. "I beg you! What are you doing?"

"Lady," the Seer looked at her wanly, "it is a lesson for your husband."

The performance was on live and the entire country was laughing at that respected man playing a dog. The prosecutor did not remember anything, but he saw the recording of his shame and could not live with that. It was especially hard after his court claim for harm to his honor and dignity was dismissed. He had
many friends and no one dared take legal action against the Seer. The prosecutor was a burnt card; he shrank into himself, retired. His kids were bullied at school and asked to bark. His wife was looked at scornfully or with sympathy which made the proud woman suffer. Soon the former prosecutor shot himself in his study.

The widow, having wept over her deceased husband, came to the Seer and he met her in cold blood. She jumped up to the host, bunching her fists, but did not dare strike her enemy,

"You have killed my husband! Broken the life of my family! He did not believe in your power! What of it? You have stomped him! And it is not only he who suffered, but our kids who are left without their good and caring father and breadwinner. Has the God bestowed power on you to take your bodily imperfections on successful and beautiful people? No! You do not act from the God! Priests are right in saying that you are a demon and spiteful sorcerer. What right have you had to destroy our world? Oh, if only I could destroy you!"

"The waiting list is too long, I'm afraid, you will have to wait long," the Seer answered indifferently. "Do you want to hear a reason or have you come to shed your pain?"

"A reason? Can there be a reason?" the widow was indignant.

"There is always a reason, but we sometimes cannot see it. But you haven't come to learn why; you have come to learn how you are going to live on. Death of your husband is a motive to approach me. Your spouse was a good father but he has never been faithful and do not raise your eyebrows, do not play with me. You must have heard about many broken lives of the people, whom your husband has sent to jail. And do not tell me that they are all criminals; some of them were absolutely innocent. Your husband made severe sentences disproportionate with crimes. Just hear the last one: a young man who was foolish enough to get into the house of a politician, stole some paper in the form of banknotes and several gold trinkets was sentenced to eight years of prison. Eight years!"

The Seer's eyes flashed. He was silent for some time, then calmed down and spoke on, "your husband, an excellent speaker, convinced judges of the threat of home burglaries and they made a sentence without second thoughts. Eight years of torture, and a spot over the entire short life, and just to please a robbed politician the prosecutor was playing golf with. And the lad had a sick mother and two sisters he had to help. I visited them and I helped them, a spiteful sorcerer. There was almost no food in the house but the mother with tears in her eyes asked me to have tea with stale bread. She kissed my hands begging to help her poor son. She showed me his splendid pictures, touching childish stories written by that talented boy and I knew that every word of the mother was true. Your husband has maimed the whole family but I will correct that and make sure the boy is set free."

"Do you mean we don't have to punish criminals?" the guest was sincerely surprised.

"All have violated some laws, if not yours, then the law of equity. Most crimes do not deserve jail. Just do not create conditions for crimes. Go into the question and have a heart. Your husband made his career on criminals who had no money to pay for lawyer services. But I haven't killed him. You could leave the country, but no, there has been no threat for you here," the Seer started to nervously pace the room. There was a feeling of a growing danger.

"And what about shame?" the woman was speaking very softly.

"You can live with that. Those, who do not climb high, do not feel pain when they fall," he recollected an old saying.

"And what about my children?" the widow asked that important question.

The Seer thought for a minute and answered,

"I can't see anything wrong. You are not going to stay lonely, have no fear, next month you will meet a nice man and forget your hatred in his hands, and without voicing it, you will remember me with gratitude."

"I will be interviewed by leading newspapers and TV," she said timidly wanting to hear his opinion.

"Tell them whatever you want, I will forgive you, have no fear. Just do not insult my talent, you cannot judge that. All the best," and the Seer made a gentlemanly gesture at the door.

Chapter 5. Boys

The widow left. The Seer was trying to explain his new uneasy feeling. He felt bad, but that had nothing to do with his recent guest. He always attentively monitored his feelings to probe events when preparing to them.

The Seer had stopped seeing visitors, although there were many willing to meet him at any cost. Just sometimes he helped his friends and acquaintances or the people who came with a recommendation from his close friends.

And suddenly he was told that there were two strange people bold enough to insist he spoke with them. The Seer got angry as he was not waiting for anyone, and his first intent was to make unwanted guests go away, but suddenly he stopped: he felt that the sense of danger was related with them. Curiosity prevailed and he decided to meet them. The gate opened and two men passed to the courtyard.

"Maybe I'll stay here to cover the rear?" asked the Soldier, examining an unknown place. He even did not try to conceal his anxiety.

"Are you afraid?" the Stranger was slightly surprised, looked his friends in the eyes and smiled.

"I don't want to be turned into a dog or worse still, in a pacifist," the Soldier whispered.

"Don't worry. Even the Seer cannot make you a pacifist. Just, warrior, do not swear even mentally," the Stranger was in good mood.

"Is it true that he can read all thoughts?" the Soldier got nervous.

"Of course, but abusive language is the easiest to read," the Stranger was trying not to laugh out loud.

"What's so funny?"

"When you were shooting you were less afraid."

"War is my elements, I feared all the time, especially at the beginning, but it is different fear. Fear that makes you stronger and sharpens your instincts, but   this one deprives you of them. Even my knees are trembling. What a mess I'm in!"

"Fear that deprives you of strength is called panic. Do not worry, hero of the war, I will protect you."

A beautiful young woman pointed out to the study. Approaching the door, the Stranger listened and said,

"It seems there is no one there. I cannot feel anything."

"You are mistaken. I'm here," a slightly croaking voice could be heard from behind the door. This voice could belong to the certain one man only.

They entered a gloomy study: bookcases were crowded with folios; there were curious artifacts on shelves, and abstract demon masks, deities, and pictures on the walls.

"It is impressive! I haven't known that you like fetishes," uttered the Stranger ironically, watching around the room attentively.

The Soldier inhaled and held his breath: the host would surely push them out for this unceremonious treatment and that was if they were lucky.

"Do not swear and don't be afraid. I respect hospitality laws. If I let you in, I will let you out," the Seer addressed the Soldier who expressively glanced at his companion and blushed.

The Stranger did not want to combat the Seer or show disrespect, but he suddenly heard a slight Wind blowing. He slowly turned his gaze earlier directed at the red and brown mask of the God of war at the host. "Can it be the Seer?" The Stranger thought and looked him directly in the eyes. Suddenly, he felt slightly dizzy, got pale, swayed, he was short of breath. But the Wind helped, it became stronger not only in the head and shoulders, but in the arms and that could happen only in special circumstances. Wind came out of him and seemed to be above him at the same time. The jaw vice which seized the Stranger weakened, but he was gradually filled with strength and nothing could harm him, even the Seer who was capable to lull a large audience or make a crowd jump on one foot in one place in unison.

"I haven't come to fight you or show my strength, I have come to speak. Trust me," the Stranger said slowly and distinctly.

The Seer was shaken. He literally pierced his guest with his stare. His eyes became wet from tears and showed fear and pain. Seeing this misery of a great man, the Soldier rejoiced. He believed. He believed the Stranger.

"I have never seen anything like that. What was that?"

The Seer was speaking with difficulty. He sat down on a chair and pointed his finger at water. The Stranger rushed to fetch him a glass of water.

"Please let's not test each other. I have come with peace," said the guest quietly. When he saw the host in that condition, he could not rejoice in his victory.

"I haven't tried to impact you to make you unconscious, I just wanted to feel you to understand what you live with. I haven't shown aggression, but drove against a powerful energy stroke. Who are you?" the Seer was externally calm and was eying the Stranger without fear but amazed.

"I need your help. Can we talk?" the Stranger asked.

"Take a seat, but I doubt I can help you," the Seer pointed at the chairs.

The Soldier was the first to take a seat; he was no less surprised than the Seer. The Stranger took his seat, too.

"I would like to know what you think about an important issue. I've heard something," he started.

"In what state were you at that time?" the Seer completely recovered. He made himself forget his weakness as a bad dream, absolutely erase from his memory.

"I climbed up the hill and tried to tune in the heavenly wave and started to speak," the Stranger hoped the Seer would understand.

"Was it a dialog?" the host's eyes shown smirk.

"It's not a theatrical performance. Why do you use such terms? Do you want to know if I can hear the Voice? Very rarely. But that requires a correct question. Sometimes I hear different voices as if I couldn't tune on to a necessary wave in a bad quality radio receiver. And still I'm not sure if I heard my subconscious voice or really entered the Source of Knowledge," it was hard for the Stranger to choose words.

"You have little experience. I have heard many voices or rather senses, since my childhood, and then learnt to translate them in human speech. But I checked myself: I came up to people and told them what they were thinking about. Sometimes I was mistaken, and the words I heard were of the person standing nearby. With time I learnt to differentiate sources," the Seer started to speak in his normal complacent voice.

"I didn't have the task to read others' thoughts. I'm interested in the rules of the universe and my actions," the Stranger explained.

The Seer was eyeing his companion with interest.

"A source of Knowledge is a kind of a large shop: there are various goods required for living and even more. There is something we cannot understand or use, at least in our time. A man who happens to be in the supermarket chooses what he needs. But sometimes takes everything he can lay his hands on, even something he cannot and will not be able to use. Give a fighter plane to a music teacher and he won't be able to start it. If you give a mobile phone to a person, living somewhere deep in the countryside, where never heard of radios or telephones, will he use it to communicate or rather hang it on his neck as decoration or use it as a hammer?"

"I understand what you are driving at. I have received something I cannot understand. But you cannot understand everything either.

Still, I think the analogy with a shop is not really suitable. A source is rather a warehouse and goods are issued by a storekeeper according to the visitor's inclinations," the Stranger said smiling.

"If a recipient does not know what it is, he should study an operation manual and understand its purpose."

"What have you seen on the hill? Repeat exactly what you have heard," asked the Seer sharply. He couldn't stand polemists and considered that he was always right and therefore was slightly irritated by lack of respect to him.

"I was told: 'Go to the City'. The voice was distinct and clear as an order. I heard it from outside. I am not crazy. And I'm no less skeptical than you, but ignoring facts is a crime."

"Have you asked something before that?" the Seer became serious and thought that something important was in the air.

"I asked how I should live. What must I do?"

"Was that all?"

"As regards the Voice, that was all. Then I have started to seek the meaning of the phrase and understood that I have to undertake an important and unsafe mission, but maybe these were the answers prompted by my soul and consciousness."

"It's good that you can tell the voice of your consciousness from another voice. But the voice of your soul can be equally true to the heavenly voice," tutored the Seer.

"Why? How can this be possible?"

"Are you ready to believe anything you hear over the radio?"

"Of course not. Do you want to tell me that I can hear an unknown voice translated from anywhere?"

"Translated by someone for unknown purposes."

"But there exists the Voice from the Source of the Truth, to explain the unclear and understand the unknown," the Stranger was slightly alarmed.

"Ok. It is hard to tell it from the voice of your sub-consciousness and more difficult from the voices outside. I'm speaking about the source of information don't have the slightest idea about. By the way, you have interesting terminology for the phenomena which are generally only hard to perceive to say nothing about describing or naming them," the Seer smiled lightly.

"It is for better understanding. Speak on, please."

"Imagine there are powerful translators high up in the sky, and all can hear a heavenly voice, but we understand that the signal is from the Earth."

"I see. You want to say that intelligence services may have sent a signal directly into my brain?" the Stranger got worried. He understood what the Seer was speaking about.

Hearing the words 'special services', the Soldier showed the signs of life with a heavy sigh, but, trained a sniper, he learned to be patient.

"Do you think I'm an idiot to believe in the omnipotence of intelligence services?" the Seer asked.

"You know what I'm thinking about."

"Ok, excuse me. Would you like some coffee? I'll ask to bring some."

"It is unimportant. But thank you," the Stranger felt uneasy: the desire to have a coffee was instantaneous and insignificant, but the Seer guessed. The host pressed the intercom button.

Several minutes later a young woman came in, holding a tray with a coffee pot, sugar pot, cups, biscuits, chocolate, and dried fruit on. The Soldier got interested and was watching a beautiful woman looking as if she stepped from a fashion magazine cover. The Stranger glanced at his bemused comrade and slightly raised his eyebrow pointing at the Seer. The Soldier took on an innocent appearance. The host was attentively watching everything going on in the room, laughed carefree and winked at the Soldier. After his guests had their coffee, he lit a cigarette.

"Sorry, I haven't understood what you meant when you were speaking about the source of the Voice?" the Stranger resumed an unfinished talk.

"Have you heard about the Adversary?" the Seer was looking at his guest cunningly.

"Yes, of course. There is a learning of a power confronting the Creator's will and making harm to people. However, the records of the earlier clairvoyants do not mention him. As if they did not see him at all. The evil similarly to the good, as early prophesy manuscript says, – is sent by the Creator who made day and night, light and darkness. And only afterwards, sages concluded that it was not the God who was the source of misfortunes or disasters, but someone else. Let's call him the Adversary. I can assume that this figure, appearing in human consciousness, is based on real circumstances. Although I think all misfortunes sent down on people are actions of the rewarding and responsibility system."

"You think that all evil, misfortunes, and agony is the doing of the reward system? And do you think it is fair and flawless? That it punishes evildoers and bestows on righteous people? Do you think the Creator is so cruel to people?"

"People make other people suffer. The Creator tries to teach us not to destroy each other but to teach in the way that does not deprive us either of autonomy or of the right of choice. Maybe the reward system is not so apparent to all because its laws overlap and it is very difficult to understand all mechanisms. We don't have much information to make the right choice," the Stranger was speaking softly and calmly, but he was tense.

"Anyone can deprive people of their autonomy. Even I can do this," the Seer looked up at a frowning companion and smiled. "Calm down I'm not using my abilities corruptly or for self-assuredness as some think. There are brain diseases that deprive people of self-control. Passions deprive us of reason and make us act crazily, so that we will regret these actions. Manufacturers of goods and advertisements impose a certain value image on us and turn us into slaves who depend on goods, which are attributes of success and happiness in the eyes of ordinary people. Tyrants, rulers, and politicians manage people's lives. Strong people try to make the weak obey, take away the right to search, independence of thinking, and destroy the right of choice... And have you ever thought why the powerful need that?" the Seer asked.

"It is not difficult to understand: money, power, and glory. All this relies on vanity, ambition, different insecurities, and sometimes just boredom and passion," the Stranger answered quickly. "Why is it allowed? There might be many traps along the path; it is a kind of preparation for those who are willing to enter the world of peace and justice."

"Then it means that confrontation with the powerful people of the world, diseases, and vices are just a race track which makes spiritual people stronger? And by the way, this training is to get ready for the war and not for peace," it was long ago when the Seer discussed those topics, and therefore despite tension in the air, was glad to have these visitors.

"It's bad that not all arrive at the finish line. And there are cases when you have to run to a certain point as there you will get your reward. You know, in order to run you have to move your legs faster. You buy a simulator, move, sweat, get exhausted, but are running in the place. People have the right to choose their way while they often serve some silly and unworthy things. They sweat as if they were running with a simulator, but senselessly. It is their choice and we do not care about it, do we? But others suffer from their actions and not all are protected against the evil," the Stranger seemed that his fate was hanging in the balance during the conversation.

The Seer was trying to recollect something.

"My camp experience proves that most people cannot withstand trials, and will break physically and morally and become inferior people. I don't understand who might need that. I have been observing ants the other day," he said as if turning it in his mind.

"They labored, hurried, stumbled against each other. A boy ran up to them and caught the first ant on the way. The kid tore off an ant foot and threw the wretched fellow away. He placed another on his palm and blew. The ant was off. While the boy was experimenting, I didn't tell him anything. Let him explore the world, however cruel the method might be, but when the brat started to stamp ants with his feet I interfered as his unreasonable actions disturbed the natural balance. The struggle for survival ended long ago, the territory was divided. Observe co-existence of creatures in the world. The boy didn't know that, was offended and ran away. He even didn't understand why it was wrong to be so cruel to living creatures and I didn't have time to explain him that. But the thing is the ants didn't understand anything either and continued their ant routine as before. They didn't and couldn't understand the service I rendered rescuing them from the boy."

"Who is this boy?"

"Boys are capable of anything. At least they have strength to tear off feet and blow off from the palm."

The Seer was attentively watching the Stranger's reaction.

"Listen:

If I remember it
And my memory doesn't sleep,
They are creators
Of the world
They do not believe
Or never cry…

…They seem to care for nothing
Captains of heaven,
Smoking in the open window
And leading by bad example…"

The Stranger laughed.

"Is this the source of your philosophy? Do you believe that the authorship of such a complex world belongs to those who do not know its laws? Those who make harm and lead astray?"

"I don't know, I think not," the Seer scratched the tip of the nose.

"But I think they exist. We are ants for them. These creatures might know nothing about compassion, cannot feel it, but they are much stronger and more experienced than we are. They have their own goals and objectives. They can use you in their own interests to no one's benefit."

The Stranger thought the Seer was not sincere and was playing cat and mouse challenging him.

"Ok," the Stranger smiled with the edges of his lips going up. He understood that the Seer could not believe he could think critically. "I know about the existence of the other world. I can sometimes feel their presence. Do you think I will have to encounter them in the City?"

"I'm not sure you need a special place, but it is dangerous for you in the City," the Seer answered and stretched a hand to fetch another cigarette.

The Stranger came up to the window and looked at a well-kept orchard with fruit trees. With his back to the Seer, he asked him the most important question:

"Have you felt the Power in me? What is it? Why do I have it?"

The Seer smoked again, was silent for several minutes. He was smoking with his eyes closed, without looking at ash falling down onto his knees, and spoke without looking at the Stranger:

"I will be honest. I have never encountered similar energy before. You are unlikely to use it to suppress people. There are other more known, simpler and no less efficient means. Certainly, this power can be used to protect against all energy impacts and even more: attack. But you won't search people who have special energy. No? That's what I have thought. And there are not many people who use their talent to make evil and so it means we have no one to fight … This might be a weapon but many-sided and very complex. A sword and a shield at the same time and God know what else. At first I thought I had something which could not be put in practice in our life. That happens. Believe me! I have faced different people, even the ones who could burn paper with their eyes from a distance of five steps. And? Who needs this when there are affordable means to make fire? I don't have information to answer. You have to tell me more."

The Stranger sighed feeling that the Seer was suspiciously interested. Rather, he thought he should not open the reason that made the Wind appear.

"I don't know why but I can't."

Suddenly the Seer looked rough.

"I understand that you do not trust me. You fear that learning the mechanism, I will deprive you of your protection. Or – more than that, acquire your ability and then you will not be the unique holder of the talent. I won't dissuade you but let me just note that it is dangerous both for you and others not to know the purpose of this complex weapon. You can't even use it at your discretion. This power shows by itself. Believe me, I'm not weak and have seen much, but I have felt uncomfortable and miserable and frightened when you showed your power. I don't know yet who controls whom: you it or it you," the Seer seemed to become tense trying hard not to lose control.

"I'm not going to fight flesh and blood. Calm down, I beg you," the Stranger was visibly afflicted.

"Do not calm me down. I don't know how I can help you. Maybe you need money?" the Seer tried to look calm and self-assured. "I can see that you are not rich."

"Thank you. Money will not help," the Stranger viewed the walls covered with expensive trinkets and looked at the host merrily. "You have much to be proud of. You have a beautiful and large house. You seem to have everything to live a happy life but you are unhappy. You have strong eyes but look like a hunted down wolf. I wanted to go to the City with you. I think we will meet something important there and you may be interested to know something new and unknown."

"I'm sorry," the wounded Seer answered coldly. A prick aimed at his guest turned against himself, "but I'm not so inquisitive to risk all for something unknown. Moreover, I can't show up in public places, especially in the City. I have too many enemies who want to become a history by sharing in my glory, who want to test me and hide behind me. I can't. I won't advise you to do this either and, even more so, to your silent friend. You can always come to me and I will do my best to help you. I wish you all the best."

The Stranger got up from his armchair and stretched his hand. The Seer answered sluggishly without looking his guest in the eyes.

Companions left the house, walked along an even path in the garden to the gate. The Soldier sighed with relief:

"Good house, nice women, lots of money, and glory. How can he leave all that and go for something unknown? The wealthy find it hard to risk," he said seriously but smirk showed in his eyes.

"Maybe. I have nothing to hold to in this world and the same is true about you, but still, have you heard his advice? Don't go to the City. I regret I let you in," the Stranger said.

"You don't know what is going on in the City," spoke the Soldier impulsively. "There are absolutely autonomous neighborhoods. Police fears to go there because there are no strangers from outside and you are an enemy for them. So many disturbing orders have appeared lately! I don't advise you to interfere with them, they hate outsiders. They won't speak with the representatives of other religions."

"I'm far from the religious representatives or communities, but I'm close to the people of spirit," the Stranger interrupted him.

"And what's the difference?" the Soldier was surprised.

"The clergy serve a certain cult, their community, and their flock. But the people of spirit serve the Truth which is above any religion or cultural and national traditions," the Stranger explained.

"I think it will be hard to explain to an enraged crowd. Teenager gangs are active in the City as vagrant dogs. They are merciless drug- addicts who lost their human dignity. Let's go together. I have decided to quit my job. I have a professional breakdown," the Soldier smiled.

"Good," the Stranger was unexpectedly fast to accept the proposal. "Let's do like this: a day after tomorrow at about eight in the morning we meet at the ticket office at the railway station. If you don't come, it means you have thought twice. I will understand it."

"And if you don't come?"

"Then you stay."

They shook their hands firmly and went their ways. The Soldier left for his home and the Stranger went to the park, as it was not cold at that time.

Next morning the Soldier was making his decision, which was

probably the most important one in all his life. "Maybe I stay; the Seer's advice cannot be ignored. I will live a normal life. Stop battling and find a normal job. Every morning I will wake up with the woman I love, have kids. That's what happiness is about…

You are lying, boy! You know yourself. You won't live a life without a sense of danger. That's how many people live and I have a chance to do something important. I have touched magic. The Stranger has found me and I have met the legend: the Seer himself. And he was afraid of the Stranger. I saw fear in his horrifying eyes. I have a chance to become a companion of the man whom the Seer himself bowed to.

What do I have to lose? How many years have I taken the risk? And what for? Destroy terrorists? But they grow in numbers every day. No, I take risk because I do not like to lead a dull life. I enjoy risk, I like to feel that I'm one of the elite, and top rulers of the country know about me. Reports on completed operations find their way to their desk. Maybe they admire me.

But I saw the light… My feats turned out to be the fruit of vanity. I happen to be no warrior of the light but a bolt in the government vehicle flying down the slope as it does not have brakes. I will become a real warrior if I follow the God's will. I have fought someone other's and senseless war. And now I want to fight for Him. He rescued me and consoled me in His church. I owe Him my life. The God saved me. Was not it for this time? And now time has come to act. By the way, why did the Stranger appoint a meeting in two days? He was anxious to get to the City. Something is wrong here. I need to lay in ambush at the railway station and wait. He might decide to go earlier without me."

Chapter 6. The Liquidator

After his guests had left, the Seer was lingering about the house aimlessly, came out into the garden, looked at trees, and smelt leaves. Having calmed down, he returned to his study and contemplated. The Seer had travelled all over the world, met people with almost fantastical abilities, but he had never seen such universal specialists as himself. He mastered telepathy, could hypnotize with his thoughts, read texts with his eyes closed, find hidden objects, lost people, shared the past in detail, never made a mistake in forecasts. However, even he did not have the power his recent guest had. It was something to think about.

"Something extraordinary is underway. It needs investigation and the sooner the better. Maybe it is necessary to prevent them from entering the City or vice versa help them. What is their purpose? Well, they don't know that themselves."

The Seer took out a cigarette and smoked. He tried to quit this vicious habit many times and did not have the right stimulus as he thought he knew what he would die of.

"First, who are they?" he contemplated. "They haven't introduced themselves. I don't think their names will tell me anything. Let's start with the silent one. What can be said about him? Slightly taller than the average, strong-built, but his muscles are trained in a natural way by many hours of trainings: he is too sinewy, lean, strong, and agile. His movements are very well coordinated and judging by his gestures, quick response, he moves cautiously and has a well-developed side vision. Is he an athlete? No, he is not an athlete; he smokes and is not young. He is at least thirty five. He kept silent all the time and tried to understand what we were talking about and wasn't catching flies. Stop! He sighed when we mentioned intelligence agencies. Is he a military?" the Seer asked listening to himself. "Yes. He is related to the army but he is not a professional Soldier. Ok, deduction and logic aside, I'm not a detective. Let's go directly to conclusions."

The Seer concentrated tuning on to the image of the silent man. He had a chain of associations: a crying and physically impaired boy, a teenager vehemently beating a suspended sack with his hands and feet, a young man in a military uniform shooting from a rifle. "He is not shooting at aims. He fought. Drills, drills," repeated the Seer. "Uneasy training, absolutely closed institution, but not for me; now I will see what they are studying… A gym. Smells of blood, sweat, or something else, oh… that's adrenaline. Full-contact fight, no protective gear. Why do they mutilate each other? Can fists play a decisive role in a modern battle where they fight with rifles striking the aim at a five-kilometer distance?"

The Seer was thinking. He was interested. "I see," he said out loud. "It's a stamina test. Those who withstand will work further. Lectures. Read by civilians: survival tactics, methods of killing, and camouflage. An optic rifle. It's clear what he has been taught. He is a liquidator and probably one of the best. Ok. What next?"

The Seer cringed in his armchair and continued, "Assignments? No need to be a clairvoyant to understand. First tasks in the group, then with a companion, and single tasks for several years. It's strange: single-man liquidation operations are not a normal practice. Why does he leave and return single? Why?"

The Seer got up from the armchair, nervously paced the room, stopped at the window and closed his eyes. "The liquidator's partners perished. He is followed by death but it does not touch him." He saw shelling: lumps of earth flow up in the air with pieces of flesh. Soldiers wailed and whined of fear. Even those who did not believe in God were praying. Young guys virtually sank their teeth in wobbling earth. Explosions smothered weeping and yelling. All died but one. "He survived when all were to be mutilated after that slaughter. Good luck? But it happened on a dozen of occasions and that means a regular pattern. He is dangerous, very dangerous."

Chapter 7. The Medium

The Stranger had long dreamed of meeting the Seer. He had many questions he wanted to discuss, but still the meeting left a painful impression. Of course, the Seer is neither an evildoer nor the son of darkness as he was described by priests, but he did not have inner light bestowing hope and inward peace, either. A searching, strong and at the same time twitchy person. And his eyes, although strong, are unhappy.

"What is happening?" the Stranger was asking himself. "Why did I meet the Seer? Did I hope he would join us? Very unlikely. I have never seen a like-minded person in him before. But the Soldier is not my brethren either, but he followed me. The Seer possesses a rare talent but he doesn't use it to explore the basics and laws of the universe. He seems to believe in the Creator but he is not searching for Him and does not try to understand His will. If he doesn't want to preach, he could at least tell the whole world what is true, what in the sacred not books comes from the Source of the Truth and what has been added and distorted. I can also detect something. I do this for myself but first, no one will believe me and second 'something' is not enough, we don't have the right to a mistake there. But they won't believe him, either. Those who worship the sacred books do not respect the Seer and they won't listen to him.

He tried to make me understand four things. First, it is not known who made me go to the City. Second, the purpose of the power inside me is unknown. Third, I can find something unusual in the City. Fourth, the Soldier will encounter a deadly danger in the City. The last must be the most important one. I need to go away without the Soldier, it's a pity but that's best for him."

The Medium

These were the Stranger's thoughts when he was slowly plodding towards the park: he was used to stay overnight in caves, on the seashore, and in gardens. He had little money and had to save it for an emergency.

Suddenly he felt a stare at his back. He turned sharply and saw a woman's silhouette about twenty paces off. A Wind breeze strengthened him and gave him confidence. He slowly approached the woman. She was staring tensely in his face and above his head. The woman made several gestures with her hand as if groping for something invisible. Coming up closer he saw how beautiful she was. His heart beat hard.

The Stranger started to drown in her hot black eyes; he almost stopped short of breath: he loved that beauty alluring and unwelcoming, unapproachable and dangerous, but he was strong enough to rouse himself.

"Look into her and feel what she lives with," the Stranger came to his senses, the Wind breath, that disappeared when his heart leaped, returned. He recognized her. No, he had never met her before, but he knew her from newspapers.

"Do you want something from me? Have you followed me from the Seer's home?" the Stranger addressed her without a traditional greeting.

"I'm Medium," she said quietly and meaningfully. "I live in the City, came to the Seer, but when I saw you and your friend I got interested in you, especially in you."

The Stranger felt that the encounter was not accidental and decided to check at once.

"I must go to the City. Is your flat big? Will you give me shelter?"

The Medium met different people, some of whom happened to be very extraordinary, and therefore she ignored the question and continued:

"Have you heard about me?"

"Very little. I'm sorry I usually do not circulate among the people who talk to the other world."

"Then you have a chance to expand your horizon," the Medium said haughtily. "Why do you need the City? Normal people, to the contrary, are leaving it now."

"Normal people..." the Stranger repeated sadly and his face was touched by a shadow,

"I don't know but I must."

"Then let's not waste time. Come to my place," the woman liked that man who was simple and complex at the same time, and she was drawn by controversies.

"No. Let's go tomorrow morning, I need to sleep well. I haven't slept two nights, and I will need to be strong in the City. Stay a night in the hotel. But I don't have money for two separate rooms, let's book one with twin beds or you book for yourself. But for the sake of saving, you can stay a night with the Seer. Sorry, I'm not so gallant."

"I have enough to book all rooms, but I want to be closer to you," she looked mischievous.

Talking and taking no heed of the time, they approached the hotel.

In the room, having enjoyed a shower, the Stranger blissfully stretched on a soft bed, but couldn't fall asleep next to beautiful woman because of excitement. He tried to instill in himself the sense of a light and pleasant breeze. He became less tense with time. Listening to a monotonous and lulling play of waves, the Stranger fell asleep. The Medium was sitting in the armchair with her legs pulled up. She felt good besides him, calm and peaceful. "I would enjoy looking at him all my life," she thought.

The Medium earned by fortunetelling and chiromancy. She told fortune in the state of a trance. But after the Seer insisted she does not change her consciousness at own will, she did it quite rarely. She treated the sick that could not be treated by traditional methods.

But she achieved the top or depth of her performance (here opinions differed) when she talked with the world of the dead. Unhappy people who lost their dear ones but could not accept the loss came to her and wished to speak with the deceased dear ones. The Medium asked the relative to give her an object of the dead or a printed photo, but not an electronic version, built a connecting channel between the object and the soul, tuned on to the image of the dead, saw contours, told about the life and habits and sometimes the last days in the body and transmitted the will or desires of the dead.

Lately, she has achieved the level of authority so high that she stopped speaking on TV, rejected interview requests and selected her visitors as she wished. She usually refused to see low-income people unless she considered the case especially interesting, although she had used to be a timid and shy girl willing to help. Fame changed her; she became haughty, proud, and obstinate: the symptoms of the star fever that the Seer, who had seen ups and downs in his life, despised. But that recent arrogance might have been a kind of a protection. The Medium was attacked by the representatives of religious orders who condemned her and continuously threatened her with punishment, but she ignored their threats and did not hire a bodyguard.

The Medium was lonely, she could not live with a man who would be weaker than she was, and could lower her head only before the Seer who treated her tenderly but patronizingly. It irritated her, tortured, and piqued, however she considered no other man more worthy than the Seer. Now she wanted just one thing: to be with the sleeping man, cuddle up to him, and there come what may. Jump in feet first.

She felt she had known him for ages. They might have met in their previous life and that happiness and joy when she saw an unknown man might be a kind of recognition of kindred. She was surprised most of all by unusual glow above his head which either appeared or disappeared. He radiated calmness and strength but his companion was a source of danger, and the Medium saw a fiery halo above him, which was inseparable from the people who had shed much blood. That was the halo of a cruel warrior, although the man did not look like an evildoer or a criminal.

The aura of the pleasant stranger whose name she had forgotten to ask was not very remarkable by itself: usually seen among believers and religious people. The Medium treated them without any respect. She respected certain ceremonies in church as well as other magical actions and even used some religious practices: read extracts from sacred books, showed religious symbols, talismans, images of saints. She thought that it was also magic, although religious but had value for her only when they contributed to her efforts.

She got up and came up to the bed where the Stranger was sleeping, sat down, took his hand tenderly and looked at the lines on the palm. Suddenly without opening his eyes, he grasped her palm, pulled it her cheek and held it there during several seconds.

"I'm sorry," the Stranger said letting her palm go. "I haven't had a woman for a long time; it was an uncontrolled reflex to the girl's fingers. Good night, medium," he said her name separating it into two words.

The woman's eyes sparkled with rage, she was quick-tempered as most of representatives of her profession which demanded very intense nervous strain. She got up quickly and left the room slamming the door.

"A hot woman," the Stranger sighed and settled down into sleep.

Chapter 8. Anomaly

After another cigarette, the Seer felt ready to get an insight in his recent strange visitor.

"He looks like an ordinary believer, you can feel this speaking with him and by the way he's glanced at my seductive servant, but he is not an adept of a religious community. Possessing such energy, anyone would insist he is guided by the godly power and by the spirit of God's ancient chosen ones and would have found a way to use the talent to the benefit of his organization or personal career development. Ok, it means he acts by himself. Such loners are harder to understand. And what if his actions are guided by a real power? Showing up, such people are precursors of disasters and catastrophes. It is difficult to understand his aim. And what's the use? I've felt the impact of his power. Fear and weakness are engulfing gradually but ruthlessly. To be fair, the man did not wish me evil, stopped on time, although it must have been hard to contain a flow of power. Hence, it can be controlled? I wonder whether his companion felt this energy. The power was against me and that was strange, as I did not show aggression. I didn't press on him. I just slightly explored him, scanned his thoughts, a normal desire. Can it be that an evil mask of the ancient god of war woke something? Strange. How can such trinkets impact? May his power show associatively? So, a believer who abides by peace principles. A rare case in our times. However, any pacifism has limits. Pacifist with a deadly weapon? Maybe that's why he is a pacifist? Or has he received it because he is a pacifist? Good intuition but nothing outstanding. The most important is the power. Others think the right question is a half-answered question, but for me it is almost an answer. Is this power independent?"

It seems to be easy: yes or no. But the Seer could not give any answer and said out loud:

"What's the matter? An inexact question?"

He listened to himself. Missed again. He lacked information.

"Does this power manifest itself at the will of its holder? The guest seemed to have intentionally held back the information on how it was the first time. This must be the key. When I assumed that the power was a kind of a weapon, he agreed. Still, the guest knows little about this himself. Let's think more. Can this power treat? Not so unambiguous. Does it treat some diseases? Seems like that. Yes, surely yes!"

Irritation passed and the Seer was inspired and decided he was approaching the solution. "What illnesses?" He asked out loud. He closed his eyes. At that moment, he saw as if highlighted on the virtual display the words 'mental disorders' and cried out, "I have it!" He extracted the word 'obsession' from list. "So, this energy can be used to treat from obsession, can't it? Exorcist? But he is not a priest. Who will go to him? Will he be hired in the mental house? Will he treat with his power? Use words to drive out demons? Ok, no one will employ him; rather make him a patient in the clinic. Doctors do not believe in demons. Will he frighten obsessed priests? Very unlikely. He is not this kind. Only in case of an accidental encounter when his power will manifest all by itself. Ok, how many charismatic priests are there?"

The Seer knew that there were two kinds of obsession. Ancient books described godly obsession with bright knowledge, prophesy, genial ideas, and prophetic dreams. Even poetry is a kind of liberation from the mind and subconscious connection to another source above human experience.

But there existed destructive obsession: passion, suicide, violence, and homicide. "Sick people think they contain someone who directs them, and there is an impression there is an anomaly which changes their identity. I think there is no anomaly. A split personality or substitution must be related to the subconscious of the sick, and it is activated under impact of special and unusual circumstances, including fear, stress, alcohol, and drugs. Most even don't suspect what might happen."

However, the word 'anomaly' made the Seer uneasy....

Chapter 9. Soul rotation

The Medium went down the hotel lounge, came up to the bar counter, and ordered a cognac, cheese, and olives. She wanted to unwind a bit. She was still drinking cognac when she saw a young man with a clouded glance, but dressed in the latest young fashion.

"What can I bring you?" he asked freely.

"If you are a waiter, get lost," the Medium proposed with expressed scorn.

"Me? You don't know who I am?" said the guy through clenched teeth filling with rage.

"Now, let's see who you are," she sharply grasped the man by his palm and attentively surveyed the life and destiny lines.

"You were born in a poor family," the Medium started to speak. She felt inspiration and anger. "You fell ill often, nearly drowned, was rescued at the last moment and maybe they shouldn't have done that. Why do we rescue villains? You have never done anything good. You have never married and never will. Your father has died recently, but you have mother and sister. Three or four years ago you received a large sum of money; either won it or received it as a gift because you were only good enough to have a dose and a couple of prostitutes. But this money is meant to kill you. You have little time left. Very little."

The man was suddenly pale, he seemed to be shocked. He turned his head around trying to become sober but did not succeed.

"H… how many years do I have left?" he asked stumbling.

"About a year, no more. Look at yourself: you are a goner," the Medium answered indifferently.

The young man took out a small box from his pocket, poured out powder directly onto the bar counter, divided it into two strips, took out a banknote, placed it at his nostril, quickly inhaled white dust, shuddered, blinked, noisily exhaled and smiling angrily winked at the prophetess.

"You won't die of sinus trouble," the Medium said and drank her cognac in one gulp. She felt no pity for the man. That was strange: several years ago she would feel compassion, give advice what to do to change the effects of the choice.

She went up to the room, quietly opened the door, and smiled seeing a sleeping man. She certainly liked him. She fetched a packet of cigarettes, went to the balcony, closed the door tight, sat on the floor, and smoked. She was not able to relax or get away from the thoughts about her new acquaintance:

"An interesting story. Who is the man? Why have I come after him? What does he need in the City? A strange halo, which either appears or disappears? There are various energy clusters above a person, especially above seriously ill people, they can be used to determine if the person will die or live. But he has totally different light above, it seems to be alive and emit power. Unclear. It seems I have known him long. May this be the experience of previous lives? It happens when you meet someone and seem to know everything about him, although you met just five minutes ago. But the most interesting thing is that I liked him from the very beginning. That feels strange. Have I fallen in love? Crap! Though…"

The door to the balcony opened.

"Hope I won't disturb you?" the subject of her thoughts whispered.

"No. On the contrary. I'm bored. Why aren't you sleeping?"

"Because I have woken up."

"Shall we speak?"

"Yes."

"What is your name?"

"The Stranger."

"Pilgrim?"

"Possibly."

"Why have you visited the Seer?"

"To speak," the Stranger answered concisely.

"And?" the Medium drew down cigarette smoke.

"We spoke."

"What do you want in the City?" the woman moved very close to him.

"I don't know yet," he whispered mysteriously.

"Have you been sent to the City?" she asked pointing out to the night sky with a cigarette spark.

"Exactly."

"Who?"

The Stranger sighed. He was joking and laughing at anything but the God.

"I hope, the Creator," he sounded a bit detached. "But the Seer doubts it."

"Why?" the Medium grew wary.

"He believes the voice is not a sufficient reason to follow."

"And what do you think?" the woman repeated.

"Time has come," he inhaled air mixed with cigarette smoke.

"What for?" she threw out the butt from the balcony.

"I hope it is for something important."

"And this important is in the City, isn't it?"

"Yes," the Stranger felt good beside that woman. He could speak up about what bothered him most.

"It happens. I have a persistent feeling that I have known you for a long time. Maybe we met in the previous life and maybe more than that," she looked in his eyes boldly.

"This would be possible if you were a woman and I was a man," the Stranger smiled. "I don't believe in previous lives. Although I know that almost all religions accept the soul rotation doctrine. Once I had to live with one tribe and study its religion and customs. The soul rotation doctrine is the most important religious principle of the community. I saw a child who told me in detail about the life of a warrior in the tribe killed in a battle, although he had died several months before the birth of the boy. I spoke with the boy and checked everything, the child made almost no mistakes, he shared even the intimate details no one but the wife of the deceased could know. Isn't it proof of the soul rotation? But it is incorrect to take into account only one version."

"Do you think the child was playing a role?" the Medium grinned.

"Absolutely impossible."

"What's the problem then?"

"The three-year old boy knew not only the deceased but other people living and dead. The child was your kin. That explains much. The chiefs used him and showed magic to reinforce religious principles and their authority to have no barriers to lead the community and send warriors to fight without fear for their life. Some think that after death of the body the soul is inseparably connected with another body and resuscitates it. Others believe that only kind souls are immortal and only the souls of kind people can have another life in other bodies, and evil ones should are foredoomed to agony. The God bestows the right to be born again upon those who adhere by commandments. There is an opinion that evil people will live a life filled with suffering in the bodies of unhappy people or animals. I can accept that in rare cases a soul can have a new life in another body. The God can do anything, even if it seems senseless. But if we didn't remember what was happening in the previous life, how would we understand the lesson and find out what has to be changed in ourselves? Here and now we have enough lessons and signs to understand our steps and correct something. Of course, it is easy to understand the misfortunes of this life by the mistakes made in the previous one. It is an attractive and easy way to go for modern theologians, but an easy way does not mean the right one! Ancient theologians who came not only to console the Sufferer but also to condemn him in his crimes and justify the divine justice never told him, 'Be patient, brother, you are paying for the crimes you have committed in past life.' They did not think of the soul rotation doctrine," the Stranger explained calmly.

"You are not right," the Medium said irritated. "There are different kinds of embodiment and it does not necessarily mean settling in human bodies, but this is not for everyone. The spiritual world is very complex. In order to see it, you need to be either born a seer or learn to see. You say we don't remember our previous bodies, but it is not necessary. We must learn to feel and follow our feelings. The soul doesn't think, it recollects and feels. The pang of conscience, intuitive knowledge of the good and the bad and even hazard, fears or, to the contrary, joys, these are indistinct memories... and lessons from previous life. The soul embedded in the body tries to save or respectfully withstand a severe and horrible trial. This is what it is for. But it is enslaved by our mind and suffers. We are weighed down by much going around and do not listen to the voice. We don't find harmony between the soul and mind."

"This is your imagination, illusionary worlds which you instill with power and make real," the Stranger muttered. "Well, if you tune on to the Source of Knowledge, you will see anything and won't be able to tell the reality from imagination. There might be no distinct border in between."

"I'm not going to argue. You are very conservative, but you are a curious man. You are unlike others," the Medium looked at him tenderly and said affectionately, "I have seen a strange light above your head and it wasn't a halo. Do you know what it is?"

The Stranger suddenly felt light tongues of the Wind.

"Can you see it now?" he asked and the Medium looked narrowly at him.

"Yes, I can see it now," she looked in the companion's eyes and saw an unknown glance, which emitted power. She felt uncomfortable. "Your eyes! What is wrong with your eyes?" she exclaimed and continued to peer at him frightened.

"Nothing threatens you," the Stranger said detachedly and the woman thought that the light above his head became brighter. "It is the Wind. He is my friend. I can see that you are connected with some energies and forces. As soon as they show they can arouse the Wind to act against them and touch you. If possible, do not try to summon spirits in my presence and don't do anything extraordinary."

"Is it bad?" the Medium lowered her head. She did not want to listen to another challenge to her abilities.

"It is also knowledge, but the source of this knowledge is doubtful. In any case, a person will not benefit from this. But I know very little about this," the Stranger did not want to hurt the woman.

"That's how I was born. I have a talent," it was important for her to justify herself.

"I'm not your judge, but they can use you. It is dangerous."

"But no, I'm using them. That's how I earn my bread," the Medium smiled.

"There are different energies which cannot be seen to normal eyes. You might see more. Animals see in a totally different system. Microscope, telescope, or X-ray can be used to see something inaccessible to human eyes. Such people as you or the Seer can see something that cannot be seen through these devices. But no talent gives access to the country of justice," the Stranger tried to speak as soft as possible.

The woman was almost on the verge of a nervous breakdown, and despite external confidence could hardly keep control.

"And what will?"

"Our endeavors, acts, and belief."

"Do you believe in the country of justice? Where is it? Over there?"

The Medium pointed her finger at stars.

"It is somewhere, far away and nearby at the same time. It might reach the Earth," the Stranger was silent and then added: "someday."

"Ok," the woman nodded eagerly. "It's a pity we won't see that."

"I won't live to these days and I won't see the time when my songs are needed... If the Creator so wishes, He can shift our substance to another medium. Do you copy important information from your computer to discs?"

"I don't copy all information to other media."

The Stranger nodded and sighed heavily:

"I'm afraid you are not the only one who does like that."

"That's personification of the soul," she found it hard to smile.

"There are heavenly shells and earthly ones..." the Stranger sank into reverie.

Silence set in. The woman seemed to be fighting a thought. Breathing out, the Medium made a decision.

"Do you want to sleep with me?" she asked sharply, even without looking in his direction.

The Stranger did not expect such a straightforward question and could not keep from smiling.

"Do you, magicians and enchanters, usually reinforce heart-to-heart talks with sex?"

"Well, no, but sex is the easiest way to get to know a person and you are a riddle to me," she looked up at him with her fiery eyes.

"Then let's postpone the learning process," the Stranger grinned. "I fear to disappoint you when you get to know me. You may deprive me of your hospitality in the City and that would be quite an unhappy occasion."

The woman smiled, looked at the Stranger playfully and thought: "And he does want me, I can see that."

The Medium went to the bathroom. She came after shower, completely naked, demonstrating her splendid figure, proudly passed the man, languidly sighed and lay down on her bed and did not cover herself with the blanket.

"There is a draught, you'll catch cold," he said yawning.

"Maybe, you are not interested in women, aren't you? Anyone in your place will be sitting at my feet."

"I'm not anyone. I thought you could see that. The strong differ from the weak not by lack of desire, but by the ability to manage and control, they know the reason to hold their passions. We had a nice talk," said the Stranger through his teeth and turned to another side.

The woman could not go to sleep. She rolled herself up in a sheet, went out to the balcony again, and smoked.

"Can I ask you a question?" the Stranger could not go to sleep either.

"Sure."

"Why do you both smoke so much?"

"Who both?" the Medium asked to clarify.

"You and the Seer. If you are able to see, you must know what harm it makes."

"As far as I know, the Seer cannot quit smoking."

"Why?"

"After his leg was crushed in the death camp, he experienced heavy depression. Have you heard about this time?"

"I have, and about a wonderful escape from the camp, too. Despite his mutilated leg, he hypnotized security guards and escaped."

"Yes, he escaped, crossed the border, returned home, did not see anyone for several months and even did not leave home. He was fed almost from a spoon. His power can break anyone, but he himself is weak and spleeny."

The Stranger was silent for some time.

"I think you haven't understood. He didn't worry about his leg or agonies in the death camp. I think he felt something was wrong. He saw imminent danger, knew he was chased and still could not avoid getting into the hands of his pursuers. And then he saw: there was something stronger than him, understood there were rules even he couldn't change. He experienced a withdrawal syndrome and that was the most difficult as it meant loss of self-confidence."

The Medium came up to the Stranger and sat beside him.

"I have bad premonitions, I have been anxious for several weeks. I have come to speak with the Seer. Maybe he understands what is going on with me," the woman took the Stranger by his hand.

"You are not the only one; all of us feel like that. We are on the threshold of amazing events and I think I will learn something important in the City. I'm drawn there as if by a magnet."

"A call?"

"This is vampire terminology. More likely, a mission. I hope, it is a mission," the Stranger softly removed her palm and went to the balcony.

"Do you enjoy looking in the sky?" the woman followed him.

"I sometimes think that the sky is looking at me, inviting me to be its guest. It illuminates the way by the stars and the Moon. You think that I've decided I'm someone very special, don't you?"

"I don't think so," the Medium interrupted him. "I believe that you can do much. But I can see how the air condenses above you. Has the Seer warned you of an imminent danger?"

"He warned my comrade."

"I've seen him. I don't like him. I strongly don't like him. I don't understand what you might have in common with a man like that."

"You don't know him. He, like many others living in the time of troubles, has another attitude to life and death."

"Could you have made a mistake with the choice of a companion?"

"We'll see when time comes. Let's go to bed. Tomorrow will be a tough day."

Chapter 10. A favor for a favor

The Seer could not get to sleep. Anxious thoughts prevented him from relaxing or getting the story out of his mind. He thought he should take some action, influence the situation, although it was not typical for him to interfere with anything not directly related to him.

"Ok, suppose, there is an anomaly in the City, and a man capable of fighting it shows up. He hears a voice, commanding him to go to the City. Tries to build a team, or?" the Seer winced. "No. They are not friends and barely know each other. Mobilized a liquidation specialist. Wanted to employ me. Funny guy. They probably go to fight. But against whom? Magicians and sorcerers? Is a black magic conference planned in the City? Most likely, no. So, what's the anomaly?" the Seer tried to concentrate. "No. Nothing fits. Maybe there is no anomaly in the City, and this man, call him the Eccentric, has power which is activated in case of...." the Seer rubbed his forehead and said at hazard: "emotional shake up of the holder. A memory of the great events of the past, history of the City can provoke an outburst of energy in the

Eccentric. A mechanism was activated for some reason and he decided he could use his ability in the City. Ok. But why does he need the Liquidator? He could feel he needed a battle tactics specialist. So, is the Eccentric dangerous? What happens if he wanders around the City. Although there are places where you better avoid. Well, it's not our problem, he is not a small boy, and he will sort it out. And what if he loses control over his energy in the City, what will happen in this case? Can't happen? Is it my imagination? But I have experienced the power of the Eccentric, and he found hard to suppress it and it nearly killed me. So, the best way is not to let him go to the City."

This thought brought him relief and his spirits improved sharply. The Seer took a non-conventional decision to call his acquaintance, named the Functionary. Several years ago the Seer made him a great favor, and that was why he dialed the Functionary's number without a twinge of conscience.

"Sorry for a night call, but my business is urgent. I hope you have recognized me?" the Seer's voice was hard and insistent.

"Oh, that's Ok," the Functionary seemed to be awake. "Glad to hear you. When would you like to see me?"

"As soon as possible. And preferably at my place, if it is not inconvenient for you."

Two hours later the Functionary was in the Seer's kitchen drinking coffee.

"It is hard for me to explain the reason for asking your help," the Seer started to speak. "I have a feeling that fulfillment of my request will benefit the country or at least postpone an imminent disaster."

"I'm sure your request is lawful as you are the example of decency and humanism. Therefore it will be an honor to fulfill it," said the Functionary in the most courteous way.

The Seer penetrated his thoughts: "What kind of a silly song is in his head? Oh... He knows that I can read thoughts and fills his head with bullshit, but I can feel his fear, distrust, and admiration, all mixed. They are strange these security officers."

"There are two people who can escalate a conflict in the City where the situation is very tense as is," the Seer came to the point. "They must be detained without violence: they are neither criminals, nor terrorists, nor rebels, but are law-abiding citizens. It is especially important to prevent one of them from entering the City."

"Do they represent an organization?" the Functionary did not believe in the power of single warriors. Then why was it necessary to take a person so late at night to settle that trifle business?

"I wouldn't disturb you if they were trifles," the Seer said strictly. "I don't know who they are related to, but I assure you it is a serious matter."

"Ok, I'll do my best. I need at least some information."

"Here are their photographs," the Seer handed him out several images. Security cameras near his house on the gate and door took pictures of the Stranger and the Soldier. The Soldier's face was closed by a cap with a long peak though, but the Stranger's face could be well seen from all views. "But I warn you, do not make them any harm. Let competent people do that. You can encounter surprises."

He took out from the case a large envelope he had prepare earlier and handed it over to the Functionary.

"Take it. To cover business expenses."

"Oh, no. I owe you so much," imitating indignation the guest rejected money.

"It's for business and to pay bonuses to your people," the Seer did not like when people were performing in his presence. "I don't want a report. I want a result. Believe, the task is not easy as it seems at first glance. These two people are not ordinary citizens. If you detain them, please do not send them to jail. Find a decent place with security. Then we'll decide what is to be done with them."

"Ok, sure," the Functionary assured him. "I'll do my best. We'll find them."

"It is not for me but for the country. We'll keep in touch."

The Functionary left the Seer's home, climbed into his car, nervously opened the envelope, counted money and shone, "Still, the Seer is an outstanding man. We will find these people without his money." He recollected four years ago when he met the Seer at one of the parties, the Seer was watching his wife attentively, then came up to him and confidingly whispered: "Your wife has cancer, at the initial stage so far, but if you don't hurry, nothing will help." The family was taken aback. She went through screenings, which showed that the woman really had the earliest signs of cancer. An operation was enough and no chemical treatment was necessary.

Now she feels fine. Remembering this story, the Functionary was on the verge of tears but he did not think of returning money.

After the security man had left, the Seer felt heart-heaviness, his forehead was covered with cold sweat: "Maybe I was wrong to set on agents? What if they do harm to the Eccentric? I wouldn't like that. It is not late to cancel everything. No, they won't do harm. They won't do harm," he assured himself. "And if they let them go? Then it can be assumed the Eccentric is really led by someone. Whom do I act against? And generally, what do I care about all this?"

The Seer was strong, very clever, and far-sighted man but at the same time mistrustful and superstitious. He managed to combine two identities. One was the result of his talent: exceptionally strong and super confident in his power. The other was weak with the soul torn by doubts and loneliness. He built a good wall around himself no stranger would pass. The Seer did not wheedle before people with power and openly despised some of them seeing their cheap identities hidden behind expensive suits that smelt of rust that could not be offset by expensive perfumes.

He tried not to interfere when he faced something which did not fit in his picture of the world and avoided questions about the God, although he was sure the universe had own Constructor. He knew spiritual laws and tried not to violate them. But the Seer could not imagine the Creator, did not tune on that Source finding it was a senseless idea to learn the global idea of the Providence and a highly foolish task to study the nature of God by own mind and morals.

He remembered the ancient people who simplified the Creator by their primitive speeches regarding His nature. The Seer thought that evolution of human mind would necessarily result in the creation of more complex theology.

Acting against recent guests, leveraging powerful people the Seer understood that he failed to follow his internal code. Moreover, he was frightened that he interfered with the course of events he could not understand.

Then still another thought depressed him: can the cause of his anxiety be in banal envy rather than care about the world?

"That can't be true. Envy the Eccentric? I have everything and he has nothing. I have the rarest abilities no one else has. I can't envy the Eccentric. It is impossible."

Chapter 11 The First Victims

Next morning the Soldier was prepared to set out. He took a small rucksack with his belongings, several chocolate bars, a plastic water bottle, and tucked money in numerous pockets. He hailed a taxi at a distance from his house, even in the peacetime he followed elementary conspirator rules. Entering the railway station building, the Soldier attentively explored the halls, went up to the second floor, sat down near the window, and started to wait for the Stranger.

Half an hour later, two cars arrived at the railway station, and strong men in official but comfortable suits with short hair got out from the cars. One of them passed around photographs to agents. The Soldier could easily distinguish a security employee in one of them, became all ears and was able to read fragmented information that they were speaking about detention of two people. He distinctly felt danger, which was possible only in case of a real and not imaginary threat. He must at all costs see those photographs and if possible take hold of them. He instantaneously made up a simple plan. He bought a bottle of cheap vodka, went to the men's room, rinsed his mouth with stinking liquid, wiped his face, and jauntily swinging the bottle, moved towards a strong guy who was carefully studying the photographs, standing near the ticket office.

"Look, buddy, we've served together. Let's drink to sort of..." the Soldier addressed the agent and as if accidentally spilt vodka over an inexpensive but good quality suit of the agent.

The agent tried to push the 'drunkard' away, but the Soldier managed to read the blow direction by the movement of the shoulder, moved in the opposite direction, and seeming to lose his balance, grasped the man with a small headphone in the ear by the hand. And he saw that...

"Sorry, buddy. A mistake. Was contused. You are kid still, couldn't have served with you," the Soldier muttered without looking at him with his head lowered.

Another security agent was approaching.

"Cheers, man," said the Soldier drunkenly, moving atilt with his bottle raised, and slowly moved toward the toilet, being fully certain that several pairs of distrustful eyes were looking at his back. Having rinsed his face with water, he took out his mobile. Found a necessary number from the list and called.

The Stranger woke up early in the morning and went to the balcony not to disturb the sleeping woman.

He startled when he heard his mobile phone ring but seeing the displayed number smiled, waited a second, and pressed the answer button.

"Hi. What's happened?"

"They are waiting for us at the railway station. They have our photos. Where are you?"

"In the Tower. Come."

The door swung open and two strong guys entered the toilet.

"Sobered up?" one of them addressed the Soldier.

They were gazing at him, these fighters ready to instantaneously attack. The agent took out photographs.

"Know them?"

The Soldier, peering in the photographs, shouted wildly:

"That's my buddy, battled together. He was killed, my trusted friend, treacherously, in the back!"

Tears were running down his face. He recollected a real case from his life and tears were almost sincere. The agents did not expect the performance, were at a loss for several seconds, and relaxed. This was enough. The agents were not wearing safety vests and the Soldier sharply made an uppercut in the celiac plexus with the maximum strength allowed by his hip and shoulder, and hit the other one who did not have time to react with his right hand on the jaw. The security employee staggered, swayed and started to fall onto his back, but the Soldier caught him to prevent him breaking his back against the tiled floor. He unfastened handcuffs from the agent's belt, cuffed their hands behind their backs fast and pushed them into a bathroom stall. Fetched the photographs and read their IDs.

"Breathe deeper, secret war warrior," he said to the agent who was convulsively swallowing air.

The Soldier ignited toilet paper, threw it in the dustbin and left the toilet shouting: "Fire! All is on fire!" People panicked, a fire siren went off. He ran outside unnoticed in that turmoil and dived in a taxi.

About half an hour later he was greeted by the worried Stranger in the Tower hotel lounge.

"You look well in pictures," the Soldier grinned slightly pointing at photograph.

"The Seer," the Stranger drawled. "Why?"

"I didn't want to go to him," the Soldier reminded gloomily.

"Just think, he set agents on us. They were in ambush directly at the railway station. After I deprived them of the right to exclusively use our photos, the railway station is a taboo."

"I hope you have killed or mutilated no one?" the Stranger did not find it funny.

"What if so!" the Soldier seemed to be mortally hurt. "I was insulted when I saw our photographs held by others. Maybe they decided to earn on our glory. It's not good. I ask, by what right? I didn't give permission to be shot. I made a scandal and they decided not to deal with me and returned the photographs without litigation."

"You must write fairy tales! Remember, violence pays back. It's not our way," the Stranger said thoughtfully. "By the way the Seer can find the hotel. We have to leave."

"Can the Seer find our location at any time?"

"I think yes. Wait here. I need to speed up someone."

"Found one more companion?"

"A woman, living in the City. She'll give us shelter," the Stranger said going out.

The Soldier followed him with his eyes, "You would never tell he is this type by looking at him."

The Stranger entered the room, sat down on the bed beside a sweetly wheezing woman.

"Time to wake up, sleeping beauty."

"Sleeping beauties are kissed to wake up," she muttered without opening her eyes.

"I'd love too, but you haven't brushed your teeth," the Stranger said moving away just in case.

"What?" the Medium jumped up pulling the blanket up.

"Well, no kiss and you are awake. My comrade has come. We have a small trouble. I'm waiting for you in the lounge. Just don't be slow."

Closing the door, he pressed against the wall: "I'm not in the City yet, and it has started. The Soldier used force to take away the photographs, most likely there are casualties. I don't like that at all and it is going to be worse." He wanted to quit and run away without looking back. Having prayed, he understood that desire was impermissible weakness and slowly went down to the lounge. The Soldier was standing near the window and looking at the road.

"Who is she?" he asked the Stranger who came up to him without turning.

"Medium."

"A medium? A guide between the world of the dead and the living?"

"No this is her name."

"So, I've heard about her. What sort of acquaintances you have," the Soldier grinned bewildered. "She is a close friend of the Seer. She can't be trusted."

"We live in the time when we cannot trust ourselves," the Stranger smiled remembering an old joke.

The Medium came up.

"This is Soldier," the Stranger introduced his comrade.

"I can see he is no general," she said drily.

"This is Medium," the Stranger uttered meaningfully.

"I can see she is not a kind fairy," despite the outer beauty of the woman, the Soldier found something repelling in her. Her eyes were strong and searching but without kindness.

"Glad you are friends now," the Stranger joked to clear the air. "Let's talk business."

The Soldier looked at the woman askance once again, displeased.

"Here are photos I have taken from the agents. The Seer knew about our plans and passed the photographs to the security with the only purpose to detain us."

"Are you sure you know what you are talking about?" the Medium looked at him surprised.

"I can answer for every word," the Soldier rapped out firmly.

"He is right," the Stranger supported him. "We'll think over the Seer's reasons later. Now we must think how to get to the City doing without the railway."

"I'll call the Seer and find out what is going on," the Medium suggested. She was apparently upset.

"People like Seer never act rashly. He knows what he is doing," the Stranger said.

"Maybe he is right and you shouldn't go to the City. The Seer really knows what he is talking about. He couldn't convince you and resorted to security agents, although I categorically against cooperation with these people," the Medium was watching him warily.

"The Seer is a great man but he is only human and thinks in human categories. And I have heard the voice other than human that is why I'm going to the City. You can leave me," the Stranger said calmly but firmly.

"Your power has shattered the Seer," the Soldier rapped out again. "I've seen it with my own eyes. I've seen you and I've seen him. I'm with you."

"I need to talk with the Seer," the Medium insisted.

"It's your right," the Stranger smiled. "Call him."

"This is silly," the Soldier whispered. "She will betray us."

"Let's step away. Let's not interfere," the Stranger asked him and added confidently: "she will not betray us. The Seer can find us without her help."

"You are too trusting," the Soldier sounded doubtful.

The Medium moved away and dialed the number, several minutes passed before the Seer answered.

"Glad to hear you, baby. I've been thinking about you. You wanted to pop in, didn't you?" he said amiably.

"Have I woken you up?"

"I'm not sleeping. What's wrong?" the Seer caught anxiety in the voice of his friend.

"Do you know the Stranger?"

"Who is this?" the Seer asked her as indifferently as possible, but his heart started to beat violently.

"He and his companion visited you yesterday."

"How do you know?"

"I saw them leave your house. Got to know one of them. The Stranger is a very interesting person. Such people are not to be hurt, it's dangerous," the Medium reminded him.

"It is he who is dangerous," the Seer said coarsely. "And he doesn't understand the weapon he has."

"And why have you set your dogs on him?"

"I have asked them not to make any harm to him. By the way, his friend has sent two agents to hospital. And that's without mentioning the Stranger's abilities. I think if he finds his way to the City, the consequences will be most unpredictable," the Seer wanted understanding.

"When did you start to care for the world's destiny?" the Medium sounded mocking.

"Don't forget who you are, girl," he stopped her. "Remember who you are talking with. I won't ask you to help to detain them, but I beg you, keep away from them."

He put down the receiver, feeling irritated. His doubts evaporated. The Seer saw a pattern.

"Why is she with him? What is going on? A mere chance? Natural development of a programmed event? A mechanism of which the Stranger is a part has been activated? But this mechanism is dangerous for people as it can trigger forces that will make many people suffer. But aren't there disasters and wars I care about no more than others? Why am I worried? What can the Stranger do? Destroy the City? No. Certainly, not. Although there were times when such people provoked the strongest earthquakes. Even so, what do I care? If the City is destined to be destroyed, let it be destroyed and no matter the reason. Why have I turned against him? No reasonable explanation," suddenly the Seer had a strange idea: "and what if I'm programmed to resist him?" This thought made him unwell. He did not want to consider that version as he thought himself an independent individual.

"Run away, run away from this land of prophets and quacks. Forget everything!"

He imagined how he left the country and forgot about the Stranger, and felt he was losing his power. Panic was slowly overwhelming him. "I can't act otherwise. I wish I could, but I can't."

He lay down on the floor and a tear of powerless despair ran down his cheek onto the cedar parquet floor.

After her conversation with the Seer, the Medium smoked a cigarette and closed her eyes.

"What's happening?" the Stranger asked.

"Strange," she said exhaling smoke. "I don't recognize the Seer. He finds you dangerous."

"For whom?"

"For me too," she drawled.

"Are you with us? Then hurry up," the Soldier interfered addressing the woman.

"I don't know yet, but definitely not against you," the Medium answered.

"First thing you must do is to change your looks, remove the beard and have your hair cut," the Soldier hinted the Stranger.

"And what about you? Grow hair and beard in several minutes. That's what you were taught?" the Stranger tried to joke but no one smiled.

"I'll handle this. Not tanned skin will show up after you shave, take her tinting cream. Do not look sullen, that's for business. You don't want to break enemies, do you? Then walk unnoticed. Can you help him at least here?" the Soldier asked the woman.

"Sure. Let's go to the room," she took the Stranger by his hand and drew him after her.

The Soldier went to the men's room in the hotel lounge. He took out a wig, put it on his close cut balding head, placed elegant spectacles with non- myopic glasses on the nose, glued on moustache and beard, took off his coat and tucked it in the bag. Took off his trousers and sharply turned them out, they were double-sided: one side was dark grey and the other light blue; he was seen wearing the first version. He stretched his shoulders.

"I need to be several centimeters shorter. Will have to slouch a bit."

Chapter 12 The Tower

After the conversation with his friend, the Seer sat down in the armchair and started to tune onto the Stranger's image trying to locate him but could not. He was either anxious, such tasks required complete confidence in own power, or the Stranger was closed, and that could happen, although rarely. The Seer easily tuned on the image of his friend and now just had to look where she was.

He saw lifts, glass doors, a bar, and rooms. "They are in a hotel. Could have guessed at once," the Seer complained. He called the servant and in a couple of minutes had a printout with all nearest hotels. There were only six hotels in the list. The Seer circled the Tower and called his acquaintance.

"Good afternoon. I know where they are. Can you dispatch your people to the Tower hotel?"

"Good afternoon, my friend," the Functionary started to peak hesitantly. "You see, it has become a bit complicated. We've found the fingerprints of the man who made a performance at the railway station. They belong to an officer of the General Army Headquarters. By the way, he is one of the best and a very distinguished man. We cannot impose administrative arrest; our authority does not apply to the people of this level. If he has a criminal record, you can call the police and they will take care of him."

"I see. I'm not interested in that one, I want the other man."

"The one with a beard?" the Functionary asked to be sure.

"Yes. I need him. If possible, detain him, but I repeat, do it gently," the Seer emphasized the last word.

"Ok. We can detain him. He is not connected with government authorities, is he? Or maybe I don't have some information?"

"No, he isn't. He can be related to some authorities higher than the government ones," the Seer answered gloomily.

"With whom? Oh, I see…" the Functionary sounded ironic. "I don't care about this. I'm sending my people to the Tower."

The Seer pressed the cancel button without bidding goodbye, irritated.

"Oh, you look nice. I've thought you are older," the Medium said admiring the Stranger.

"I'll be old again soon. Let's go, have a look at the Soldier," the Stranger touched his smooth cheeks with his hands. He left some hair on his chin and above the upper lip and made his hair in a braid.

They went down and could hardly recognize their comrade: a cultural dark-haired man was looking at them through spectacles.

"You haven't changed your boots," the Stranger pointed at his footwear.

"Have you recognized me at once?" the Soldier asked dissatisfied.

"Recognition does not necessarily imply seeing with your eyes, feeling is enough," the Stranger stated and added, "you have excellently changed your appearance."

"But you don't look like a law-abiding citizen anyway, you smell of blood and death," the Medium said scornfully.

"My dear lady, could you be as kind as to do me a favor?" the Soldier addressed the woman. He did not like it when he was reminded of his work and all the more so, when he was judged.

She nodded and said smiling:

"It seems like this phrase is the most difficult in transformation. I'm all ears, my gallant knight."

He said slowly and harshly looking in her eyes:

"Fuck you, stinking witch…"

The woman's eyes filled with rage. She made fists and stepped towards the grinning Soldier.

The Stranger caught her hands.

"Stay calm," he whispered. "Do not be hurt. You have insulted him. And you are wrong. There would be more evil without the ones of his kind. You know nothing about him."

"Fuck you all!" she broke away from him and almost ran to the exit.

The Soldier made a false remorse grimace and looked at the Stranger.

The Medium almost ran into a man in sports clothes at the main entrance. He was followed by two more people wearing official suits. One of them silently approached the headwaiter sitting at the table, showed his ID, and took out a photograph from his pocket. The Medium halted. Her face became tense and attentive.

The Soldier gave the Stranger a packet of cigarettes and said under his breath:

"Stay calm. They can't see us yet. Hope this bitch will not betray us. Take a cigarette."

"I don't smoke. Look here's a Don't Smoke sign," the Stranger said impassively.

"Right. I'll quit soon. Do take it. I know what I'm talking about."

"Gentlemen," they heard a hotel employee say. "Smoking is prohibited here. Go outside."

"Oh, sorry, we didn't mean that! We will go in the open air," the Soldier apologized and whispered, "when you are passing the agents, breathe out more smoke. Come."

A security agent was closely watching the Stranger.

"Wait! Come up to me!"

"Don't turn around, go on. Hail a taxi and leave fast. I'll call you. I'll handle them."

The Soldier slowly approached the agent.

"Sorry, what's the problem? What do you want?"

"I am not after you. Call your friend."

"I know him!" the Medium exclaimed suddenly pointing her long finger at the photograph, which the man in the suit was showing to hotel guests. "This is my fiancé. Where have you taken his photograph?"

"Oh, yes," the hotel employee confirmed. "This woman with the man in the photo checked-in last evening."

"Where is he now?" the agent asked coarsely.

"In our room taking a bath," the Medium answered and looked at the Soldier.

"What is the room number?" the security employee snapped.

"I'm not going to tell you that," the woman showed her deepest scorn in the phrase. "Wait half an hour until he goes downstairs."

"Room number!" the agent croaked piercing the hotel administrator with his stare.

"Just a moment. Room's number forty," the hotel employee chummed.

"Keys, hurry up!" the agent stretched his hand towards the woman.

The Medium showed a vulgar sign demonstrating her rude refusal to obey.

"Stay with her!" the agent shouted to his companion and ran to fetch a reserve key the hotel administrator gave him. "You, come with me!" he told the guy wearing a sports uniform and then turned to the woman, "and you, slut, wait until I come back."

The Medium looked up at the Soldier and showed him an equally rude gesture to get lost.

But he would not.

"What a beautiful woman!" the Soldier exclaimed and went towards her. He came level with the security officer glancing at the woman, went around him, and sharply hit him on the neck with a fist. He instantaneously turned the agent around and hit him in the groin with the knee. The Agent bent moaned tunelessly wide-eyed and fell onto the floor shuddering with pain. The Medium looked up at the Soldier satisfied. He took her hand and ran to the exit.

The Stranger was waiting for them at the hotel.

"Why haven't you left?" the Soldier asked him when they were driving away in the car.

"I knew you would be out soon."

"And your girlfriend did a good job. Excellent performance."

"I'm not his girlfriend," the Medium said gruffly.

"We know whose girlfriend you are. No pass," the Soldier grinned. "But you really did a good job. You haven't lost your composure. By the way, Stranger, she called you her fiancé. A nice couple you are: he with a white glow and she in the dark mist. A paradox."

Chapter 13. Prophesy

The Functionary called the Seer and reported the incident in the hotel:

"The Stranger had accomplices, a man and a woman, who helped him to escape. One of our employees was severely wounded."

"That's too sad. Specify the account details of the injured I'll pay compensation."

"I don't mean that," the Functionary waved his hand. "They are to blame, that haven't recognized the Soldier in his new dress-up, rose to the woman. We have lost three agents during the day. These are very serious incidents. I won't be able to control field agents if they decide to avenge their comrades. And then, we really need a solid basis for detention of the people, otherwise, we might be involved in a scandal."

"Three injured agents are not grounds for detention?" The Seer's mood was rapidly fading.

"No. We can't make this incident public, journalists learn about this and we'll be in trouble. And what if we have interfered with the operation of our colleagues from another agency?"

"I see," the Seer said gloomily. "Thank you for everything. Sorry for bothering you. All the best."

"Wait," the Functionary hurried to say. "There is another way."

"Speak up."

"You can go to private agencies. But it is not going to be cheap," the Functionary breathed out.

"Ok. Thank you for your advice. I'll think about it," the Seer said dismissively and hung up.

He did not doubt that the woman the Functionary mentioned was the Medium. He was displeased that she had disobeyed, had not followed his advice and, more than that, she helped the person who was a potential threat to people like her. The Seer understood that many people were a danger but was it a sufficient reason to attack? A seeing person can tell a real threat from an imaginary one and should take preventive measures only in case of a real danger.

But his decisiveness was limited by the boundaries he would not cross. The Seer did not think twice and rejected the idea of hiring private detectives as he feared their non-professional actions would harm the Stranger. What then? Will his good intentions bring death to the Stranger? Will they add agony to hardships?

The Seer was trying to visualize what would happen when the Stranger would come in the City, but in vain. He still felt the urge to do something. First thing, he decided to separate his friend from the Stranger. It is not banal jealousy, rather fear: if the anomalous abilities of the Medium provoke the Stranger, the consequences of an energy blow can be disastrous. The Seer understood that and started to act without a twinge of conscience and even enthusiastically. He sat down in the armchair and concentrated. He rarely made people to act against their will. But this is a special case and requires special measures …

A taxi drove the companions from the dangerous place. The Stranger asked to halt near the park. He liked to walk along the alleys, feel leaves, and freshly mown grass. The passengers got out of the car, walked around the garden, came up to a small pond emitting freshness and easily found an empty bench in the shadow of a shaggy oak.

"I will go to the railway alone to see what is going on," the Soldier suggested.

"We'll go together. I think there is no threat at the railway," the Stranger said.

"Why? Aren't you are wanted?" the Medium asked.

"They are probably looking for us but I can't feel danger," the Stranger answered.

"However strange that may sound, me either, and I am also used to trust my feelings," the Soldier was thoughtful. "But agents never forgive insults and always repay debts. We do the same not to take revenge but to teach others so that it does not become a habit."

"You may be right but do not forget: they are intelligence acting against us and if they want, they will catch you in any other place in the City if not at the railway," the Medium said in an indifferent and exhausted voice.

"Quite probable," the Soldier supported her version. "To keep a seizure group at the railway station is expensive, the more so that they don't know when we are going to show up. The group must consist of at least six people. The easiest way is to have two observers, one will watch the ticket office and the other will be at the railway platform, and take pictures of everything suspicious. These images will be analyzed and checked with special software. If they are identical, an armed agent group will be sent to detain us as soon as we leave the rail car. 24-hour survey security cameras can also be installed. Then these cameras will be everywhere, even in the can. We don't know about the scope of the operation but I think the agents did not take it seriously and sent few people to detain us. It's sad. No cordon, amateurship …"

"Calm down," the Stranger interrupted him mildly. "They are not police. They are security. I think they don't take us for criminals. Although these people are manically distrustful, they are no fools. The Seer probably asked his friend to detain us and that is why the operation scope is limited."

"You are right," the Medium interfered. "It is the Seer who wants to detain you. He believes that your energy will show up in the City and will be a threat to City residents. Moreover the agent in the hotel showed around your photograph only," the woman looked up and down the skinny Stranger. "And three people are too many to detain you. I don't know what the right way to choose is. Understand me; the Seer is a very intelligent and far-sighted man. He knows what he is doing..."

Suddenly the woman's eyes sparkled and perspiration showed on her forehead. The Stranger looked into her eyes, felt something, and listened attentively, while she continued:

"Don't go to the City. Your power is free to destroy," the Medium seemed to have lost control of her, she was breathing heavily, and falteringly. "You will be our judge. Who will resist your spirit, who will be able to fight? I know who you are. He has sent you and who is able to withstand the arrival of your Prince? Who will survive when he appears?" the Medium was in a trance, her countenance sharpened, she had a slightly croaky voice, and her pupils widened.

The Stranger got up from the bench. He felt the Wind. He felt how the skin on his head was getting numb impacted by that power, as if needles pierced his head, or to the contrary, protruded from it. Human consciousness was going away… The Wind took hold of the Stranger's will.

"Do not speak," he commanded. "Do not speak. I prohibit you to do this," the Stranger put one of his hands on the woman's nape and the second on the forehead and uttered slowly: "do not worry her anymore."

The Medium shuddered from head to toes, her hands were shaking, and she became very pale. She was nauseated.

"I feel bad, very bad… Let me go."

"That's fine. It's better like this. You will feel better," the Stranger said, caressing her black hair. At the last movement he saw how the Power was breaking the woman. Some more time and it would crush her. So, he let the power go. The Medium pressed against his chest and wept.

The Soldier turned away, took out a cigarette from a pack, looked at it, crumpled it, and threw away. Tears welled in his eyes. The Soldier was rejoicing as a kid. He believed that he faced miracle again: the Stranger won from the Seer, drove a demon out of the Medium. Now he is on the right side, among the warriors of the light. No one will be able to stop him now.

Chapter 14. Husband and wife

The Functionary sprawled on the sofa in his two-level apartment and was sipping twenty-year cognac from a glass and smoking a cigar rolled on the bodies of black beauties, at least that was the supplier's version. The Functionary was relaxing. He was disturbed that he could not satisfy the request of the man who was so important to his family.

"What's wrong, darling?" his spouse came up, sat down beside him, and covered his hand with hers.

The Functionary often shared with her government-level rumors and secrets and thus maintained his authority in her eyes. He did not know if he should tell her about his conversation with the Seer and its consequences or conceal it, being aware that the whole case was unflattering. But he wanted to share and learn her opinion which could help to make another decision. He exhaled another jet of smoke:

"I'd like to tell you something. I think you might find it interesting. Do you remember the night when I had to leave unexpectedly?"

"Yes, darling. Sure, I do. I'm used to it. That's your work. Where have you been?"

"I visited the Seer."

She became nervous and took a sip from his glass.

"He called and asked for an unusual request," the Functionary fell silent again.

"Don't keep me waiting," his wife's eyes opened with curiosity. She understood that the visit to the Seer had nothing to do with her.

"He asked me to detain two people whom he found to be a menace to the society. I sent my guys twice to hunt and to no avail, they failed. I have decided to roll the operation back because one of the suspects works for a powerful government authority. I don't have power to detain a man of this level. I've broken the rules."

"Whose task are these people carrying through? Do you know what their purpose is?"

"No," the Functionary shrugged. "They are eager to get to the City, but no one helps them. They seem to be all by themselves. I think the Seer doesn't know what to expect from them or knows this, but hides this information thoroughly. One thing is certain. He is interested in catching them."

"Can't you do something for him?" his wife asked compassionately.

"I suggested that he should go to a private company; he listened to me and hung up. Of course, this problem can be solved without his approval, the more so that the Seer has allocated some money to detain them …"

He should not have said the last sentence.

"And you took the money?" she raised her voice. "Have you forgotten everything?"

"How could I refuse when he stuck a packet in my hands! The Seer hypnotized me," the Functionary was not sure if his wife would believe that smart story. "The Seer is a strange man: some people hypnotize to take something, while he does this to give you something. Who can understand an unworldly man?"

She calmed down a bit.

"You must help him," she squeezed his hand. "Hire people. If you don't have enough money, we'll pay extra. Maybe he has noticed danger and tries to do something before something horrible happens? Your responsibility is the security of the society. That's your job."

"You see, darling… It's two different things: to pursue a criminal that all people are anxious to see jailed or detain someone who has not offended the law. Charge a person without direct or indirect evidence? Make him a criminal based on a tip-off? It's very dangerous. Witch-hunting was the darkest and most horrible times in human history. A crowd, that believes any slander, will agree to the actions of such clairvoyants as the Seer, but no normal court will condemn a person for an uncommitted crime. Can you judge a person based on clairvoyant premonitions? Do you know about a changeable psychological factor and why court wouldn't accept the evidence from a lie detector? Because an experienced criminal can cheat, while a frightened innocent person can condemn himself. Even if the Seer is right many times, but without direct evidence, DNA test, fingerprints, appearance or voice check, or witnesses our society will be in the darkness drowning in anarchy with a quick to judge court."

"And if someone is going to offend the law?"

"This is to be proven. And how would you do this? Suppose police detains a suspicious person in front of the bank. He is searched, and a gun, stocking, and a bag are found. Can we pursue him for robbery? No. For attempted robbery? No, either."

"What about the gun, stocking, and the bag?" his wife would not agree.

"He can be pursued for carrying unregistered arms, but the suspect can say that he has just found it and is carrying it to the police station. A stocking happens to be in the pocket by accident and the bag is for shopping. Unless he confesses and admits an attempted robbery, they'll have to let him go. The same with a foreteller, everything seems clear, he describes the appearance and habits of the suspect, crime details, but does not provide evidence or proof."

"But there are administrative arrests. No charge is needed to jail a person in this case."

"Administrative arrests are typically based on accusations of trusted persons. The investigator must find evidence and make the suspect confess as soon as possible. If he lingers and evidence is not found, the detained person is released. But we even have not been tipped off. We are not police. We cannot plant drugs, weapons, provoke a fight or hire a prostitute to have the suspect charged with rape. There are dozens of ways how to put a man in jail, but our service is engaged in investigating real crimes," the Functionary explained proudly.

"Hire people to at least follow him! Sure, it's not the whim or eccentricity of the Seer. If he warns about a threat, there is danger."

"I'll do that. Good advice," the Functionary assured her. "But I don't think it is a threat to the society. The Seer has never warned of pending terrorist's acts or asked to detain a criminal. His acquaintances happened to warn about acts of terrorism when he told them not to go to certain places. We always treat such messages with care."

"Have you asked him to cooperate?"

"A couple of times. But he always answered that he belonged to the whole world. The Seer is a cosmopolite and helps politicians only with personal matters. Today he is with us, and tomorrow with another agency or in another country, which is our enemy. All are willing to receive him, all have problems."

"Then why has he asked to detain them."

"I don't know. Maybe they are a danger to him or his friends? I believe the clue is in the City. What do you think; shall I give them a chance to get to the City?" the Functionary said cautiously.

"You tried to detain them and failed, but you can pursue them. Hire people."

"I am afraid my guys can not only pursue, but also leave traces. Rumors of injured comrades spread fast and it will be hard to prevent our guys from violence," the Functionary sighed.

"Then don't lose time, darling."

The Functionary was pleased: everything seemed to be more or less comfortable. He was torn by curiosity and wanted to know the reason why the Seer resorted to him.

"Many people are waiting for the Seer's fall," the Functionary was thinking. "I hope, someone will take him down somewhat. And what if this person is the Stranger? The Seer seems to fear him. I can use this to make an interesting game called the 'counterbalance' and besides earn points for an excellent idea. Now I don't have time to lose, I must act."

Chapter 15. Keys

Two men and a woman entered the cafe. They had coffee in silence and headed for the railway. The Soldier was still wearing the wig, but took off his spectacles. The Medium was sighing all the time. She seemed to have difficulty walking. The Stranger was thoughtful and sometimes looked up at the woman who felt unwell and finally decided to ask her,

"Do you feel unwell?"

"I can't walk. Legs can barely support me. I'll give you keys from my home and come later."

"The Seer," the Stranger whispered unheard.

"Go away. I'll come in a couple of days," she could not look in his eyes.

The Stranger fetched the keys, tossed them, caught deftly, held them in his hands as if weighing.

"We'll find shelter. We don't need them."

The Medium smiled apologetically, looked askance, and took her keys back.

The Soldier stretched his hand.

"I'll be glad to see you."

The woman pressed the hand with the tips of her fingers, drew the Soldier against her chest and whispered in his ear, "Take care of him."

She looked into the Stranger's eyes.

"We'll see each other soon," she said hugging him.

"I also think so," he said with a forced smile.

The Medium stretched her hand to hail a taxi. A car appeared at once as if ordered. The woman took the seat near the driver, opened the window and turned to the Stranger. The taxi started and was soon out of sight.

"It's good you haven't taken the keys. People in ambush are hard to dodge…" the Soldier grinned.

"I was thinking about something else. She won't set agents on us."

"But she can leak information. If two know, know all pigs about. So, are we going to the railway station?" the Soldier asked doubtfully.

"Who has a good sense of danger? Why don't you ask yourself?" the Stranger evaded an answer.

"Feels Ok. No pressure. Where is she going?" the Soldier nodded at the leaving taxi.

"To the Seer, I think. He has called her," the Stranger said quietly.

"After everything she's been through?"

"Calm down. She is not against us. It's not as simple as it seems at first glance. Have you ever been in a strong sea current?"

"I have," the Soldier frowned.

"What did you do?"

"Relaxed, saved my strength, I was swimming in waves until I was beyond the current."

"Were you taken away far from the shore?"

"Yes."

"What then?"

"I swam to the shore. I was swimming underwater almost all the time and surfaced only to breathe in some fresh air. I was fast carried by waves and very soon sprawled on the sand. So, what?"

"It is the same offshore or onshore," the Stranger answered mysteriously.

"Explain. I don't get it."

"There is a dangerous current both onshore and offshore. It takes you away
away from your goal. You cannot fight it but can just watch. The most important thing is to feel the time when it weakens to get out and proceed to your goal."

"How can you feel that?"

"A developed and trained body excellently responds to temperature changes, starting a thermal regulation process. The same with your soul: develop it, making respond to changes. Then you will find and feel a favorable current which will take you to the saving shore."

The taxi halted at the Seer's house. The Medium came up to the gate but did not dare to call. She was standing and waiting patiently. A couple of minutes later the gate opened and she walked along the path of colored bricks along the alley. Having approached the nearest bench, she sat down exhausted.

Soon she heard hasty steps of the host. He was almost running, pulling his mutilated leg.

"I've been waiting for you," the Seer cautiously sat down nearby. "I'm very glad you have come. Would you like some tea or coffee?"

"Yes, later. Sit down, be with me," she took his hand and pressed it hard.

"You can't be with him. His power is mortal for you. It can deprive you of your talent, weaken you and make you a nonentity," the Seer was consoling her.

"It's late," the Medium said dully.

"What's happened? What? Tell me!"

"I don't know. I was in a trance. It happened against my will and very fast. I started to prophesy something."

"What were you saying?"

"I don't really remember," she was looking in one point. "Initially I was speaking about you. Suddenly I felt that I was engulfed, taken away. I was knocked down and can remember only fragments of what I said then. I think I was saying something about the Stranger and the Prince but I don't remember the details. Then I felt the Stranger's hand touching my head, I was clamped and felt fear. I was nauseated as if I were sick. Then it let me go, I felt good, quiet and light. I wept, maybe because I felt happy: I saw the world with other eyes as if I were a kid long ago, but then I felt sad again and understood how scary it was to lose the world you were used to. I panicked and here I am with you. I feel so sad, on the verge of moaning."

"You need sleep, dear girl," he stroked her hair. "I will put you to sleep, you will relax and then we'll discuss everything."

"I won't be able to go to sleep now."

"My dear, once I managed to put to sleep an audience of about three hundred people, and I will surely handle one small tired girl. Don't worry: I'll put you to sleep."

"You can put me to sleep forever," she tried to smile.

"Silly one," the Seer said taking the woman by the elbow. "You'll sleep two or three hours, that'll be enough to come to. Then we'll think what is to be done. I don't mean bad to the Stranger, believe me."

The woman lay down on the sofa. The Seer covered her with a rug blanket, touched her forehead and said quietly, "You are going to sleep, you feel good and calm, all your troubles are going away. Sleep fast." The Medium fell to sleep almost immediately.

The Seer was beside her for some time, then fetched the telephone, and dialed the number:

"I cancel my order; do not even keep track of them."

"Ok," the Functionary agreed lightly. "We won't follow these people anymore. If you want something else, I'll be glad to help. Now I'm in a hurry, sorry."

"Good bye, all the best," the Seer answered mechanically and turned off the phone. He felt a lie.

"Where is deception here? The Functionary mentioned three things. He does not follow these people. Offered help. Told me he was in a hurry. Will help, no way out, but won't enjoy that and won't be eager to please. He does not lie that he is in a hurry. We don't follow these people," the Seer repeated the last phrase he heard twice. "That's a lie. Oh, that's more than a lie. Maybe I still have time to reverse the situation."

The Seer dialed the Functionary again, but no one answered. He paced the room: "That's all right, that's all right, and I'll find a way."

Chapter 16. Versions

The Functionary was in a hurry, he had time to give necessary instructions to his non-staff agents, deliver instructions to conduct concealed observation, and send photographs. It was necessary to increase the number of operations members but that required special sanctions and the Functionary decided to receive them notifying his line commander of the events. He understood how difficult it would be to receive the permit as there was nothing criminal in a journey to the City and almost anyone was entitled to go there. The Seer's warnings were not enough. The Functionary decided to act and claim that the operation was aimed against the employee of another agency.

Several chief officers were present in the office of the security commander. After he had shaken hands with everyone, the Functionary cautiously took his seat.

"Do you have an urgent matter?"

"Yes, I think so."

"Do you prefer to talk in private?" the Chief inquired.

"No, this information is not so secret. Last night the Seer called me," when that name was mentioned, tense silence set in. "He asked me to see him. You know how much I owe him."

"It's not good to be indebted to anyone, especially in our work," the Chief noted. "No offence. Speak on."

"The Seer asked me, without explaining his reasons, to detain two law-abiding citizens of the country and prevent them from entering the City. He thinks that once they are in the City, these guys will escalate a conflict."

"I believe the reason is absolutely clear. The Seer does not want the fragile and temporary peace between different groups of population to end," one of the employees ventured to say.

"Do not interrupt. We will think later," the Chief checked him. "Speak on."

"I dispatched several security agents. Before they had time to disperse across the railway station building, a person came up to one of the employees, soaked him in vodka, saw the photographs, and ran to the men's room. Two of our agents decided to check but he unexpectedly attacked them. We took his fingerprints," the Functionary made a pause. "It is the Soldier, known in certain circles," he pointed his finger up. "He is a professional liquidator, one of the best or maybe the best of his kind. I explained the Seer that we could not arrest that person. Then he asked to catch the other. It is a Stranger. He managed to escape from the hotel and again with the Soldier's help. Here's a detailed report of our agents. If you are interested in this case, we can expand the number of observers to include the City in the scope of the operations," the Functionary kept silent for several minutes. "This is about all I was going to report."

"It's interesting. Do you have versions?" the Chief addressed his officers.

"It can be assumed," one of his employees started, "that the Seer thought it was necessary to warn us of a pending conflict in the City provoked by the persons involved. But there are two questions in this case: who are they and whose task does the Soldier fulfill? If the information on the Soldier is correct, we know the customer. It's a political order or an army operation. We should think if we want to interfere with the operation of another agency."

"And how a conflict situation in the City can be provoked by one person?" the Functionary asked.

"It is clear that you are not an operations officer," his colleague commented. "For instance, sacred objects can be desecrated. It is enough to show your ass during a public prayer. The City is a kind of a tinderbox now, you just throw a match and it is on fire. The Soldier can be sent to destroy one of political or religious leaders."

"We can assume the Soldier aims at destruction of the object that harms the country," another employee ventured his observation, "rather than escalation of a conflict."

"Other versions?" the Chief asked. Silence set in.

"I see that the situation is unclear," the Chief summed up. "The Seer can play own game, his personal game. And use us while keeping in the dark. And he won't rescue any religious leader. By the way, why does the Soldier need the Stranger? I've heard about the Soldier, he works alone and does not carry out political orders. He shoots terrorists, militants, and rebels. That's his qualifications. Why would he be assigned other tasks? It is not a custom, you can't teach old dog new tricks. The City is generally out of his scope, as far as I know no liquidator has been involved there lately. And why has the Seer asked to catch the Stranger? The Soldier can't complete the operation without him, can he? It means the Stranger plays a role, doesn't he? Maybe no less important than the role of the Soldier. Why have they decided to take the train when there are other opportunities to get to the City? Military intelligence couldn't equip a plane? Who is going on a task by train? Nonsense. Too many questions and I don't like this. We should send experienced agents to the City and spy secretly. Find all information about the Stranger and report to me. And do not try to detain the Soldier. Owing to your ill-thought actions," he glanced at the Functionary sternly, "we can spoil the relations with the General Staff, which are quite tense now, and a complex operation we know nothing about. Possibly, there is no
operation at all. Friends decided to go to the City and bad men do not allow them to enjoy the right of a citizen: move freely. You all can go."

The Functionary was leaving the director's office in a bad mood. He assumed that the commander would not challenge that the Soldier acted upon instructions of the General Staff and would not miss the chance of using that in the secret war between security agencies and was one of the main stimuli for their high performance. One thing has become clear: they will not allow him to lead the case. Superior commanders consider the Seer's abilities as a threat to national security. The man, who, if he desired so, could disclose any secret, was very dangerous. And the agency had many secrets.

The Functionary decided to inform the Seer that the case would be under official control. He dialed the number.

"Hello," a familiar voice said.

"It's me again. Can we meet?" the Functionary asked cautiously.

"I called you earlier, but you didn't answer. It continues, doesn't it?"

"I haven't heard the telephone call," he said surprised and the Seer felt that his interlocutor was not lying. "Are you interested in discussing the situation?"

"Come to my place. I'm waiting for you."

Chapter 17. Stereotype

The companions were approaching the railway station. The Stranger asked the Soldier:

"What do you think why have I been instructed to meet you?"

"And you had such instructions, hadn't you?" the Soldier was surprised.

"I hope so."

"How?"

"I understood that I need a man who can discover a deadly threat in a heap of identical stones and neutralize it. I found you using the map with my eyes closed and came to the mentioned territory. I wandered a bit and saw two young men. I thought they were threatened. Something heavy overhung them. I came up closer, and looked in their faces and understood who they were. I wanted to pass by but couldn't," the Stranger fell silent and reluctantly continued several minutes later, "I told them the road they chose would lead them to death. And they believed me."

"Why?"

"I spoke with the presence of the Power and they were jittery and susceptible, and understood at once. Sometime later, I met a gloomy man in ragged jeans and understood that was the person I was looking for."

"You did," the Soldier drawled and smiled gloomily, "but not the right one."

"How come?"

"I haven't found a land mine among stones. All in all, I've found different mine. It's not as difficult as it seems at first glance, especially if you know your surroundings well. But I don't disarm them. I communicate with the operations army facility and they send mine pickers."

"And can you disarm an explosive device?" the Stranger thought he asked a very important question.

"Once several years ago I saw or rather felt danger. I looked around and saw an AP mine hanging from the tree. I shot and neutralized the mobile device, which served as a detonator. Local residents, mostly teenagers ran up hearing the shot, surrounded the place and the bomb exploded," the Soldier was silent for some time. "It turned out to have two detonators, or the mobile phone was a false detonator; the second one was a chain: you step on it and wires close and… No amateurship since that time."

The Stranger amicably poked the frowning Soldier in the shoulder.

"That's all right. People often get in the trap of their stereotypes. First, they build a model and if the events do not fit in with the stereotype, instead of trying to understand what is happening, they destroy everything. The Prince was not accepted in his times because his actions and thoughts did not fit in with the stereotype resulting from incorrect understanding of ancient prophesies."

"I've heard about the Prince," the Soldier became thoughtful. "He was a good preacher. I liked some of his conversations. Especially, when he had a go at priests, preachers, well, all. He accused them of spiritual bankruptcy and showed them who they were and who he was. The Prince was declared an outlaw, was promised an award for his capture, all were hunting for him. This rabble caught him assisted by an informer, slaughtered without trial or record and left his corpse in the City to be seen by everyone. People were made to pass by and spit on him. Those who refused were beaten up and jailed.

Then as far as I remember, the legend says that angels came to the square at night and resurrected him. Of course, there were people who stated and even swore that they saw him alive, and almost at the same time, in different places, some of which were located at a distance from each other. They were tortured to recant from their words.

Several years later a riot happened in the country. Priests, preachers, and sorcerers were killed especially cruelly. Rebels found a motive to avenge the Prince and they are still taking revenge against anyone who does not honor him. Now he has many worshippers all over the world among pacifists and terrorists. The irony of fate, when alive he was considered mad and when he died, he became a sage. And his offspring still receive donations, a home museum was setup: here's the stone the Prince used to sit on, and here's the cup he used to drink from. Well, do I know the history and religion, what you'd say?" the Soldier boasted.

"You don't know the most important thing."

"What is the most important thing?"

"The Prince has the power to change the world by changing the man."

"Why hasn't he changed it? Look, there's still as much shit as there used to be."

"He changes it but it isn't so perceptible. Without him, humankind would develop in another way, a much worse way. Still, there is much shit, that's true, because the way proposed by the Prince was rejected by most."

"You are speaking of him as if he were alive. Do you think he is alive? Do you believe he was resurrected by angels? This is the rebels' belief."

"Resurrected, reanimated… supreme forces   can do more than that. He is alive, Soldier, he is alive. He was dead but came back to life," the Stranger said confidently, fell silent and asked, "and would you spit on his body?"

The Soldier shrugged his shoulders.

"I fought against rebels, but I rather like the Prince," he explained.

"The rebels have nothing to do with the Prince, they are not his servants. They just used his name for their purposes: power overthrow, tyranny, and destruction of their political enemies. They distorted the Prince's teachings and degraded his name."

"You think I am the person you need in the City, don't you?" the Soldier looked at the Stranger slightly squinting.

"I don't know why I am going to the City, but I am unlikely to get there without you. And God knows what happens."

"Here's the railway station," the Soldier nodded towards a three-storied building. "Briefing first. We enter the building one by one, you go first. You enter, walk like all others, come up to the cafeteria, buy something and sit down with your face towards the counter. Don't turn around, eat and drink calmly. If you are caught, I'll find a way to take you out. Good luck."

"Don't worry," the Stranger seemed calm. "We are not alone. The Heaven is with us."

The Soldier was attentively watching the Stranger; he did not like that almost all passengers stopped at the gate to listen to the musician singing about an unhappy love. The Stranger also halted. The Soldier came up closer; he could hear the words of the songs of a street singer.

"The musician is a decoy bird. The voice is too good and he plays too professionally," the Soldier was thinking. "It will be hard to make the object out, especially if he looks different than in the photograph. No doubt, they are watching."

The Stranger was standing nearby for some time, then asked the singer to give him the guitar and started to play with the strings. He sang a rhythmical song in quite a pleasant voice. The Soldier did not believe his eyes but understood that he had to use the chance. His companion attracted the agent's attention. The Soldier moved towards the gate. He was ready to fight. Listening to the words of the song, he was even more surprised.

Evil autumn at the prospect
Is carrying around dead leaves.
I'm roaming around the city,
Now I'm lonely.
I come up to the store
To buy wine and margarine,
But I can't understand,
Why I need the margarine.
And you had gone, you had gone
But again remind of you
On the bottle of chip wine
Any letter – W

Having repeated the refrain, the Stranger looked the Soldier in the eyes. The Soldier slowed down, he seemed to hear the order 'Listen!' in his head, and the Stranger sang louder:
We've been chatting about the life

With my homie all the time,
Drinking wine and frying chips…
He said: "Stop fretting,
We'll go and gat girls now!
It's not bad as is:
There are many chicks at the railway here
But there's much infection there,
Where would I get a normal one?

When the Stranger was expressively singing 'There are many chicks at the railway', the Soldier understood everything.

"It's not you who must cover me, I must cover you. Stop it! I won't let anyone draw fire." The Soldier remembered his army friends who had been killed or mutilated trying to save him. He headed for the ticket offices: "Why do I have to run or hide in my own country? I have served it a lot. Why does the person like the Stranger have to perform a concert to these nonentities? That's enough, let them tamper and I'll tear them to pieces."

"Two tickets to the City," he said loudly.

The Soldier deduced an agent: he had a caption on his T-shirt "Kill yourself and save the world" and callous slightly swollen knuckles, palm ribs with muscles as a person going in for battle arts would have. That was totally out of place given his drug-addict pacifist image.

Having fetched the tickets, the Soldier approached the agent and felt (his intuition sharpened at the moments of danger) that two stocky guys separated from the crowd and made several steps towards him.

"Hey, bro, give me a cigarette."

The young man stiffened, turned with his side to the man and answered loudly,

"I don't smoke brother."

"And the legend says you should. You are a bad conspirator," the Soldier said instructively and quietly and moved towards the Stranger.

"The train is in forty minutes, let's go and have a bite."

"You are not worried that several pairs of eyes will be watching you closely while you are feasting?" the Stranger asked.

"Not anymore. If I understand it correctly, they detected us long ago and did not take any measures to detain. It means we have a good chance to eat calmly and even take the train," the Soldier's jaw muscles moved.

"Their instructions changed," the Stranger scratched his forehead.

"When you don't know your adversaries' plan, be ready to see events develop in any way. I think this time they treat it much more seriously."

"You are right, but their readiness to act will not mar my dinner," the Stranger grumbled and headed for the cafeteria.

The comrades ordered cheese buns and tea.

"I've bought tickets, and agents know our seats. Spray gas in the compartment and we won't get to the City, but first bug us to gather intelligence. Most likely they will catch us on the train or when we get out in the City," the Soldier was thoughtful and then asked, "do we have time?"

"I don't know. You propose to detour? We are not lonely. We have help."

"Do you mean heavenly protectors? And so we need to go as an icebreaker?"

"No. This is always a bad idea. Icebreaker breaks, and I do not want to break."

"There are sideways leading to the City and I can guide you. We will change routes, hitchhike, go across the desert, and mountain paths. I warn you, the way to the City will be difficult, but we will reach the goal. And if we go now in this comfortable train, going the direct way, we'll land directly in a trap."

"You couldn't be more right," the Stranger smiled.

The Soldier stood up and said loudly,

"Wait here I need to pee."

"Spare me the details, especially during lunch," the Stranger grumbled and resumed eating.

In the men's room, the Soldier asked a cultured-looking but down-dressed man to buy him two tickets to the train from the station called the Oblivion Hill to a small settlement of Victory, the last station before their destination point, the City. The Soldier made up a story fast telling the man about a jealous wife who hired private detectives to follow him, persuaded the man to take a modest payment for his service, and asked him to place the tickets in the toilet booth rather than give them to him directly. The Soldier came up to the Stranger and almost inaudibly told him:

"When I scratch my nose, you will go to the men's room, the left booth, take out tickets from the toilet paper roll and go back at once."

Sometime later, the Stranger recollected, "I'll go pee."

The Soldier only sighed.

They came into the railcar and closed the compartment door. The Soldier put his finger to his lips, carefully inspected the walls, shelves, and a small table, but found nothing, sat down, and shook his head. The Stranger pointed out with his finger at the ceiling. The Soldier blinked: his eyes ached; the light did not allow seeing properly. He stood up on the table, discovered a small hump on the ceiling near the lamp, nodded to the Stranger and raised his thumb in approval.

"Make yourself comfortable, relax. We'll be in the city in about eight hours, and I'll look for our guys," the Soldier decided to set the agents on the wrong track. If they work on a false version, they will lose time and will hardly enforce actions, if they believe that there are support fighters nearby.

The Soldier left the compartment to watch movements. In case of an attack in confined space, there was a chance to straggle. A young pretty girl was standing in the corridor, looking in the window and rhythmically wagging her head: she was probably listening to music in her headphones.

He came up to her to a disrespectful distance and immediately felt her fear.

"It's a long way, would you like to chat? Make the way shorter?" he proposed to the girl smiling good-heartedly. The girl went pale, pursed her mouth but turning towards him answered calmly:

"I'm tired of conversations. Leave me alone."

And without saying anything else, she returned to the nearest compartment where the Soldier noticed a young woman and a guy.

The girl closed the door behind her.

"What has happened? Why have you left your post?" the man from the compartment was indignant.

"The object tried to speak with me. I don't have instructions what to do in this case," she answered falteringly.

"You can speak with him, but I warn you again, this man is extremely dangerous. Do not betray yourself and us. Now go back. No, you go," the agent nodded at the other employee.

The Soldier dropped by for a minute to warn the Stranger.

"We get out in half an hour. Three agents are in the compartment nearby, one of them is in front of the door," he explained in gestures and mimicry. The Stranger shook his head showing that he is categorically against violence and left for the corridor. He stopped near the girl and scrutinized her.

"I can tell you fortune by your hand," the Stranger almost whispered to the girl and added, "absolutely free of charge."

The girl looked at him surprised, smiled, and hiding her palms behind her back asked him:

"Which hand, left or right?"

"Doesn't matter," the Stranger answered indifferently. "Let's just step aside."

She stretched her right hand. The Stranger was not a chiromancer, he was not even sure that the palm showed fate. But he gently took her hand and concentrated. He thought he could see something hidden, information came to his head in fragments, and he was to put into words his visions and feelings.

The most important thing is not to think too much and say whatever comes to your mind first and needs to be expressed.

"You are from a family with strong family traditions, a well-to-do family," he started. "You have two sisters and a younger brother. Your father is a military, retired, but he seems to be working somewhere, but it is not written on your hand. Your mother is an excellent woman; she suffered much at your father's hands but never stopped loving him or caring for him. By the way, tell her that she requires cardiologic screening, she has high blood pressure. She worries about you and doesn't want you to work in this organization," the Stranger looked in her eyes.

"What organization?" the girl said in a trembling voice.

"Your mother's right, nothing good awaits you here," the Stranger ignored her question. "You have a choice: stay or leave. Possibly, you can work on there but you'll see so much dirt that you will drown in it and lose your soul. Go study to be a medical doctor. You have dreamed about that since you were small. That's your mission."

The girl's lips trembled.

"How do you know all this? Do you know me? Most unlikely," she was peering in his face as if he were a ghost.

"I know that, and that's enough. The God opens this to me," the Stranger assured her. "We have to get off soon, please do not turn around. They will necessarily ask you, you won't lie if you don't turn around. Service to the God is more important than government service."

The Stranger returned to the compartment and made a gesture with his hand, "We get off now, you do nothing."

The Soldier nodded and asked out loudly:

"Do you have a lighter? I'm going out to smoke."

"Take it."

The Soldier opened the door and went directly to the girl. The Stranger took him by the collar of the coat and pulled to the exit as he would pull a disobedient dog. The Soldier did not resist.

"She won't turn around, I've spoken to her."

"I need to tell her something."

The Soldier came up to the girl and whispered: "You'll tell them you saw me leave the compartment with a pack of cigarettes, look at the pack and remember. Good luck. Thank you."

The agent briefly glanced at him and pressed her lips to keep from crying. She was very much frightened.

They silently left, slowly got off the train at the station, sat down onto an empty bench, and waited for the next train, which arrived soon.

"What do you think will happen with the girl?" the Stranger asked.

"I don't know, they may fire her," the Soldier showed indifference on his face. "I've advised her something. Let them think hard. If they run the girl through the detector, which scans brains and identifies areas responsible for lies, even then everything will look true and they won't give her truth drugs, she is not a traitor. The girl really did not see you leave the compartment and go to the entrance. She noticed only me: that is why she will surely pass the inspection. How have you managed to persuade her to let us go?"

"The same I did to make you follow me."

"Well, Ok," the Soldier agreed. "I can smell great deeds awaiting us. You are the massager of the God and fulfill His assignment. I am ready to leave everything and help such a man. I owe much to the God. Without belief, working in my job, you can become a psychopath, go on drugs or alcohol. The God has always helped me. I escaped in absolutely mortal situations: was under shelling, caught in traps, surrounded by the enemy was pursued, and several days wandered in the desert without water. Just imagine, it was ten years ago. I left the army car to pee a bit. And hear a car driving fast in my direction, I turn around and it is in front of me. And suddenly time changes, I can clearly see how two muzzles slowly go out of open windows and start firing at me. They are at close range, two meters, but since time moved slowly, I understood where to move and did not get a scratch. It seemed I even saw bullets."

"An interesting story," the Stranger said. "Only the time did not change, your perception of the time changed. Probably, this is how birds or flies perceive time. They fly at a high speed without any accidents."

"So, it means I turned into a fly?" the Soldier guffawed. "But, if the God wishes to turn me into a man-fly to save me, I have nothing against it."

"Maybe, that's so. But the body of some people in mortal danger or stress is capable of something you could never guess," the Stranger was looking through the window all the time.

"You don't think it was a miracle, do you?" the Soldier was somewhat perplexed.

"Of course, it is a miracle, if you use this word to describe something unusual which still remains unexplained."

"And is there explanation to everything?"

"I'm sure, there is. I think that secrets and miracles are shown to us so that we could try to solve them… The cognition process develops us. With time, humankind can find answers to many questions. Someone wants us to develop."

"Who? God?"

"If it serves the purpose of the good, then it is surely God. But the knowledge of the matter without the knowledge of spiritual rules is a way to a great disaster. People use knowledge for mass massacres and destructions. They have neared a very dangerous edge which when crossed, can bring total destruction."

"What do you think, why has God created humankind at all and provided it with the right of choice?" the Soldier was in the mood to continue a philosophical conversation.

"And why does a poet write poems, a painter paints, and a builder builds?" the Stranger asked.

"It's a kind of means to express their abilities."

"If we assume God has abilities, for example to create, then creation of the world is a kind of expression of His abilities. However, I don't think this is the only correct interpretation. Possibly, we are part of a global process where humankind must play a certain role."

"And why does a person need the right of choice? Maybe, it doesn't have it at all. All of us have a role and we play it regardless of our will. If the future is known, it means it is defined."

"There is a difference between something known and something defined," the Stranger did not agree and tried to explain:

"Suppose, the Seer can foretell someone's actions or can mentally make someone take actions. Can you see the difference?"

"Looks like that," the Soldier hesitated. "For example, God knew I would be a warrior but he was not pulling me by the hand to enroll in the army and did not force me to sign a contract."

The Stranger made an indefinite gesture.

"Although, I assume that sometimes a man is really pulled by the hand. The Creator made the most complex creature provided with an autonomous program, the right of choice. But He wants to help His creatures, bring them to senses, protect from incorrect actions without disturbing independent development of the man."

"And haven't you lost your independence? Do you act guided by your own principles or not?" the Soldier was looking at him attentively.

"I hope so," the Stranger's voice faltered. "So far my actions have not conflicted with my beliefs."

"And what about mine?"

"Your actions do not conflict with your beliefs, but conflict with mine quite often," the second part of the phrase was spoken by the Stranger sternly.

"Ah... You are against violence, aren't you?" the Soldier drawled and skeptically nodded his head. "I see. I can't imagine how you can protect yourself and your dear ones without violent actions or physical impact. You have seen the victims of terrorists, haven't you? Those mutilated children whose only joy is pain killers? Mothers who have shed tears over the children they lost, handicapped fathers who can do nothing to earn bread for their families? Yes, you can stay aside, you can remain free from blood but that's all until a disaster enters your home."

"The actions you take will not bring consolation to the unhappy," the Stranger answered. "There is another way; there is another solution, not blood for blood which results in eternal hatred and war. I believe in humankind`s change, in returning to spiritual laws, and this change will benefit people and stop wars and violence. This is the way shown by the Prince."

"Well. Suppose, you are a highly spiritual person, but your neighbor is a scoundrel. And he builds on your decency for his corrupt purposes. And if you have a wife, children, property, and you are not ready to protect them, this neighbor will take everything from you. And outrage over your wife and children to please his vile heart. And you think that the right way is not to wipe him up the floor but forgive him and allow further brutalization? And he always hunts for the kind and meek ones. He is not strong enough to handle the strong. You can't be a sheep in this world!"

The Stranger was silent for some time and then spoke:

"There are different types of protection. Fists are not the only means. If your neighbors are armed with rifles, and you have a stick, then only your desire to protect your dear ones is not enough. Understand, that God is a reality and no one will be able to resists Him and His power, and no guns will help. Your belief is stronger than all guns, but if it is time, you need to leave as the Prince did feeling pity to his murderers as his way is to eternal glory and they will go to oblivion and darkness. If we could see the entire picture of the creation and not only a minor portion of it, we would change our priorities, but as is, we only have to believe. But belief is one of the conditions to enter the country of justice. It's a pity that I don't have enough words or arguments," the Stranger was visibly upset. He turned away from the Soldier and watched landscapes passing by in the window.

"How do you manage to persuade people," the Soldier suddenly spoke peacefully and gently.

The Stranger smiled.

"I don't persuade, but sometimes, when I'm speaking, the Power shows up and changes the creed of people and persuades them of the rightness of my words. No logical arguments are required anymore."

"Maybe the Power shows when you are right and when you are wrong, you don't have it, may this be true? No, you haven't managed to really persuade me," the Soldier grinned.

"That is not so," the Stranger said sharply. "When are we getting off?"

"Get as close to the City as possible and then walk across the desert. If we reach the goal, they won't risk chasing us. I don't fear for myself, they won't touch me, though I am not sure. If necessary, they won't spare me. But I don't know the instructions the Seer gave them with regard to you," the Soldier said.

"I don't believe the Seer wants my death. I don't believe the Medium will intentionally act against me."

"I don't know, I don't know," the Soldier said quickly. "The Seer contacted the security service. He has exposed you to risk. Maybe he wanted to understand your power. He has never encountered anything of the sort earlier and you refused to talk with him. I don't know. But the service will play its own game and by its rules. They can do anything needed to reach their goal and anything that will benefit them. They will step over not only me, but over you and the Seer and will enjoy that. I know many people who have a grudge against him. People will remember long his exposure of the provocations initiated by the security service broadcasted live. Have you seen the Masks Off talk show where he appeared once? However, that was the first and the last time when he interfered in a dangerous game. Do you remember someone from the audience asking him how one of rebel leaders, chased during many years, managed to escape the army cordon? Who provided him with a corridor, led through all posts and helped to cross to another country?"

"Yes," the Stranger recollected that and nodded. "The Seer then thought several seconds and blurted out: people above the law, with a headphone in the ear."

"And those people above the law did not suffer but a very competent person was fired from the army intelligence for letting the rebel boss escape," the Soldier gritted his teeth.

The dismissed man was the boss who thought very highly of him. After this incident, there were personnel rotations, which pushed the Soldier back. A new director got rid of the former team, which was loyal to the former boss. The Soldier was assigned insignificant and dangerous tasks for several years, he worked without support or companions, therefore he had been thinking of resigning for a long time.

"I think that was the purpose of the operation," after several minutes of silence the Stranger said. "But I don't have proof and my word does not bear the same authority as that of the Seer's. Accept it as a version and forget. We must not interfere with these games."

"It is important for me to know the reasons," the Soldier did not agree with him. "I believe you and will have no regrets if I go off my course."

Chapter 18.Torch

The Seer woke the woman up by tenderly stroking her wild hair.

"I haven't enjoyed such a balmy sleep for years," she said with a stretch.

"A friend of mine, a security man, will come soon. Do you want to be in at our talking?" the Seer asked.

"Sure. After all, you will speak of the Stranger?" she guessed.

"Did you like him?" the Seer was playing with her curls.

"Aren't you jealous?" the woman smiled raising herself upon elbow.

"Not at all," he smiled ironically. "I cannot imagine you together. You need to match each other, but none of you can make a compromise. He has not it in him to love ardently. His feelings are aimed at something else; he is not a man to peddle on love to woman. And you cannot live without passion. I see, you need an interesting person, and he is exactly the one. But he doesn't need a woman like you. However, if you are ready to give up your activity, change your principles and your mindset for the sake of love, he will take this sacrifice. You see, dear, if the Stranger has a mission, indeed, he will go immediately when he performs the task. They won't let him lead a quiet life. The System surrounds the messengers with aura of mystery, and people compose legends about them. Here's a PR campaign. But what is the point of family life? Who composes a legend about a good husband or father, even though to be the same is no less heroic than to be a hero in the battlefield? There is kind of regularity: the more important a mission is, the quicker the man goes. Some exceptions may occur, but these are people who manage to find the golden mean, and this does not apply to the Stranger. I liked him too, I feel sorry for him, and that is why I want to help him. It is important to make sense of his mission, before it's too late, until striking mechanism is activated, until the guarded fire flares up."

"You know, I do not want to conjure dipping in the world of the dead and ghosts. Something has changed in my inner world. I can see the reality differently. I don't know, maybe it will pass," the woman smiled recollecting something.

"That's the Stanger's job," paused the Seer discontented.

"Is he in danger? Can we help him?"

"I am trying. He came to me for help himself."

"And you said no. Why on earth?" asked the Medium reproachfully.

"I did not say no. I asked him to clarify something, but the Stranger suddenly went to his shell. He thought me to be a danger to him. I found this unfair."

"So, you decided to take revenge by setting the dogs at him? Maybe, he could understand that you are equal to something like this, and so, he went to his shell?"

"It's not all that simple," the Seer shook his head fiercely. "I just asked to stop him gently, provide with the best accommodation, feed properly and take care of him. When the belly is full the bones would be at rest. I would talk with him, and we might make the best of a bad job. Mind you, I wish him no ill, while in the City he will die and ruin the others. Can one carry out the mission he hasn't the slightest idea of, possessing powerful weapon that could be revealed with no X-ray? I wish we would make sense of it all together with him," the Seer was calm and convincing.

"What is that to you? Maybe, he does not have any mission at all. Let him go to the City to fully realize his powerlessness. He'll see that nothing happens. And if the mission does exists, who are you make head against? You say: I'm afraid for him, I want to warn him… But what's he to you? Why are you so sympathizing with a person you've seen once in a lifetime?" the woman was talking hotly, being all yes.

The Seer saw that she did not believe him, started from the sofa, walking about the room nervously.

"You are silly!" he raised voice. "Do you even realize what he possesses? Do you know the limits of his abilities? What powers of darkness he can rouse? The City is the very place to give way to this energy to the fullest extent! The atmosphere is too favorable. Could he suppress it? Tell me, why this man does go to the City?"

"Do you bear him no malice, indeed? And you do not envy him, don't you?"

"I bear the Stranger no malice. Can one envy him?"

"Well. Look then," the Medium nodded readily. "He called his force 'Wind'. Its power may change. The Stranger said that was the weapon to respond to any occult acts, magic or witchery, even hypnosis. And something else: it seemed to me that the power comes with the Stranger's emotions."

"Wind, wind…" the Seer repeated thoughtfully. "Why not Spirit? Well, we'll see… So, the Wind comes from outside, not lives in him? Are you sure?"

"I could see just light. It was emitted slightly… sometimes more intensely… or disappeared altogether."

The Seer did not trust in such phantoms. It is in human imagination to create illusory objects, and even make other people feel and see them. He knew that to use imaginative power to hypnotize people. Once, when a young man, he was walking home late at night from a party with a girl on his arm he had lately acquainted with, and happened to be scoffed at by two elevated youngsters. Instantly, his imagination drew a horrible monster with fiery eyes and huge tusky chap. The created monster was broken upon the young people, and he moved towards them, with his fists clenched. The outcome exceeded expectations: one of the youngsters fell to the ground and, screaming with wild horror, urinated on himself. Probably, he went off his head. Another one was more courageous, he could gather himself up to run away in fear. The girl went into raptures for her knight who waded single-handed into two gorillas, and he was awarded for bravery the same night.

The Seer was listening to the woman's blundering account.

"Do not tell anybody about this, even more so, special service agents, if only you do not want to ruin him. I think, you are not right, this power lives in him, and he can release this power. However, not always at his will. But this is quite curious; after all, you also believe it depends on the Stranger's emotions. This is very interesting and very strange," the Seer repeated once again. "Now, the guest will come, do not trust him."

"I trust myself not always, how can I trust a dog?" the Medium uttered with a superior and independent air. She could not bear any security service agents calling them scornfully 'dogs'.

Later, the Functionary arrived. He gave the woman a cold nod, although he recognized her, and greeted the Seer warmly. After having a cup of coffee, the guest began to talk about the purpose of his visit:

"An unpleasant thing occurred: our services have taken interest in the Stranger and Soldier..."

"Sorry for interrupting, but who is of major interest? The Stranger or Soldier?"

"The Soldier, of course."

"What can such interest lead to? Why the Soldier?" the Seer kept on querying.

"I think it is caused by his professional activity. It seems to our superiors that the Soldier and his assistant, the Stranger, perform the task of their command."

"Are you serious? Well, sorry," the Seer looked at his guest with surprise.

"What harm this may do to the Stranger?" the Medium interrupted worriedly.

"Do you know him?" the Functionary asked.

"Very closely," she threw off defiantly.

"I see. You helped him in the Tower," the Functionary nodded as if he was turning it every way in mind.

"Our agents collect information keeping a close watch on them. Perhaps, they will be permitted to approach the City freely."

"And what's next?" the Medium grew suspicious.

"The decision depends on the information we obtain."

"It is clear," the Seer ticked off. "They are waited for in the City."

"I don't think that our officers are going to arrest the Soldier."

"And what about the Stranger?" the Medium asked.

"Quite possible. We and you know that nobody is at the back of him, so, nobody will come to the defend him. It is not me who decide. I am sorry. But I have dropped out of the game."

"Can you inform me about everything concerned with the Stranger?" the Seer inquired.

"I'll try to do my best."

When the guest went, the Seer made a reach for a cigarette.

"He is a liar. The Stranger and the Soldier have come to the attention of the authorities on his tip, and the Stranger is of greater interest to them than the Soldier. I am sorry that I have got in touch with him. Ooh, an old fool," sighed the Seer.

"It cannot be so serious. It is absurd. A mighty special service starts hunting for two little persons for nothing. What a thing to do!"

"People are nothing but string puppets," the Seer kept silence for a while.

"I have arrived at this conclusion not that long ago. Little people are governed by strong forces that prefer to stay in the background, and change history using little people. Our independency is very limited. We are captivated, nothing more."

"Are you serious? Captivated by whom? Maybe, you know a way to release from prison?" asked the Medium incredulously.

"No," uttered the Seer sadly. "The Stranger may know. But even if he shows the way, the direction is sure to be misinterpreted. Everything is as usually."

"Does he know more than you? Or, you cannot learn what the Stranger knows? After all, there must exist a shared learning field! All we need is to focus on it. And if someone knows something, this cannot be a secret for you," the Medium was surprised a lot.

"Shared does not mean accessible for all. There is a channel, and it is protected by kind of bright light. Nobody can penetrate it, it is impenetrable. Perhaps, the information about global events, riddles of the Universe is stored there, and this light breathing touches the Stranger? He has something I do not have," said the Seer sullenly. "I would give my all for feeling the same."

"You envy him," uttered the Medium disappointedly.

"No, I don't. His life is not easy. I've seen something. He is suffering, yearn is getting him down. He cannot keep still. It has been for several years already. He was betrayed by the nearest. He hasn't broken down, but has been hardened, instead. The Stranger is a man of iron will. And will of iron is cruel-hearted and unforgiving if stacked against enemies. Enemies are not always people; these may be demons wringing heartstrings. Don't take this the wrong way, but I do not believe in demons, evil spirits, or other hellish stuff. Myths hide the psychology and struggle of a person with vice. Myths need understanding. The Stranger chops the heads away, but he must know that the neck must be branded so that the new heads could not grow. Now, he is happy with carrying out the mission. However, after all, the mission will have been completed. Sooner or later, everything comes to an end under the Sun, you know. How will he get? Sitting in the rocking-chair thinking of old times? Writing memoires?" the Seer ironically smiled. "He is like a meteorite, he flies, flames, but he burns himself out. He is like a torch left off..." the Seer hesitated for a word. "The torch was used not only for lighting, but also for arson. See?"

"Not exactly," said the Medium perplexed.

"I think I know who governs him. He is the man haunted by the world. He decided to take revenge."

Large heat drops were running down the Seer's wrinkled forehead.

"You mean the Stranger?" the Medium looked at him in horror. In such instances, the Seer was fear awaking.

"Do you remember speaking of some ruler? Who is he, do you think?" gasped the Seer.

"Maybe, God?" the Medium shuttered.

"No, he is a man. This is so called Prince. The Lord of rioters, hermits, and other scums of the earth. For curiosity, I dipped into the past to look at this wandering healer. Now, I know one thing: we cannot play against this vagrant preacher. Apparently, the Stranger knows that too, so he has taken his side."

The Seer wiped his forehead and fell heavily into the chair.

"Well then, what can be done?" the Medium asked again.

"I do not know. Sometimes, the least done the better. Maybe, to leave the country is the best way. I haven't made up my mind yet."

"The dogs will catch up the Stranger, do you think?"

"If so, I could get him out. I would rather not be anxious about it," the Seer paused weighing different scenarios and listening to his feelings. "No. They could not catch up the Stranger even if they send all their agents against him."

Chapter 19. Report

The Chief of the internal security service received a report on disappearance of the Soldier and Stranger, and immediately called the head of the hunt group on the carpet.

"How come?" he stared at his subordinate.

"I have made a report on all our actions," uttered the latter guiltily.

"Tell me in your own words!"

"We set the hunt group at the station entry, held the conference call…"

"I need all details," the Chief interrupted him.

"Two officers at the entry, an additional observation post on the second floor. A group next to the ticket office. A musician was attracted on purpose. Set a direct line with the ticket office computer. At about twelve, two suspected persons were observed. One of them directed steps to the station, where he was taken a picture of, while the other remained on the spot. The checkup identified him as our object, the Stranger. He came up to the station arch, looked around, and gave a wink to our agent."

"Why did he wink?" the Chief frowned. "How, on earth, he realized that this was a security staff member?"

"I do not know. This was a professional; he looked quite ordinarily, like a tourist."

"Go on," the Chief saw that the case was much more complicated it seemed at first glance.

"Then, something quite unexpected happened. The Stranger asked the musician for the guitar to sign a song."

"What a song?" the director was surprised. The officer held forth the note with a text. Having read the words of the song, he directed burst laughing:

"But this guy has a sense of humor. You, bullheads, couldn't see what 'there are wenches at the station' means?"

"You mean the Stranger wanted to warn the Soldier in such an original manner?"

"I'll bet."

"Well, say it were true. I cannot believe that an amateur could lay open our group," the officer's voice was scornful of sarcasm. "But, above all, the Soldier quite openly bought tickets and met with his accomplice inside the building."

"And where are they now?" the Chief was ready to burst with range. "You have underestimated them. They twisted you around the finger. What was next?"

"We bought two next door compartments, fixed wires."

"The wire data! Straight away! What is here?"

"Nothing out of the common. They almost were not talking. The Soldier went out to the corridor, and spoke to our agent, a young pretty officer. Shortly, he went to smoke. Our agent who replaced the first girl and was permitted to get in contact with the object saw him. She was immediately sent to control her. All clear, she doesn't lie. The Stranger remained in the compartment. The tape shows some sounds, but we couldn't identify them. Perhaps, some technical defects. When, in forty minutes, the Soldier did not return, our agents checked up the compartment, then the entire train set, but found nobody. And this is an enigma."

"Did you monitor everything?"

"Yes, even the ticket office of the station, where the Soldier was likely to get out the train. He couldn't shape the invisible."

"Well, say it is true. The Soldier gets out at the station and somehow disappears. He is a professional. But what about the Stranger? Where? You say he was remaining in the compartment? Has the taping shown the door slam after the Soldier left the compartment?"

"No. Nothing of the kind. The Stranger did not leave the compartment. We lost them, but if you give us the warrant to arrest, we shall find them soon, after all, then we can involve the police, they have their eyes and ears everywhere," the agent tried to find excuses.

"Well, but without the warrant. We shall operate on our own," the Chief has made a decision. "The minute you find the Stranger, take him and bring to me, I will examine him myself. Do not let the Soldier get into the City, you can do what you like, but do not cripple him! Interrogate the 'tail' once again, especially, the maiden. Put through it! There must be a catch somewhere. The Stranger could not slip through. I cannot believe this."

"Sorry, but we cannot interrogate the girl. She handed resignation and went somewhere, her mobile phone number is unavailable. Sure, we can find her, but should we waste time and efforts? And why, indeed?"

The Chief half stood, kept silence for an instance, and threw off: "Dismissed."

He understood that nobody supports the Soldier and Stranger, and put his foot down. The Soldier was suspended from serious tasks after change of the leadership, and several scenarios were in the making. The best one is to recruit the guy, although the shift from one service to another one was not in common practice, this was considered to be betrayal.

The Stranger is not connected with any service at all, but to work with him will be difficult. It is hardly possible to overplay the man who can read thoughts and practices hypnotism, after all, somehow he escaped observation. "But never mind, be sure, we shall make him talk."

Chapter 20. The Sense

The Soldier was thoughtful and silent, the Stranger was calm. As approaching the City, he felt stronger, filling with knowledge unknown before. It seemed to him that he is gaining authorities: to give orders, bring under his control, or even punish. This conflicted with his views and led inevitably to inner conflict. On the one hand, he is a weapon of Providence, yet he is also peaceful man not wishing to inflict suffering even on hostile people.

Educational methods are permitted if they are fruitful. But if not? Then these methods turn into punishment, revenge... But, after all, God says: "I will revenge you". Some people said: "The God will revenge on those who are stronger then we are, but it is useless to bother him needlessly, once we are able to stand up for ourselves", and those who said this, slaughtered even their enemies' children until their fragile teeth turn into fangs to revenge their fathers.

The Stranger realized that if the war begins, the millstones will grind more and more people. He felt its coming. Perception of reality was changing in him. The Stranger was getting very attentive and ready to respond instantly to any threatening motion.

"Tell me, how you feel the sense of struggle?" he addressed to his friend, stroking his neck.

The Soldier looked at him in surprise:

"If you are going to fight, this means that things look black. It is useless to rely on fists in the City. Well, let find a pair of guns. Can you shoot?"

"To fight does not always mean to strike out wildly. Tell me!" the Stranger demanded.

"There is a difference before the hand-to-hand fighting and fire-fighting," the Soldier took his mind off sore thoughts.

"Tell me about hand-to-hand fighting."

The Soldier's eyes gleamed for a moment.

"When taking up the battle, you must feel confident, absolutely confident. Above all is to get rid of fear. To achieve this feeling I should be aware of my doing by rights. I must 'read' my enemy as an 'open book', and foresee all his movements, combinations, and maneuvers, that is have total control over him. Since before the enemy strikes at me, I know the path of the blow, so I can easily dodge or block the attack, or deliver a counterattack. I have to see the weak points, or make the enemy reveal them. A fighter must be trained as close as possible to the true combat conditions. Dangerous and painful training instills confidence, depriving of fear in a real battle."

"OK. But I enquired for something else. I asked: how it is that you anticipate fighting?"

"I see," the Soldier felt flattered with the Stranger's interest in his art. "In the very beginning I feel slightly anxious. It doesn't hinder me but makes me mobilize all resources. Then I set myself up for fighting. I try to calm myself down, concentrate, and envision my victory. Yet, sometimes I feel panic-stricken, not anxiety, and it was time to avoid struggling. Whenever I couldn't escape, my confidence sank. At that moment, I did nervously and not always successfully. Why have you talked of that?"

"I have started feeling like that, but I don't know, why. My war is not against sons of men..."   all of a sudden he felt power, stopped talking, and turned to the window.

"I cannot grip what you mean, but I feel not quite the thing," the Soldier looked at the Stranger frowningly with caution.

"I cannot grip it myself, sorry," the latter responded not facing the Soldier.

Chapter 21. The Archeologist

The Chief of the Security service called the Functionary to account. After some insignificant questions he enquired as if incidentally:

"How is the Seer?"

"Not bad. Truth be told, he is a too closed-mouthed person to talk about himself," the Functionary followed the principle: what can be checked cannot be disputed.

"Did he inquire about the matter?" the Chief made no bones about it.

"The Seer is not so curious," the subordinate bit back politely.

"What is his interest in this affair?" the Chief stared at him.

The Functionary could stand the steely glance and answered calmly,

"He is interested in the Stranger. Nothing more."

"Why?"

"I haven't the slightest idea, but I'm sure that he has a reason for this."

"OK. Make him help us to find with the Stranger, we have lost him once again. He has dropped the mob in the train. It is too expensive to make scale arrangements for detention of a former archeologist. We have enough on our plate, which is far more important than searching for the now tramp."

"I have looked through his dossier. He is neither a mere archeologist nor a tramp," the Functionary objected. "He has a number of papers on field archeology, major research in study of scriptures. He is an expert in ancient manuscripts and dead languages. A famous person in certain circles. He is a follower of the so called Prince. Eight years ago, the Stranger was squeezed out from the scientific environment after he published the results of his research into sacred book prophesies and lately found ancient manuscripts. The Stranger tried to prove that the ancient prophets of all times, who lived long before the Prince, had anticipated his advent. After that, the Stranger was hunted. He was accused of contacts with riots, the information wasn't justified though. We could trace the thread leading to the Hermit: about thirty years ago, he was famous as much as the Seer. The Stranger often visited him, and the Hermit is not a man to welcome around. He is also an adept of the Prince, but in contrast to the riots, had never incited people to armed struggle. We have lost him out of sight for a long time, it was hasty of us: such people need thorough watch or care.

After all, the Stranger was brought to trial. Based on crime information, his house was searched. The items were revealed that were found at archeological diggings of purportedly great historical value, but no reported to the Institute of antiquities. He stated that went to the length of crime since he had wished to bring to public the importance of the discoveries. He accused the Institute of antiquities of hiding valuable information for the benefit of the established opinion. He got a term: two years of imprisonment. The public Prosecutor, now deceased, you know who, considered the archeologist to pose a threat to public because of his extreme views, so he suggested that the court sentenced the accused to solitary confinement. His wife did not wait for him. Hardly had he was imprisoned, she filed for divorce, forbade their children to meet with the father. By the way, they are three. After emerging from jail (just in a year, since the manuscripts revealed were recognized faked), he was engaged in day-labor, and to the date, he has not been found to do anything suspicious."

"Why did the prosecutor think the Stranger dangerous for society?" the Chief got that the tides turned.

"Not clear," the Functionary shrugged his shoulders. "Maybe, something happened at the proceedings. We should find those who were present there, for, thanks to the Seer, we cannot ask him directly. I think the Stranger to have been sentenced wrong. He has numerous merits in his field. He used to find jars filled with gold and silver coins, but gave in everything to the government, living plainly. Perhaps, he could not afford a lawyer; at least, a defense attorney was not present in the court. When in army, he was a male nurse, participated in military actions, extricated casualties. Awarded for heroism. Tell the truth, the guy rejected all the awards."

"I wonder," the Chief was thoughtful for a while. Suddenly, he turned pale, feeling dry in the mouth, his fingers numb, severe pain pierced his breast, but he strung himself up to utter: "find out what happened at the proceedings, talk to the Seer, make him help us to find them."

The Functionary left the building, and walking down the square dialed the number.

"Hello," the croaking voice was annoyed.

"We need your help with a matter that is of interest for you too."

"I see. There is no point in talking too much," the Seer interrupted him. "You don't know where the Stranger is, and want me to point at his location."

"Yes. My commander wishes you to do this."

"I won't help your service. My request was of personal nature, I just wanted not to let the Stranger in the City, where deadly danger is reserved for him. Yet, even that was too much, we had no right to do this. Now, you have conspired unfair game, I do not play such games. And you would rather not!"

The Medium was satisfied with the Seer's refusing to help the dogs and his harsh tone. She came up to him, and gave him a hug.

"Can we take action at last?"

"Not yet, I'm not ready. Let's wait."

The Seer tiptoed to kiss her on the neck.

Chapter 22. High price

They got out on the Victory station, the last stop before the City.

"We can't stay in a prominent place. We'll have a snack somewhere in the café and hitch a lift to the Silencers' desert, cross it by foot, then through the mountains and we will come to the City," the Soldier said looking about.

"Two days," the Stranger said thoughtfully. "I know this region quite well; we can walk the short cut."

"Maybe, we are safe now? What do you think?" the Soldier asked.

The Stranger listened to himself and had an unpleasant feeling as if the storm clouds amassed above his head.

"And closing my eyes I feel: the whole world is marching against me."

"I think the same," the Soldier spitted on the ground. "Do you believe the Seer is helping them?"

"No. We've been on the lam too long."

They walked down to the tunnel and went out to the marketplace. Near the countless small shops there were young and middle-aged men sitting, making a row, gesticulating, playing dice, tables, and cards.

"Unemployment," the Stranger sighed.

"Don't worry for them. This town is the center of drug dealing, stolen articles sale and other unpleasant things. Just don't look anybody in the eyes, here it is considered to be an aggression and challenge. As if they were beasts. I need a gun, really need it!" complained the Soldier. "The locals must think we are on business here, but not some mere curious idlers. God forbid if they take us for undercover cops. We should buy something."

"Let's buy a couple of knives, it is almost legal, here it is cheap."

"Good idea, we have come to buy good and cheap blades. What for do you need a knife?"

"We are going on the war-path, we shouldn't be unarmed," said the Stranger with eyes predatory slit.

The Soldier looked at him uncomprehendingly.

"Calm down. It is not the kind of war where they shoot and cut with knives. Knife is a symbol," explained the Stranger quickly.

"For us is a cover," clarified the Soldier.

"By the way, this small town has its own story. Many centuries ago, a famous saint named the Winner was born here. He was a general, a desperate warrior who had never lost a battle, but one day his life changed. He met the disciple of the Prince and followed him; he abandoned all his posts, honors, belongings. The authorities captured him and tortured for a week. Any other person would have died on the first day of such torments, but not the Winner..." the Stranger stopped speaking.

"What befell him?"

"He's got his head cut."

"I've heard something about him. Some legends," said the Soldier incredulously.

"Fables always follow the legendary people; every myth has a prototype in reality. I got to read the scroll which was found in this land not so long ago. It was written a bit later after the life of the Winner and by some miracle remained intact in one cave. All the tortures he was put to were described in detail; he was decapitated because they were not able to kill him with torments. His firmness and endurance inspired a lot of people to become the disciples of the Prince."

The Soldier shrugged.

They went to café, sat to the far corner near the wall: complete overview and covering of the back in case of the assault.

As they began eating, a pretty, slim girl with black eye-rims on the pale face, set down to their table.

"Got a cigarette?" she said and added quietly, "cheap service."

"Take the whole pack, beauty," the Soldier gave her the cigarettes. "And get out."

"You're a boor!" the girl shouted but took the pack.

Suddenly a short dark guy appeared.

"Sister, did they offend you?" the boy asked, flexing his muscles.

"To the very heart," the fair-skinned girl confirmed.

"I didn't know 'beauty' was an offensive word," the Soldier said calmly.

The Stranger looked at her absent-mindedly. There seemed, he was disturbed.

"You should pay," the boy said through his teeth.

The Soldier sneered, his eyelids narrowed. The Stranger decided to recapture the initiative, until it's too late, stared at the boy and slowly started to speak:

"Young man, if you want to live and stay safe and sound, do not interrupt our dinner. We are on business here. The girl will stay."

The novice bandit looked at them perplexedly and stammered:

"Should I... go?"

The Stranger nodded lazily. The girl got scared too, but after taking a glance at him, calmed down instantly. Instead of fear a new feeling appeared, a feeling of kinship, as if she met an old friend.

"What do you want?" she asked with her eyes cast down.

"There is a lot of dirt in your life, but your heart is still kind. I want to help you. Come with us."

"They won't let me go. I owe a lot, I have to work out."

"We will settle this question," the Stranger said, looking at the Soldier who shook his head.

Outside the café they saw the familiar guy and some scowled people.

"If I start first now and with no mercy, I can deck them in few seconds. We can't allow them to pull out the knives and start waving them around. Take their car and get out of here," the Soldier whispered.

"Don't do anything!" the Stranger prohibited. "I see, you are the head," he started speaking, referring to an unshaven man. "I have a talk."

"Who are you?"

"I am the Stranger. Have you heard about me?"

"I don't recall," the criminal answered cautiously.

"Phone the Serpent or you don't recall him as well?"

The unshaved man sneered.

"If you're bulling, we'll bury you in the garden," he pulled his hands out of the pockets. "I'll call him, but in case the Serpent doesn't recall you, you'll breeze no more, you're alive no more.

Change your mind, until it's too late, pay the amends. I see you don't have the needed sum with you, but you can go home and bring it, while your friend stays here for some time…"

"You talk too much," the Stranger interrupted. "Give me the phone."

"Don't have money to buy your own?" the bandit said through his teeth with a grin but passed him the mobile phone. The Stranger thought to himself for a moment, dialed the number and turned the loudspeaker on.

"Would you be so kind to calm your guys down?"

The criminal took the phone carefully and said respectfully:

"This is Bumblebee, there's some Stranger here and we don't know him. Behaves like a big cheese and looks like a tramp."

"I know him," answered the phone. "Pass him the mobile."

The Soldier has just gone into the state of fight: there is no chance of fixing up with such jackals. While negotiations are carried, it is time to attack.

"Problems?" asked the Serpent.

"Always problems. It's good they didn't go worse," the Stranger answered. "Here is the girl, young and slim, she works for your Bumblebee, I need her, want to buy her."

"We don't sell our people, we buy them. Sorry, bro, she is ours and we need her. She is a valuable worker. Go, they won't touch you. No need to thank."

"Listen," the Stranger's voice became husky with anger. "There is ours and nobody takes what is ours. Give back what you had taken."

"You are not in state to make terms with me," hissing sounds for which he got his name appeared in the speech of the criminal. The Serpent spoke no more.

The Bumblebee gave a nod: the audience was over. The Soldier looked at his friend, sighed and whispered into his ear:

"Let's go out from here. We did everything we could. Do you want me to interfere? Shall we left the bodies and take the slut?"

The Stranger stood still; he felt he couldn't leave without the girl. He cannot leave her here.

He delved in the pocket of the old jacket and pulled out a small worn leather baggie. He untied the ribbons and carefully took out a shiny small stone.

"This is a diamond. Three carats. Crystal. More than enough for the girl's debts."

"Thanks," thanked the Bumblebee with a grin and took the diamond. "But you've heard the Serpent, he doesn't let her go."

Anger filled the Stranger. "Come, Wind, Power of my God, show up!" he called on and felt the faint breeze of the Wind on his head, but it was not enough to subdue a few stoned people. He was not able to control the power. "I really need it, help!" Useless. The Stranger tossed inside, it seemed he was going to burst into tears under the insult. He tried again and again. As if he was trying to start a car, but the starter didn't work. He looked up to the sky in despair and saw it darkened. He peered and noticed that some building has been burning. Heavy black smoke went up high into the sky.

The Stranger felt the power approaching. The Wind got stronger. He took it happily and didn't think of any limits. For a moment he realized that the Wind had changed him completely, but it was too late. The Stranger didn't feel like himself anymore. Consciousness was thrown away.

"The woman goes with us," he started slowly. "This place will be committed to flames which will burn your wickedness. You all," the Stranger said suddenly with a totally hoarse voice, "cannot enter the land of Eternity and you will not last long here. You," he turned to the Bumblebee, "slaughtered a teenager when you were seventeen; at twenty you raped a girl despite her cries. You robbed and tortured. You escaped punishment, and you didn't repent, you didn't value the great mercy that you hadn't been destroyed like some stinking trash, but you enhanced your wrong-doing. But you will not escape the judgment of the Justice, it is here."

From afar to the consciousness of the Stranger glimmering has come: a few more words and the criminal will die. He turned to the other bandits. He looked in the eyes of each of them.

"You, on your knees! Pray to stay alive. The keys, now!"

One of them obsequiously passed him the car keys with shivering hands and his eyes bent on the ground. The Bumblebee stood waggling. He saw himself in the abyss and there were no escape. Crimes arose in his mind, laid as heavy as stones.

The Stranger nodded to the girl, pointed on the car. He got behind the wheel, depressed the clutch, started up the ignition, put the transmission lever in first position, pulled away slowly.

"The God has visited us, the sinners," the Soldier said reverently. "Let me drive, take some rest."

The Wind was still here but the Stranger began to realize the reality. He stopped the car, asked for a chocolate bar; the Soldier pulled it out of the bag in a hurry. The Stranger divided it into three pieces and shared with his companions.

The Soldier pulled away with a screech.

"What should we do with her? We can't take her with us; she will not be able to climb the mountains."

"Have you been at war?" the Stranger asked.

"I have…"

"Do you know the rule: never leave the wounded man on the battlefield?"

"Yes, I do. But the professionals destroy the firing posts first and then take care about the wounded comrades."

"She will help us. If she can't walk, we'll carry her."

"What has happened? What have you done to them?" the Girl nipped in.

"Me? It was not me," the Stranger answered dimly.

The Soldier turned back for a moment and screamed delightedly:

"It was great, really great! You smashed them. I believe in you, Stranger! God is in you! We will turn this shitty world upside down! We will clear it out!"

"Don't be too excited," the Stranger didn't seem to be pleased, if anything. "It's a pity we couldn't understand each other. The only good thing: we took the girl without blood. And may be those people will come to reason."

"Are you happy? And what about me? Soon I'll get withdrawals, it's time," the girl spoke trough set teeth.

The Stranger looked at her arms.

"You don't main-line, do you? Do you smoke grass?"

"Special grass. Few times a day. I haven't smoked today yet, haven't earned."

"I will detox you," the Stranger promised.

"What do you want from me?"

"Good question," the Soldier responded. "But it seems that even your savior can't give an answer."

"He is right. Soldier, do you trust me?"

"I do. I have never trusted anyone more than you."

"I saw her soul. I hope, you'll understand. The future depends on the present. The choice made today will influence the fate tomorrow. I don't know if this meeting was for good or for ill, but we couldn't pass by. Excuse me, I need some rest."

The Stranger closed his eyes. "I need to distract; the breath of the Wind is still here. I was not able to call it, until my consciousness changed. I saw the fire, and the strong Wind appeared immediately. What turns it on? I didn't pace myself. I can hardly remember what I said. I found myself in due time. I hope. Though they deserve punishment for their crimes, I am not a hangman and not a judge. How can I control the Wind when I don't feel me? What is it?" he opened his eyes and looked at the shivering girl.

"Are you OK?"

"No," she snapped.

"How come you know the Serpent?" the Soldier asked the Stranger.

"I dragged him from under the heavy shooting, it was long ago... Sometimes I regret it. His hands are in blood."

"They won't leave you alone. You have taken me, the car, these people don't forgive debts," the girl warned.

"I have paid the high price and I owe them nothing. We have more serious enemies," the Stranger said in calm voice. "We are rushing into the war, where secret services and criminals are the less dangerous enemies."

"The Seer? Are you talking about him?" the Soldier asked.

"The Seer is not an enemy, he is just a man."

Chapter 23. Interrogation

The accident near the café was gathering like a snowball, and twenty minutes later, the story reached the security service. But only after some details were clarified, and the participants' appearance was described, the case was believed to be something extraordinary. A brigade of field agents was sent, a police checkpoint was arranged on the way towards the Silencers' desert, and the Chief himself showed his willingness to interrogate the detained on his own.

He got down to a special room for interrogating. Special lighting was hiding the interrogator's face, while the suspected person, on the contrary, was lit excellent to watch the prisoner's facial expression.

Experienced interrogators can see through the trick, that is why hard core criminals prefer to keep silence. The interrogator himself controls the recording. Sometimes, through torments, it is interrupted, it must be said though that torturers refer to their job more elliptically: 'special means', or 'special measures'. A prisoner is exposed to tortures only in cases of emergency, when it is necessary to fish for information about terrorist attacks being prepared. If there is no hurry, the prisoner just is not allowed to sleep, and on the fifth day, the majority of the arrested persons agree to cooperate with police. However, pursued by hallucinations, they can hardly tell reality from dreams, which make interrogation more complicated.

In the center of the room, in the chair, the Bumblebee was sitting, tied by the leg. He took two doses of strong sedative drugs, but even that did not sleek him ruffled piece of mind.

The Chief nodded towards him, looked at the gloomy investigator and said in a chummy manner:

"Come on, Bumblebee, why droop head? That was ordinary hypnosis. Didn't you hear of such things?"

The criminal shifted his lost glance onto him and whispered:

"What the fuck hypnosis, boss! God visited us, the sinner."

The director gave a sigh: it makes no sense to talk with a madman. The Bumblebee does not pretend, enough to look into his eyes to see this.

"Have you junked up? You met with a hypnotizer. Not a big deal, have a rest for a couple of hours with us, and then we'll go on."

The next prisoner was much more tranquil.

"Tell! I have no time to listen to lies. Tell nothing but the truth," the Chief ordered.

"Well," the criminal began, "we were waiting for them…"

"For whom?"

"I don't know. I was told: stay near the Bumblebee when the one starts talking."

"What talking? What was in question?"

"I don't know. I was told to stay. I was staying."

"What next?"

"Then that… whatsename… yeah… the Stranger… began preaching, the Bumblebee and I were touched and moved to tears."

"The Bumblebee is still crying," the Chief interrupted.

"To cry befits a right man," the criminal mentored.

"What was next?"

"That's all. The preacher's gone; the brother Bumblebee couldn't get off the ground, was standing and crying. I stayed with him until your people came and took us," he finished his short narration, shifting his glance. That man could control his feelings despite being suppressed and frightened.

The Chief was listening to his unpretentious narration with undisguised contempt:

"That's it. Take an hour to write down all details. I don't want you to describe your dirty deeds. I don't care about it. You will put down everything you know about this story. Otherwise, you will leave the house heels foremost with severe heart attack, or suicide. I'll consult friends to decide on how to kill you best of all. Do you believe me?"

The criminal nodded grinding his teeth. This is not the police: nobody will look for the reason for his early death.

Talking to witnesses has clarified the situation more or less: the Stranger and the Soldier were confronted by the Bumblebee's gang-band for some young woman. The Stranger tried to ransom her offering a precious stone. The gangsters took the stone but stood him up. Then, somewhat baffling thing happened. The Stranger accused the Bumblebee of crimes threatening with terrible scourge. The word struck down the band, however surprising it might seem. Having examined the case, the Chief of the Service understood, why it was the Stranger, not the Soldier, that came under the Seer's notice.

Chapter 24. The Bird

Despite the delight raging in his soul, the Soldier did not forget to listen out for his inner indicator: anxiety replaced slight strain, his palms sweating. In the rear-view mirror was the Stranger's austere face.

"Stop here, we mustn't keep driving. We have an ambush ahead of us, and a trap at the back..." the Soldier nodded towards the road.

THE BIRD

"Let's leave the car over here and cross the field, there are hills, we can wait out and move on to the Silencers' desert," the Stranger suggested.

"We mustn't. They will catch us in a shake, we have no time to cross the field. But what if they are ordered to shoot to kill? Would you blow them down that far?"

"This doesn't work like that," the Stranger shook his head. "We should go, and then it's all in God's hands."

"I see. Get out of the car!" the Soldier gasped. The Stranger understood his friend's intention, smiled guiltily, and shook his head again. The Soldier put money in his pocket, gave a wink, turned the car round, and rushed backward.

"Let's go," the Stranger took the girl along. In a short while, he stopped and strained ears:

"We have to hide ourselves." He dug a trench quickly, and erected a small hill. The fugitives flattened themselves against the ground. "Now they'll pass by," whispered the Stranger.

The girl was silent, she felt shivery. Soon, they heard a car roaring. The off-roader drove to the field, two young men got out to examine the terrain thoroughly.

"Nobody is here, nobody is here, nobody..." the Stranger harped on. He repeated those words as an incantation. The Agents stood looking around for a minute, then got into the car. It jerked away raising wet clouds.

"I feel sick," the girls whispered. "Help me."

"Don't worry. Now, you'll feel easier."

The Stranger closed his eyes, felt the Wind almost at once, and not only on his head, but also in the palms. He laid his palms onto the girl's eyes and rolled, "Get purged!" Then he put one hand to the back of her head, another hand to her heart, and heard 'Free!' in himself. The girl was in a slight faint. The Stranger was carefully wetting her face with water. She opened her eyes.

"Nice! I feel light and free, like a bird, I can fly..."

"I'll call you the Bird. Nice name."

They were lying on the ground looking into the eternal sky so difficult to make sense of.

Chapter 25.Cuffs

Hearing the order to stop, the Soldier picked up the speed by giving full throttle. "Above all is to take them away from the field. For myself, I'll come through. Not a big deal, I've worked with worse." In ten minutes of the rush, he saw the road blocked, yet he remained satisfied: the Stranger is likely to have already been at the green hills.

He got out of the car calmly, sneering at the guns facing him.

"Hi, colleagues. Who dares to chain me?" he asked, stretching his shoulders, wrists and neck. "By the way, what's the reason for the detention?"

"Car theft," one of the agents answered with a fixed smile.

"That's right, your brain is good-for-nothing but dealing with car theft," the Soldier was teasing them on purpose, to keep on the safe side, for security, to fill in time. Besides, he wanted to take out his rage onto the people who drove him apart from the Stranger and miracles he had looked forward to see.

"We need only Stranger," said the man who apparently was a leader of the group. "Give answer and you may go even in the theft car."

The Soldier spat out. The safety lock clicked. The agent slowly raised his hand with a gun.

"Cheap bluff," the Soldier said quietly, without a trace of fear. "I'll speak to your boss only. The operation we are conducting now is beyond your scope. I hope, you're aware of my position in the General staff?"

"You will speak to the boss; you must be in cuffs now, though. But first, we'll pay you back," a strong agent gave a nod to a tall guy, and they made a move towards the Soldier.

He was ready to fighting, and even was glad. He stepped aside to be shut by one of the assaulters from the other one. The first enemy jumped up to him trying to kick his hip. To start fight with kicking is mortal amateurship. The Soldier was disappointed. He responded to the blow easily by slightly raising the knee bent, but he decided not to play with the opponent. Just a sudden lunge with a left hand. The man who attacked first was able to spring back, but lost balance. The second hop blow that was sideswiped fell to the lower cheek-bone. The head jerked, and the man fell backwards.

The Soldier rushed to the second fighter's feet escaping his giant fist. He clenched the enemy under the knee and knocked him down with a lunge. Then, quickly rising up and at the same time pulling sharply the agent towards himself, the Soldier countered him at the head. Out of the corner of his eye he caught the motion of another fighter, rolled over aside, and rushed to his feet, grasped at the ankle, and giving a sharp twist turned out the foot. The agent lost balance, fell down fours. The Soldier jumped up and hit him at the nose with his knee, blood spattered. They did not come up to the Soldier any more. Contented with the fight, he stood smiling with a gracious wry smile.

"Guys, I don't give in," he took a deep breath repeatedly to recover breathing.

The leader of the group took an electric gun. The Soldier got tensed when he saw the weapon and turned pale shutting lips tight.

"It's fifty thousand volts. Hold still, I haven't decided yet whether to apply it or not. I do not want to carry you unconscious.

Let's do it on a good note: put on the cuffs, and let's go. Nobody will lay a finger on you, you have my word."

The Soldier looked around, and called to mind the Stranger and his words:

"If your neighbors are armed and numerous... God is the Reality. He is the Protection". The Soldier made up his mind to appeal to this reality. He looked up into the sky and shouted,

"God of the Stranger, help me! Give me power too! May my enemies fall!"

The security agents looked around, some burst laughing: the joke was apt to relax the atmosphere.

"Stop screwing," the commander threw the cuffs under his feet.

The Soldier looked at the sky reproachfully, did up the bracelets at his wrists, sat up front and said through his teeth: "Let's go."

The agents gave their commander a questioning look: a detained may not sit front, but the commander permitted and took to the wheel himself. The task to recruit the Soldier, or, at least, to pave the way for recruitment failed. He had not 'defend' the Soldier from furious agents. The world-old game in good and evil policemen had no effect.

The Soldier was disappointed as well. He called to the God sincerely, but all in waste, he failed to be heard.

"Do not think, do not think of anything," he tried to impress on himself. "I'm a good brick, they won't catch the Stranger, and this is above all things now. Keep quiet. I'll think later. Now, I have to calm down. Everything what's happening is nothing but a performance, with everybody playing its own part." He called to mind happy and joyful moments, his safe and proven method for composing and making sound decisions not burden with negative emotions.

"How's with you, Soldier?" the process of self-composing was interrupted.

"Has been fine till met you. What a bad habit with your people to poke nose into else's business? What is that to you? I mean the Stranger and me. Are we enemies of the state? Terrorists? What's wrong with what we have done? Who can forbid us to arrive in the City?"

"Don't you know?" the agent paused on the word. "The Seer."

"Who is he?" the Soldier was simmering with anger. "Why does he order else's destiny? Why do you obey his orders? Does he pay to you? The Seer is your commander now, huh? A sponsor?"

"We are trying to tackle. We also want to see the reason why he has turned to us. You see, Soldier, we sympathize with you, we have the common goal, and we don't mean harm to the Stranger. But if we don't help the Seer, what will he do next?"

"You mean he would turn to somebody else?" the Soldier turned sulky.

"Sure. The Seer can hire anybody: he has the means. They can do such hunting; there'll be hell to pay. In the City, our service is action-constrained. But the hired guns feel at home. The Stranger is in danger."

"You're the only ones to hunt us for now. The Stranger can stick up for himself," the Soldier said unflinchingly.

"We've already got it. He has a good command of hypnosis. But can he send into a trance, say, a sniper? Can he deal with professional mercenaries? Sorry, but they are not the criminal drug users to be sent into a trance by any hypnotist, for they already have their brain freeze. Our service has collected sufficient data on people with psychic powers. There are few who know anything about them, even in our service, only the select have access to the information. There is a special department established to study people like the Stranger. And you know what our experience shows: they get sick and die like ordinary mortals, if not more frequently: 'he knew too much, so, the God took him too early'. They have to be protected against hostile special services, criminals, or religious fanatics. Do you remember the story from sacred books about the prophet by the name of the Wonderworker who used to retrieve a king from certain death by warning him about ambushes and traps? Enemies suggested leakage of information, but later, they arrive at the conclusion that it was the Wonderworker that saved the king, so they made up mind to kill the prophet. Don't you think something has changed now? They are always hunted for. If you do want to help your friend, let's do it
together."

The Soldier kept silence, he wanted to tell the talker about the Stranger very much. To find him and escort as before, and to take these guys to guard him. However, he saw the agent play a game, telling all right, though. You mustn't believe agents, preachers, policemen and advertisement. This is an axiom the Soldier has already learnt when taking special courses. It's fine to play with the agent, showing that you give credit to him, about giving credit... Let him believe you to be in his trap. Agents are pretentious and vain, they trust in their being chosen and gifted with power.

"Have you any constructive suggestion to make?" the Soldier asked somewhat perplexedly.

"I do have, still it's up to you to decide," the agent was leading his part with care.

"For example?"

"We can go back to find the Stranger. If you don't confide in me, let's drive in one car, say, only three of us, but you have to be in cuffs. Sorry, old boy, you are more dangerous to us than we are for you. If you wish, let's go to our office. You'll talk to the Chief to make a sound decision. The Stranger cannot do without assistance. Do you know where to look for him?"

"I do not know. We haven't discussed it yet. Had no time."

"Now you can see. We can be late. We must find him now till he is not dissolved in the City," the agent's voice sounded tensed and threatening.

"I need to be left alone," the Soldier scratched his chin. "Stop the car. I'll go out to think."

Chapter 26. Faith

The Stranger and the Bird climbed up the hill. The girl recovered her breath and asked:

"What is so special about me? I'm a burden for you. Don't you see I am the same as others, even worse?"

"You are not a burden," he resented sincerely. "I'm sure you are gifted, you have some special ability."

"Which one?" the girl smiled like a child.

"I haven't realized yet, but I feel I need you. It is you who help me, not I help you. I can't explain it now."

Indeed, he could not understand why he would take a companion who brings more harm than good at first sight, but having defended her he felt a surge of energy. Perhaps, he enjoyed being the superman? What if that was the responsibility for the girl that made his senses more acute?

The Stranger thought about the Soldier. He realized that the Soldier had not changed dramatically; his principles were the same, only the accents shifted. The Soldier believes him; maybe he is the only one who does. Faith is his greatest merit and it is not for nothing. He has left to distract attention of the pursuers from them, he takes risk to save some person he hardly knows and now it is the obligation of the Stranger to help his friend.

The Stranger got to the very top of the hill, concentrated on the image of the Soldier and called: "Soldier, it is me, your friend. Soldier, do hear me... God, protect him, please," the Stranger begged, "he helps to fulfill Your task. Will he suffer because of me?"

The Soldier got out of the car to take in the difficult situation. "What am I to do?" he moved his lips soundlessly. "I don't trust them, but I can't leave him in the desert, in the City, alone against everyone. What a hard choice." At this moment he felt that scales fell from his eyes, earplugs left his ears and he heard the clear voice of the Stranger:

"Go... we'll see each other in the City... trust in the God only. He will not leave you. Plan is ready."

The Soldier understood: the command had come to a decision and his task was to follow an order.

"Let's go. I don't know where the Stranger is. I will find him in the City."

"Do you know where he is?" the agent asked drily.

"I know who knows," the confidence was returning to him gradually.

"Whom are you talking about?"

"The Seer. I have to meet him and sort everything out."

"Good. Let's go. It's up to you to decide," the commander answered as kindly as possible, trying to hide his disappointment. He believed that the trap had been set perfectly and he even used hypnosis, he was rather good at it.

"Don't be offended, bro," the Soldier's guess was right. "Tell me about the people with transcendent capacities. But I don't need disinformation, I read tabloids. I know enough about the vampires, werewolves and extraterrestrial beings inseminating our women. Do you know the real facts or does your department lavish the tax money?"

"Facts are verified, though sometimes rather strange. Let's do it this way: you tell me about the Stranger, I tell you about anyone, even the Seer."

The Soldier made a wry face:

"I don't know much. He didn't tell me about himself. But I know one thing for sure. The Stranger has got the real power. When it comes, he changes completely: the eyes, the voice. A totally different person."

"And he doesn't keep silent, does he? There was a whole preach for those scumbags. His words hurt them. Right?"

"Indeed hurt. What do you mean?" the Soldier looked at him with interest.

"That's the way the hypnotist works."

"But he didn't tell anything to the Seer, he kept silent and stared at him, the Seer even started to stagger, turned pale and barely fainted."

The agent paused to think, the obscure smile glancing on his face and disappearing immediately.

"Looks like an energetic strike. Your friend turned out to be stronger. I wish we knew the backstory earlier..."

"The Seer is a real hypnotist. The Stranger is completely different," the Soldier stood his ground.

"The Seer can give a mental order remotely. But we know that people even as experienced as he can't demonstrate their abilities at their will. Some special mood, power-up, drive, if we can call it like this, is needed for it. The artist can't create a masterpiece when he feels no inspiration. The poet can't find the words for a heavenly poem when his Muse is away. Anyway, let put lyrics aside. Do you see now why the Seer asked us to help? There is a new star on our skies, as bright as he is. Pity, if it will set soon."

The Soldier just grated teeth.

The Bird approached the Stranger. She wanted to hug him but she didn't have the heart to.

"We have to cross the desert at night," he said.

"I can't. I'm totally exhausted," she answered guiltily.

The Stranger made a wry face as if he turned something every way in mind, pulled out of the backpack warm clothes for the girl and spread his jacket on the ground.

"Sleep. It will help you recover."

He thought: "We have two hours but then we need to move on. We can't sleep in the desert, it's too cold. It's dangerous to light up a fire, somebody can see us."

The Stranger knew the Silencers' desert well. He visited it many times and remembered the way to the ancient tunnel leading to the City. He felt that he was late and they could start without him, he must hurry.

Chapter 27. Intention

The Seer strolled in the garden, breathed the leaves' freshness, enjoying silence. The Functionary phoned and told him about the incident on the Pobeda station.

"It has begun," the Seer was rubbing his forehead hard. "The Power emerges. What next? Soon he will come to the City. Who will stop him? Could he be not a harbinger of the disaster, but a person that can save and protect us? Why did he take the girl with him? She was the reason for the conflict. What if he just wanted the fight and tested the power? Subconsciously?"

The Seer remembered about the Soldier, caught the information, "Will we see each other soon? Yes, very soon. Now he is not afraid of me", then he grinned and said aloud: "I will find you myself."

Incredulously he looked at his big beautiful house, lovely garden, well-groomed trees, flowers, and said through his teeth:

"All that's missing is peacocks".

The Soldier was brought into the office.

"The key, quickly," the Chief ordered to his assistant. "Give order to bring us some food."

He unlocked the manacles himself, apologized for the rudeness of his people.

"I've heard a lot of good about you. It's an honor for me to see you here. I wish the circumstances were different," he nodded on the manacles.

"No offence. I understand," the Soldier said good-naturedly.

"Great. Let's eat, drink some brandy."

"Call the girls," the Soldier continued.

The Chief laughed carelessly. "That's my boy. Made the old man smile… To the Stranger!" he declaimed rising the glass of brandy.

The Soldier sneered: "Overacting", but nodded and emptied the glass. They ate and drank unhurriedly. Having finished the meal, the Chief asked,

"Do you want to read the dossier of your friend?"

The Soldier assented by a nod. Reading the information he realized that the Stranger was not a naïve dreamer with a mysterious power, but a person that went through the mill and knows life. Though the profile was based on the facts, the details were changed, that's why it formed the different vision of the Stranger. He looked like a martyr, his opposites like villains. The recent events were mentioned too, as well as persons responsible for them: the Seer and the Functionary, the inner investigation being initiated against the latter.

"What do you say?" the Chief asked, following closely the Soldier's reaction. He was pleased with the effect.

"What do I say?" the Soldier repeated. "The world is unfair. The Stranger has the same gift, but he doesn't boast of it. The Seer broken the laws of hospitality, he attacked my friend but met the rebuff. The Stranger took mercy on him. The Seer has everything. This man has bought the world. And he decided to finish the Stranger, the pariah, with your hands, because he was not able to beat him."

"I agree with you. The Stranger is a unique person, but he is alone and the Seer has everyone in hands. It's unfair. Believe me, we bear him no malice."

"I need to see him."

"Whom?"

"The Seer. I have to talk to him."

"Can you persuade him not to persecute the Stranger?"

"I will try," the Soldier looked at the Chief meaningfully.

"We will not help you."

"Just don't interfere."

"We have no right to arrest you. Have some rest, think it over. Then, if you like, we'll continue this talk. I'll show you the way."

The chief was very happy and gave the Soldier a hug at parting. He believed that they had a chance to get the better hand in the long and exhaustible confrontation of the two legendary special services.

The job requiring a lot of preparations was reserved for the Soldier, but first of all is sleeping. He was on the verge. He came home, took hot shower, ate a sleeping pill that he could not go without for a long time and drowned in a leaden nervous sleep.

Chapter 28. The Silencers' desert

The Stranger was sitting near the sleeping girl. "It's time to wake her up. What has the City reserved for me? Still it is good that she is beside. How are things with the Soldier, I wonder…" the Stranger took thought. Suddenly, he felt severe trouble. "What's up with him? Is he in danger? No," answered to himself. "Is he up to something awful? Yes".

He got nervous, his hands trembling. "God, have mercy upon us! Why it is so? I cannot let the Soldier conduct atrocity for me". The Stranger raised himself up, made several steps and called: "Soldier… Soldier, do nothing, nothing… It doesn't work out, he cannot hear me… The Seer. He is not an enemy. He must help", it has dawned upon the Stranger, and he whispered, "Seer. A turn to you…"

The Seer was contemplating the leaves that turned yellow, stroking the trees, and talking to them. Suddenly, somebody called for him, he looked around and a moment later he understood, and smiled.

"You have learnt something. Do you need help?"

"Find the Soldier and make him give up his plan," the Stranger asked while being at a distance of several thousand kilometers. He was sure: he was heard.

"The Soldier wants to kill me," the Seer uttered sadly.

"Excuse me. What is the Soldier up to?" the Stranger was distracted because he failed to translate the language of senses into verbal language.

"Kill me," the Seer snapped.

"Remove, erase, move aside?" the Stranger asked again. An association with some obstacle to be moved or thrown away.

It looked like a poor connection, and the Seer sighed,

"I'll help."

The Stranger couldn't hear words but felt joyful. He came down to earth. Tears were running down his face to take away fatigue, stress and embarrassment.

"O Lord, why have you endued me with power? I do not want to make war. I'm alone now. You were the only one to support me, so, give me support now again. I am Your servant, and I can see You. There is no my will, but there is Yours, there is no my way, but there is Yours. And if it is so, let me take Your will as if it were mine. Let me understand and take your ways. Give me piece of mind. But whether one can feel peaceful when the world goes down the road of death? Your creatures are blind. What can be done? And what can I do?"

The Stranger heard the low Voice in himself soft as a waft of wind:

"I know all creatures. Do what you must". Strains accumulated over the past days have disappeared completely. He came back to the Bird and woke her up.

"Wakey!"

"I haven't been so tight asleep for years," she smiled.

The girl sprang to feet, stretched her arms and gave a cry:

"Say: it is light, and life is light,
And you can see the close sky.
We both are sitting at the clouds
As if we were picked up in arms.
One day the smoke, then it is snow.
And we are here to stay forever."

The Stranger burst out laughing.

"It is nice here, but we have to go."

The Bird took a deep breath and nodded fatefully.

They descended the hill to start towards the famous Silencers' desert.

In ancient times, travelers were afraid to walk on this land without amulets. People of different sort escaped to the desert: slaves and kings, bandits and victims of lawlessness, weak and strong... Since the old days, a belief has been existed that only the righteous people of very distinct character can survive there. The caves of holy sites were occupied by monks and followers of religious orders who hoped to gain an insight. At the hills, heights traces of stone altars were seen. Here, the soldiers of special divisions of the Salvation Army, and riots for whom to sneak into the training camp of the enemy, steal ammunition, and escape was bravery of special kind. The getters were met with songs, circle dances, and sweets. The most beautiful girls whispered to one another, giving soulful sighs and burning the young heroes through with impassioned glances.

The stars were shining brightly, cool wind blowing. The Stranger loved the desert, dissolved in it becoming a part of it and felt free and powerful.

"How much longer we have to walk?" the girl broke the silence.

"Not so long. The way will take about seven hours, but we're halt soon," the Stranger calmed her down.

"I cannot walk for so long. I've never walked so much in my life!" she was perplexed.

"Even if I have to carry you, we must reach the tunnel before daylight. I don't know why, but we must hurry," the Stranger stared at the sky.

"What tunnel?"

"A concealed mine. In ancient times, the habitants escaped through the tunnel out of the besieged City," he explained. "Are you afraid of closed space?"

"I am."

"Never mind. I'll take your hand, and when passing through a checkpoint grip hold of my shirt and pass on with your eyes closed."

"It was a joke. For one who did not live it is not frightful to die, but one who lives will never die," she cited a saying by one of the Prince's follower.

"Have you heard of the Prince?" the Stranger was surprised.

"Everybody's heard. I like him, though not always understand. Tell me, why he didn't take pay for curing sick people, though he had often no money on him? Why did he risk life? Why didn't he use violence against his enemies? Why didn't he break out of the country? After all, he could do that, but met death, which he was very afraid of. I've read, he even was crying before he died. Who stole his body? Or, he revived, indeed? Why are so many villains amongst his followers?"

While listening, the Stranger slackened the pace.

"Indeed," he shook his head. "You have read books, to put it mildly, not recommended for average reader."

"I used to read a lot, loved poetry.

'I'm ashamed that I believed in God
Bitter to me that I do not believe now…'

This is about me. I believed in God, but through folly got in touch with the Snake, fell in love with him, but he got me hooked on drugs and got me a place with the Bumblebee to cheat mugs. There was no God. But you can't think me on the street to make love with any gutters. Can you tell me about the Prince?"

"Sure. But first, I'll answer your questions. The Prince was a healer and helped everybody without charge. Doctors did not treat beggar, but he proved to the world that the poor will receive healing the rich cannot buy for money. The Prince cured with power, with gift from above. And gift should be given for nothing. Isn't it? Risked life, because he had a mission. It is far more important than life itself. Your former companions ran the risk too. A drunkard and a drug user risk not half! For what? For a dubious pleasure leading to hung-over? And he ran a danger for the sake of the truth and rescue of people. He could not leave the country because he exemplified courage and faith. The murder of the Prince shocked and shook many people. This is the God's plan. Do you know how many feats followed the suit? And he comprehended something very important under torture and execution, gained experience that helps to understand pain and fear the other people suffer. He was left face to face with this world, without divine shelter. He couldn't feel presence of God, while for such people this is the end of the world. That is why he was crying. Still, the Prince roughed it. His body was not stolen, rather it was changed, maybe replaced by more perfect one, and, of course, not people, however, I'm not aware of technical. All that I know for sure is that he is alive and acting. Villains… doesn't matter how they call themselves, or how the others call them. Their essence matters. Their thoughts and deeds speak for the only thing: not only they are not his followers, but enemies. And when he comes, purification will start with the house under the sign 'Prince's House'."

The travelers talked away time, they walking having thrown fatigue to the wind. All of a sudden, the Stranger stopped and seized the girl by the arm. He looked somewhere into the distance and saw strange shadow figures. Tall extended forms were moving fast and smoothly dead towards them.

The Stranger stood motionless trying to find whether it was a mirage. He had been to the desert a great many of times, but seen nothing of the kind. Reality lost its shape, the sky hung out over him, the air got dense, sand viscous. The Stranger looked towards the moving figures and could not believe in the events. He found the right state: you mustn't be afraid; instead, you should take another reality for a dream, not to 'hover', but pass by as if you were a passer-by, a spectator, so as not to go mad. But if you seek more, you should go beyond the limits of your consciousness, believe that you belong to other reality, and then you will be a participant rather than a spectator.

"I'm not afraid!" he said to himself and made several steps towards the horror.

"Who is that?" the girl asked cuddling to him.

"She can see them too. May not withstand", the Stranger thought, his blood running cold.

He already could see the well-defined silhouettes: three very tall figures of almost the same height. Clothing (apparently, making the integral whole with the bodies) was of unusual style, black or dark grey. They were approaching inexorably. Troublesome music sounded in his temples. The Stranger remembered about amulets and numerous altars in the Silencers' desert. Whether those legends of yore about daemons of the desert were based on reality?

"I'm scared, I'm scared so much. I cannot move," the girl whispered, trembling all over.

"Close your eyes," the Stranger said stiffly. "Don't look. Do not look at them under any circumstance. They intend no harm on us. They are just a desert mirage. Don't be afraid. Do not be afraid of nothing. God's power is on me."

He took her by hand and stared at them. He felt interest; curiosity is not a vice, but very dangerous trait.

"No fear. No fear. His power with me. Wind, come! Creator, give me powers, do not leave me!" He felt just faint breathing of the Wind, but that was enough to look at them fearlessly.

The girl closed her eyes tightly and buried herself in the Stranger's shirt, convulsively throwing her arms around him.

The Stranger saw one of them cast a glance on him: a scornful masque on a pale yellow, unnatural, inhuman face. The rest even did not take a look towards them and walked by right off.

He was torn by conflicting emotions. He couldn't explain what he saw. That was not a mirage, but unexplainable terrifying reality. And you must either forget about it and erase out of memory, or take it for fact. Certainly, the Stranger chose the latter, but his unprepared mentality could not cope with the ordeal that fell to him: he felt like screaming and running for his life from that place. He looked back and at the sight of the girl lying low on the sand he felt ashamed. The Bird opened her eyes and muttered:

"I cannot go, leave me here."

Chapter 29.The Hermit

THE HERMIT

In the Silencers' desert a legendary old man lived. They called him the Hermit. Many years ago, he left the world to occupy one of the caves of the mountain hermitage. People in the vicinity venerated him as if he were a man of God. The Stranger met him by chance: he walked into the Hermit's dwelling when examining the caves in search of ancient artifacts.

He was met by an austere wrinkled, very tall old man with white beard.

"Peace to Thee, wanderer!" he said. "Go up to mine. I've prepared tea for you to give strength and vigor."

"And peace to you. How could you see me? I've come from outside the mountain," the Stranger was surprised.

"I've seen you long before," and without another word, he threw down a rope ladder…

The Hermit always met the Stranger with sweet-scented tea, in a mysterious way knowing the time when the guest visited him even after several years of absence. And the Stranger had no better place to have a rest, though sometimes he used to stay in expensive hotels. Their meetings were always fruitful. The Hermit showed him hidden caves, masked tunnels, crawlways, helped him to find invaluable artifacts and treasures. In the evenings, the friends lighted fuses of lamps handmade of clay and filled with oil, prayed, discussed sacred books. The Stranger often argued against the Hermit, still holding him in respect. The Hermit always cried when was saying good-by to the guest and asked for visiting more often.

After release from prison, the Stranger came to the Hermit; there were nobody who waited for him. Every day, while imprisoned in a one-man cell, he recollected the old man's prophecy. "You will be alone for a year, you'll be speaking to yourself, because you'll have no person to talk to, still the God hears you and he won't leave you, and after those days you'll become a great person. You'll be a man of spirit to see the Truth. The Stranger of the last way inspired by the God's breathing will come to the City to implement the ancient destiny. He will be in glory and power to drive away horror and fear".

For two hours, he was carrying the girl on his back, washed out came up to the cave of his best and, in the event, the only friend.

"Hermit, it's me! I need your help. Help me!" the Stranger called out.

A familiar form was not slow to emerge in the opening.

"I have been waiting for you, Stranger. I have been waiting… your tea is ready. Climb up!" the old man responded joyfully.

"I'm not alone, I've brought a girl, and she feels bad," the Stranger slapped her slightly in the cheek. "Bird! We must get up."

She mumbled something in response. The Stranger jumped onto the rope ladder holding the girl's hand tight. The Hermit threw down the rope with straps to help her get up.

The Stranger, faint with fatigue, laid the Bird onto the wooden bed, and fell down the floor, burying himself in fresh sheepskins emitting sharp odor. His heart was beating frantically, his head swirling. "Now, it's going to be all right", he tried to persuade himself.

The old man brought the tea smelling of smoke, cakes, and thick honey. He looked at the girl, sighed heavily, raised slightly her head and gave her to drink the hot tea. The Stranger who came to life recovered his breath and thanked the God for bread (he did not want to offend the man safeguarding blessings jealously) and attacked the food.

The old man looked at him with sympathetic tenderness, then dropped:

"You have changed, Stranger. Much wisdom and much grief in you, man."

"Waters of life were flowing, Hermit, many things were taken away, many things were brought."

"I have been waiting for you. Now, you're a man of spirit."

"I'm just a leaf in the wind. It is not my coming to be waited for, but our Prince. He is to come. He promised."

The Hermit's eyes were dimmed with tears, and he shook his head sadly.

"Can I see him? I wish I would live to see."

"Sooner or later, you will see him. Do not hurry, my friend, everything is God's will. I need to get to the City. Your prophecy is coming true. But I go not for fame or greatness. Fame and death go hand in hand, but I want to live. I love life whatever it is. But I'm a servant of God, and my fate is in His hands. I'll do everything I must... May I leave the girl with you? She shouldn't go with me until she gains strength. She is scared to death, and, in earnest, I got a fright too."

"Have seen something?" the old man screwed up his eyes cunningly. "Spirits of the desert? You have never believe in them, and even chaffed with me."

"They were not spirits, Hermit," the Stranger stared at one point.

"So, who they were? People? You were frightened by children of bones, haven't you?" the Hermit looked at him attentively.

"They were not people, Hermit. They were not people, yet, I don't know who they were," he shuddered and shook off all stupor.

The old man was gimleting him with gaze, then started back abruptly, turned pale, leaned against the cold wall of the cave, kept silence for a minute, and then uttered in a low voice,

"They're already here."

"Who?"

"Alien people. The predictions of great prophets are being fulfilled, which vaticinated invasion of aliens," the rhetorical language of sacred books confused the Stranger who preferred modern speech patterns. The Hermit often was talking to the characters of ancient scriptures as if they lived in his cave. He admired them, held up as an example, or even reproached some of them.

"What does it mean, Hermit?" the Stranger asked.

"You'll see this in the City," the old man answered mystically.

"I'm not strong enough to stand against them. Nobody can withstand them."

"A man cannot, but God can. You have a gift, you can win with it. But you must know: if you don't hold power, they'll destroy you, and the defeat will tell on the result of the coming battle between light and darkness."

"What dreadful words you say! If I can influence anything, then we're sure to lose!" the Stranger exclaimed. "I cannot govern this power. I call for it, sometimes it responds to certain words, and manifests itself, but sometimes these words do not work out like an obsolete code. I never know for sure, whether it will come or not. Sometimes, the Wind appears itself, without any apparent reason. If I face them, I have to find the right code instantly, otherwise I'll be powerless."

"Code is an idea, word, vision, event, or something else. You have a big choice. Do not be afraid! I believe that the Spirit ought to appear in danger to protect you," the Hermit said enthusiastically.

The Stranger smiled sadly.

"And what about the girl? I've called her the Bird."

"She lost her wings," the old man replied. "Do you remember a book of poems you brought to me? I liked some of them very much:

'And if the building's in fire,
We'll die without the wings
The wings so precious to me'."

"Never mind, Hermit, her wings will grow again, and she'll fly. Let her stay with you," the Stranger asked.

"Are you going to the City? I'm ready to follow you. Stay here for a while, at least have a rest, and then, let's go. For your sake, I'm ready to leave the desert," the Hermit said.

"No, I'll go alone. Help the Bird. I'm hunted by the great. I put my trust in the Seer, but he let the dogs loose on me. A friend of mine who had trusted in me helped me, but now he is in their hands".

"People won't be able to help you, Stranger. And it's not people whom you should be afraid of. Our war is not against flesh and blood. Oh, Seer, Seer," the old man fetched a deep sigh. "There's something wrong about it, Stranger, something wrong. He wouldn't do hurt to you."

"What are you talking about, Hermit? We're not the enemies with him, not we are kindred, though. What did he want? I couldn't guess. Is it possible that the Seer got a fright?"

"He didn't want you to come to the City," the Hermit answered in an assertive tone.

"Why do you think so?"

The old man glanced at the friend wit reproof.

"Sorry, I'm tired; I'm just being thick today," the Stranger smiled.

"I've discovered the Seer," the Hermit sighed. "I've found a puny boy with fiery eyes, seen his gift and helped him be developed. I was a famous telepathist and healer. I had not to stay in this world amongst people. I could hear thoughts and see the true essence of a person, his past, and felt sick. I could see the future: death and pain, and felt like crying. Such capacity brings grief, and my skin was as thin as letter paper. I perceived else's pain as if it were mine. The patient has a headache, and I have, he's hung over, and I have that morning after-feeling. He suffers from loss of his loved one, and my heart is breaking. That's why I'm here, and long ago. And the Seer was able to find himself in the world of hypocrisy, seeking lucre, and violence. He has adopted somehow, gained fame and respect. Yet, people like him try not to do hurt to righteous people. They know the worth of such a crime. I believe, he's undertaken to take care of you, in a strange way, though. The Seer has his head in the clouds, but he's got accustomed to this world, even struck his root deep. Sooner or later, he'll sober up."

"Why did the Seer refuse aid?"

"He saw danger for people if you come to the City now."

"Do you believe that I pose hazard to people?"

"You're the torch. You give light to kind people while burning malevolent ones. You know, the Prince possessed power that not only saved but killed. Once, when he was hungry and exhausted, he was angered by emptiness and unbelief of people and could not suppress the power that arisen in him. Then he directed it towards a tree so as not to hurt sons of men... the tree burst into flames as straw. Believe me, it is the most difficult thing to possess power but not to resource to. And you'll also find it difficult to refrain; still it is you who decide."

"Hermit, who is good? Who is bad one?" the Stranger gave in. "Why are you here, not with good people? Where are they, the good ones? Well, they probably exist, but why are they good, have you an idea of it? The answer is simple: biology, genetics… this is their nature, not merit. But what's about the bad? After all, they are ill, prisoned, with their mind struck blind, their feelings closed. You cannot burn snakes and scorpions! They are no ways to blame for being born with poison! There is military situation, and there is time of peace, both have their own laws and rules. Sometimes a man does well, sometimes he is wrong, it depends on circumstances. Men of God fight not against people, but against human errors. Anyway, I believe, people can change, but under certain circumstances, and this happens rarely if ever. Mostly, people cannot change, even if they'll change their clothes, bare essence of them will remain unchanged. What can I do, and for whom? It is not rare that I need help myself, sometimes I feel blue, though, I know it's too silly of me. I'm nothing alone. It seems to me that I'm just a cheap bottle for expensive wine; the bottle will be cast off no sooner than the wine dries up."

"My poor friend! Love has cooled down in your heart. I'm afraid you're not ready yet to go to the City. You're over the hill. I can see it is not wine to soothe and cheer up that you carry, but a sword, and you are eager to unsheathe the sword. The Prince was not like you."

The Stranger stood up. He felt sharp rage of the Wind. He didn't find the reason that drew to power, but noted, "Wine, sword. Remember another code. Maybe, it'll work one day".

"The Prince was pierced, and I'm a sword now. The world keeps on killing him every day," the Stranger was under the influence of the Wind and didn't understand what he was telling about.

He turned away trying to calm down. Then he came up to the old man who was keeping head down, and offered his hand,

"Thank you for everything, my friend. I'll be pleased to see you in the City."

Coming to the edge of the cave, he jumped down, flied over several meters to land softly onto the sound. Then he stood up straight and stepped out not looking back. The Hermit was looking at the Stranger's figure moving away, heavy tears running down his seamed face to vanish in his white beard.

Part two

The City

Chapter 30. The guardians of the tunnel

The desert was freezing cold. In a hurry, the Stranger left the bag with the possessions with the Hermit and, light-handed, was now walking quickly. He was not thinking about anything, he only wanted to melt into the desert. Sometimes a strong wind started and threw sand at him. When the Stranger got tired he stopped and looked at the huge bright stars shining from the bluish black sky. With the dark the desert started to wake: the yellow eyes of predators flashed here and there, jackals howled, animals and birds hooted and chawed. The desert was now filled with the sounds that drove mad the ancient travelers who at night climbed the branchy heads of trees to avoid being caught by the wild animals, spread their cloaks and waited for the dawn. But he had no time to wait as he no longer belonged to himself. He had no fear: on the contrary, there was a desire to fight.

He remembered meeting with the three wayfarers dressed in black, the mask-like face of one of them who deigned to look his way, the scorn that flickered in his inhuman eyes and could feel the Wind that helped him to survive.

The Stranger drank in the Wind and felt protected: without water, weapons, even without a stick to frighten away the beasts and throw off the snakes. He could only rely upon the Creator.

Early in the morning he reached the tunnel and found the entrance covered with stones. Without hesitation the Stranger began to turn the rocks and throw them away. He could barely finish the work when he turned his head to see two stout armed men with beards. At once, he understood they were the adepts of some religious order and talking to them would be hard.

"We are the Guardians of the holy gates. A stranger shall not enter the tunnel. Get out of here or we'll cut you to ribbons!" said one of them and slowly, as if posing, took out a thin knife.

"Wait," said the second guardian and, gazing at the Stranger asked him, "how do you know about the tunnel?"

"I know about the tunnel. You have no right to hold me off. The tunnel belongs to everybody. You are like a snake guarding its gold."

The guardian held a knife to the neck of the darer, but saw no more than a sneer in his eyes.

"Put down the knife, quick!" ordered the second one, staring hard at the Stranger. "Who are you, man?"

After this question the Stranger felt the breath of the Wind: the anger that was suppressed with such a difficulty still hasn't passed.

"You'd better not know this. Help me or get away, or I'll crush you!"

The man with the knife trembled, lowered his head and sank to his knees.

"Forgive me, Prince, I haven't recognized you. Forgive me!" he looked at the Stranger with admiration and devotion.

"I am not the Prince, I was only sent by him," the Stranger lifted him. "Help me."

The guardians exchanged glances and willingly nodded their heads. Altogether they started to clear the entrance.

"Careful! We've put a trip wire," warned one of the desert warriors.

The mine was placed with one branch of the trip wire, attached by pegs and rose about 15 centimeters above the land surface. The guardian took his sharp knife and quickly cut the strained strip, removed the camouflage layer around the igniter set and out pieces of wire into the openings of the pin slapper rods. Then he picked the side of a small mine with his knife and, turning the igniter set counter clockwise, carefully unscrewed it.

"Who are you?" asked the Stranger with hardly concealed irritation. He could hardly have expected that the tunnel would be full of such surprises.

"We are the warriors of the desert. We have a contract with the governors who have given us the right to guard the tunnel," answered a guardian with great dignity.

"Why do you need the tunnel? And what has happened with the entrance?"

"The tunnel is one of the main sacred places, according to the prophecy: 'Give the Prince the entrance and give his messenger the exit, and no strange person shall pass them or tread the bullets of our God, as no evil man will walk along His roads and anyone plotting evil will die'. We do believe that the Prince or his messenger will get to the City exactly through this tunnel. And this is where his ascension to glory will begin."

"So you've decided to fulfill the spiritual prophecy this way, by making so many traps in the tunnel, and you think that if a sincere person goes here, nothing will happen to him, and one shouldn't be sorry for a sinner, right?"

The Stranger understood: he won't be able not only to destroy the traps, but even to spot them. That was the thing the Soldier was needed for. He sat at the entrance and started to pray.

"The sons of Men make it all so much harder. They kill others and themselves without understanding the sense of the ancient prophecies, and the pastors use them in their interests disorienting their parish. And now, do try to clean up all that mess! I cannot go through the tunnel. If only a messenger of God was here with me, as the legend about the young men who were thrown into a boiling copper trap said it. I'm in the same trap now. What shall I do? Return? Take a train? But they're looking for me. I can go over the mountains, but it's a long and dangerous way, and I should be quick. If I don't arrive in time, it'll be a trouble. So, what can I do?" the Stranger turned his thoughts to Heaven. And inside his head he heard a voice: "The help will come, wait".

"Do you know how to go through the tunnel avoiding the traps?" the Stranger attentively looked at the guardian.

"No. Nobody knows it now. The one who put them is no longer with us."

"I get it," the Stranger saw that the desert warrior was not lying. "I heard a voice that told me to wait here. The help will come."

The guardian looked at him with disappointment and regret. An experienced warrior of the desert liked this newcomer and it even seemed to him that he possesses some divine power and spirit, but he still had to be killed if he refused to go through the tunnel.

The Stranger felt the fatigue only then. He closed his eyes trying to take a nap, but he could not: every time he fell asleep, he was overcome with fear. Where was the Wind that gave courage, confidence and bravery? He had to search the codes.

He remembered the courtroom, the charge of illicit possession of the ancient artifacts, and with a difficulty his speech: at some moment, he lost control of himself. The Wind took over him, and he started to predict sorrows to all those who were in the room. Later on, the Stranger was horrified by what he had said but comforted himself by deciding that he was not inflicting miseries, he was just foretelling them. After all, a news presenter is not guilty for the bad announcements, he only reads the text displayed to him.

Chapter 31. The bitter decoction

The Hermit had made a healing decoction and was patiently waiting for the guest to wake up. Soon it happened, she half-rose from the bench, saw the dozing man and yelped,

"Where am I?"

The Hermit opened his eyes.

"I am the Stranger's friend. You didn't feel well, and he asked me to look after you," he explained.

"Why am I here? Where is he?"

"The Stranger has brought you to me and left for the City. Now I am responsible for your life," the old man answered coldly.

"I must catch up with him! Which direction has he taken? I will not stay here without him," the Bird said determinately.

The old man stroke the beard with his hand.

"I need to speak with God and will give you my answer soon," he rose and put the healing decoction to her lips. "Drink! It will give you the energy."

The Bird sipped a little and almost got sick.

"How terrible! How bitter it is!"

"If you don't drink it all, I won't even ask. It will take you too much time to get better, and you will stay here for long."

She looked at the clay cup with a great doubt, then pinched her nose and drank the bitter liquid smelling of herbs at just one swallow.

"Don't you dare vomit this!" the Hermit said sharply. "Endure it!"

The eyes of the girl filled with tears, she jerkily tried to inhale. The old man understood that she was not going to bear it, remembered the taste of a sweet ripe apple and threw the impression to her. She calmed down practically at once. The taste of the decoction, as bitter as wormwood, was exchanged for the taste of apple juice. The girl felt a surge of energy, vivacity, a desire to move and even some kind of delight.

"Thank you! You know herbs really well. Can I go now? I have so much energy."

He approached the side of the cave, looked at the sky, silently moved his lips, listened to something and pronounced: "We will go together. If you want to be with him, you'll have to go the way of death. Are you ready?"

"I don't see any sense in my life without him," and she told how she had met the Stranger.

The old man listened to her attentively, nodded and lay down on the sheepskin. The Bird looked at the lights of the clay lamp for a long time. She felt so cozy and protected inside the cave that the tears of tenderness welled in her eyes. With all that, she was a little afraid of the Hermit, the very look of which resembled the ancient prophets from the works of great painters. From time to time he threw a glance at her and shook his head with disapproval.

It seemed to the girl that his sharp eyes reflecting the little sparks of fire reached the deepest parts of her heart. She smiled guiltily looking by steal at the old man.

"May I ask you a question?" the girl started. The old man nodded propitiously. "Why hasn't he taken me with him? And has given them the diamond?"

"He could not do other than he did. The Stranger has embarked on the course of war, and to survive he needs the armor of purity. Heaven welcomes mercy and kindness. But probably you will also help him in need," the Hermit was silent for a little while. "He had three stones: a carbuncle, a sapphire and a diamond. I found them in a hiding place in one of the caves and made him promise he would not give the stones to the governors and would use them only to save lives. He gave away the carbuncle when he needed to buy out his companion captured by the rebels. The sapphire was for his ex-wife to take care of herself and the children. And the diamond, his

last stone, was for you. But when the misfortune came they betrayed him: according to the testament of the saved friend, the Stranger was accused of the concealment of ancient manuscripts, and his wife
showed the secret places where he had hidden the scriptures. The precious stones were wasted on the wrong people. Stand up, woman, it's time to go."

Chapter 32. The eastern direction

The Soldier slept nervously and keenly. He saw the Prophet in his dream.

"Your friend needs your help. We need to meet. I am sitting at your entrance. Get up." The Soldier woke up, opened his eyes as he heard the loud and distinct voice. He went into the bathroom, washed his face with cold water. "That is insane", he thought, totally waking up and looking into the entryway. He became weak in his knees: there was the Seer sitting on the steps. He put the finger to his lips and whispered, "Let's go. We can't talk here."

The Soldier gathered everything quickly. While leaving the entrance, the Seer nodded to the van parked nearby:

"There are agents. Sleeping soundly," and the Seer threw the keys to his companion. "Take the wheel. I don't like driving."

Starting the car and taking off slowly, the Soldier shook his head few times, as if throwing off the stupor.

When the oppressive silence reached its peaks, the Seer decided to give the explanations:

"I am not against the Stranger. Remember this. He asked me to help you. For I know, what you have in mind, but you are wrong. The agents showed you wrong direction. We are going to the Silencers' desert now and we will find the Stranger there. Do you believe it?"

The Soldier gave a nod. The most important is to find him and then act according to the circumstances.

"Tell me, what has happened to you."

The Soldier took a breath and started from the very beginning. The Prophet was listening very attentively without interrupting, but he asked to tell about the conflict with the criminals in all the details. He tried to see the last events in the eyes of the Soldier.

"What's this fire?" suddenly, the Seer interrupted his narration.

"What fire?" the Soldier looked both sides in surprise.

"You saw the flame, lots of black smoke. You didn't tell about it," the Seer seemed to be looking at an unseen screen.

"Yes. That's right. There was a fire, it was some factory burning, I think. How is it connected?"

"I don't know yet. Did the Stranger look at the fire?"

"I think he did."

"Did he strike the criminals with the words?"

"Yes. It's not hypnosis, was it?" the Soldier didn't want to believe the agents.

"No, it wasn't the hypnosis. It was something different. Let's say for now it was some miracle," the Seer named as a miracle the phenomenon that modern science couldn't find explanation to so far due to the lack of scientific experience and knowledge. "No, not hypnosis. It was something else."

"Then what was it?"

"Probably, it was the discharge of directed energy," said the Seer slowly.

He had no doubts any more that this fire has somehow helped the strength to come out.

"The Stranger needs inspiration, or impulse to open himself for this energy," the Seer made this conclusion. "But it's hard to understand this occurrence that doesn't have any analogy, at least in my practice." Anyway, he came close to the solution of the origin of this mysterious power that the Stranger calls as the Wind.

They reached the Silencers' desert by the morning, passing the block stations. The Seer impressed the soldiers and the officers with the thought that it a high military rank passing by and they let the van go without any problem. Only at the last block station, one captain was very insisting asking to provide escort for them, arguing that they can't approach the closed zone with the battles going on to liquidate the terrorists. The Seer had to "show" armored troop carrier that was waiting for them in a few dozens of meters. Pointing to the huge stone, he sent the captain the contours of a battle ship, hardly knowing himself how it should look like. The captain looked at the rock for a long time in total amazement and even tried to come closer to see the new miracle of engineering. The Seer could hardly calm down the zealous soldier. The officer softened, saluted and wished a good trip.

The Seer left the van, stretching the numb muscles, breathed the dry air of the desert tiredly, he hadn't worked that hard for a long time. He looked into the horizon, reached his hand in eastern direction,

"The Stranger is there. Something is going on. There is haze over the city. It's a trouble. It's a huge trouble for the City."

"It's dangerous. It's very dangerous," the Soldier forced a smile.

"Maybe let's go back?" offered the Seer and gave him a keenly look.

"No. I am ok. I am not afraid; I just feel that there is danger ahead."

"Get some rest. I will drive."

In an hour and a half of driving slowly, the Seer stopped the car.

"The van can't go further, and I can't. I will be waiting for you here. Persuade the Stranger to come back. I will find a way to send you to the City. You will cross the hills and go to the highest mountain, you will see him there."

"Tell me, will we survive?" the Soldier saw only death ahead, but after finding out about a backup, calmed down a little.

The Seer looked wearily at him.

"A wrong question has the wrong answer. Go there and persuade him to come back. If you can't persuade, come back alone. Do you understand me? Do you understand it well enough?" he asked with some pressure in his voice.

The Soldier nodded and hastened to the hills. His body treacherously trembled, but he walked further, biting on his lips. The danger sensor beeped nonstop, the increasing fear bound his feet, weakened his hands and shadowed his mind. The Soldier gathered his strength in his fist. He started to run, he wanted to shout loudly but mostly he had a desire to hind, dig into the sand, hide himself in a crack, narrow his eyes.

Only not to be walking forward: to meet his death.

Chapter 33. The tunnel of death

The rumor that there is a stranger has spread around quickly, the warriors of the desert and the followers of the other war religious orders drew up to the tunnel. The Stranger was sitting on a stone. There were about a few dozens of people, lying around him, calmly but with the weapons in their hands. The Stranger spoke quietly and smoothly, not like other preachers who are skilled to transfer from angrily shouts to a whisper, from curses to tears.

"Brothers, the time of horror and fear comes, the time of troubles and diseases. The time when people lose their heavily protection and become the booty of the Alien people, who know no mercy or compassion, the people that you can't stand against. We will rush to appeal to the Heaven, but it won't listen to us, for we refused His Voice at a certain point. We killed innocent, shed blood as if it was mere water, indulged in lust and nasty things. We chose our god: Money; but this god has no power when the trouble comes. The real God, the Lord of life, we refused him, killed his servants and chased him away. The Prince, who brought us all a hope, was killed and his testament was trampled. And now the time of the court and justice comes and this is the time of sorrow. But God is merciful. We will repent, while we are alive and, probably, He will have mercy on us, He will give us protection and will accept us in His dwelling place."

The warriors silently listened to him. Some of them nodded as if agreeing with him.

"I see you know what you are talking about," the elder of the community turned to him, "and there is a power in you. But are you ready to pass our trial? Can you pass through the death tunnel?"

"Why test the power of somebody else and endanger each other?" the Stranger tried to persuade them. "Are you searching for a sign? You are searching for a sign because your hearts are silent, your eyes are blind and that's why you turn to the ancient books and look through somebody's eyes."

"The ancient books are the revelation and teaching to the future generations. Isn't it so?" objected the elder.

"The ancient books are the experience of the ancient's and it's very useful for us, I don't deny this. But can a man become full just by reading cookery recipes? The revelations are directions but not the final destination. Learn God, be sincere and kind and then He will be opened to you, He will protect and lead you by your hand. You don't understand the prophecy about the 'entrance' and 'exit' correctly.

You expose the dreamers who think that they are prophets to a death danger. It is not right. The Prince would never have something like that in his mind."

"So we will check if God leads you by your hand or you are just pulling the wool over our eyes. If you survive, we'll believe you. You die, and we will pray for you. It's doesn't matter if we understand the prophecy correctly or not. The tunnel like life is full of traps: you can't remove them but you can avoid them. You speak very well. It's impressive but can you do more than just speak? We don't trust the words. I repeat: if sent by the Prince, you'll escape unhurt, but if you are a mere dreamer, then the tunnel will become your grave. A man, who sincerely thinks he is a prophet, but who isn't a real one, is a false prophet and he has to die."

"Has anyone ever tried to go through the tunnel?" asked the Stranger. He understood that it's impossible to persuade people that trust only in their signs and codes.

"After we have explained that this place is mined nobody even tried. You said that you are sent by the Prince. Don't refuse your words. You saw our faces, you know the place, you can't just leave," the elder looked at his weapon with some meaning.

The Stranger felt his throat squeezed, he felt fear: there is no way back.

"I can't show my fear to this people. They are like predators: as soon as they feel the blood, nothing can stop them. As soon as they feel the fear, they will get into a fight. The only law of theirs is the strength. I need the Wind so much but my fear doesn't let it come. I do need the Power!" he prayed and tried to remember: "The sword of truth is in my hands." A slight hope showed up, he listened: no, wrong code. Suddenly the Stranger remembered the desert and the three travelers... and felt the Wind blowing. "The Alien people! I have to hold it. I will not be afraid and I will be protected."

The Wind grew stronger. "It's time!" decided the Stranger.

"Warriors of the desert!" he exclaimed. "You have overtaken the authority that you weren't given, and you will be responsible for that. I am not afraid of you, His Power is with me. Your weapons have no strength; your hands will not be able to hold them. I will pass through the tunnel and after that you will bury your weapons deep inside the send and will go to the Hermit, the man of peace and kindness, for your weapons have no use in the upcoming war and it will only lead to destruction. You will want to buy off but the money will become like sand in the desert. You think that your faith will save you and that God will not leave you? But you are not protecting the faith. It can't be protected by mines and tortures. You say that you are the only ones who have the truth? Is it in the desert? But is the truth just saline land and thorns, rocks and sands? Isn't it everywhere, and mostly in our souls? You say that fasting and washing away cleanse our souls. But can famine and water cleanse the heart? Fashionable models exhaust themselves by hunger, prostitutes soak in bathtubs and Jacuzzi but this doesn't make them righteous. You say that you have seen miracles in this desert? May be, I won't argue. But what is a miracle? A rare phenomenon? You had the honor to be in a special zone, and you, leaning on your weapon are telling about your anointment? A man, who has lived his whole life in a grotto, who is used to cold stones, darkness and who comes out to the light and sees the sun...will he be surprised by its qualities. But this is only in the beginning because later on he will get adjusted to this just like you got adjusted to the desert and its miracles..."

When seeing the Stranger surrounded by warriors, the Soldier took a few seconds to slap himself on his chest, shoulders and belt: it was a mere reflex in front of armed people, but he didn't even have a knife with him. He fell flat on the ground and looked into the sky.

May be there is still some hope, and the miracle will happen again and they will come out of this alive. He raised himself and slowly came down the hill and as soon as he stepped on an open area, the warriors have taken aim at him.

"I am not armed! Don't be nervous!" he shouted. "I came to my friend."

Two warriors jumped up to him, one put the gun to his temple, the other one kicked him with his gun between his shoulder blades.

"This is my friend. Take your weapons away!" demanded the Stranger.

The elder nodded and the warriors put their weapons down.

The Soldier gave the Stranger a hug and whispered into his ear,

"Let's go and let's do it fast. The Seer is waiting for us about two hours away from here."

"No, my friend, I can't leave. I have to pass the death tunnel," and he pointed to the dark entrance.

The Soldier peeped into the dark corridors and got scared, an unconcealed fear showed on his face.

"This is the death tunnel. It's mined, full of traps. They won't give you a mine detector, will they? I doubt it would even help. They are the desert sons and we are on a truce with them, they demanded to exchange this tunnel to stopping the acts of terror. May be they will let us go? Let's leave this place!" begged the Soldier.

"Why don't you want to come with me? You are the mine searcher. Your skills are especially for this. Let's go together, step in step," persuaded him the Stranger, but he already saw the Soldier seized by fear, not sure about his strength, broken down, and so, he will lose.

"We will die there, we don't have special equipment, and you can't do it in the darkness by touch, I don't even have a flash light with me! We won't even see the mine wire. I can feel one mine, may be two but not more than that. The warriors of the desert use charging and discharging mines. You have been in the army, you know what it means. It's silly to die like that. The Seer can help us get into the City; he is with us now, just as you wanted. This is a great miracle," whispered the Soldier.

"Time can't wait," intruded the elder. "Are you coming with him? We have an agreement: he passes through the tunnel and we go to the Hermit. If he doesn't pass it, we will pray for him."

"What Hermit are you talking about?" exclaimed the Soldier. "No one can pass through this tunnel. Please, let him go, begging you, he doesn't know what he is talking about."

The desert warrior looked at him with despise. The Stranger stood there stunned. He rejoiced when he saw the Soldier: here is the help.

And again everything went not as he thought it would.

"I counted on you. I thought you could feel the trap," he said with disappointment, still trying to persuade the friend.

"No, Stranger, there is death there. I can see it. The one will get on a mine, the other will die. We can't go there. There is death, I can see it. It's our death."

"You are right. I will meet you in the City. Go. Just do it," said the Stranger in a deep voice and turned away. He didn't expect this blow.

"I can't watch this. Please, forgive me. God protect you! I am leaving, the Seer said so," hardly keeping his tears whispered the Soldier and started moving backward.

"You can't leave. You've seen our faces," said the elder.

The Soldier looked at the warriors. He had a thought: it's better to die with his friend, than from the bull of these jackals. But the Stranger intruded:

"Leave him alone! This man is not dangerous for you. I am responsible to my words. I will pass the tunnel, just let him leave. The agreement is still in force."

"Go!" he told his friend sharply. "God protect me."

The chief of the warriors gave a sign to his team, and the Soldier was allowed to leave.

Chapter 34. The Lantern

The Stranger stood near the mouth of the tunnel hesitantly and peered at its fearsome arches.

"The fear of death," he told himself. "When will I get rid of it? How long will it follow me? Where is my belief? I cannot die until my mission is completed. I should see it as a game: it's hard, it's scary, but nothing can harm. It's important to understand the rules, options and the system of the game. But how am I to go through the tunnel? The Wind is not supposed to search the mines. Should I search by the feeling of danger? But the fear gives too much of false references, I will be all mussed up. Why the Soldier got scared, though his gift destined for such situations? The reality doesn't fall into our pattern, does it? You think you've understood and got the point but it appears that your conclusions were wrong; you didn't take into account all nuances. Could the Seer go through the tunnel? Perhaps, he could, but no, he's got bad leg... What if there are taut wires? He would need to crawl or jump. He is incapable. Why didn't the Soldier go? Why? Could this be connected with the prophecy? The Soldier cannot be the messenger. His hands are covered with blood, a bad example for the followers. The Soldier doesn't believe that the Prince was the chosen one, how can he be his messenger? But on the other hand, the warriors of the desert worship the Prince, but what is the good of it? However, they worship the other Prince, created by their sick perverted imagination. They would have killed the true one. And who am I?"

The Stranger heard: "Shield and sword".

"Whom am I to protect? Show me these people. Are they the warriors of the desert? But it is me who needs protection against them," the man standing near the entrance to the death tunnel thought with sad irony.

He heard the metallic clangs of the bolts and turned back. Joy crashed on his heart like a wave; he recognized the tall figure of the Hermit and the slender silhouette of his new friend. "Why did he take her with him?"

The old man approached him, holding the girl's hand and paying no attention to the noise and shouts. The bandits seemed to recognize him and made a lane for him respectfully.

The elder one came up to the Stranger.

"Will the Hermit go with you?"

The Stranger smiled but said nothing. He shook the Hermit's hand and kissed the girl. The Bird ran into his arms willingly and squeezed him. They stepped aside from the gunmen.

"Are you better now?" he patted the girl's rough hair and turned to his friend. "I hope you are here not to talk me out of going there?"

"I brought your things. I questioned," the old man answered serenely.

"And..?" the Stranger tightened.

The Hermit kept silent.

"Shall we go together?" the Stranger asked eagerly.

The old man shook his head.

"Shall I go alone?" the Stranger peered into the Hermit's face. "No. What then?"

"Just don't get nervous. I will go with you," the Bird nipped in.

"What? Are you joking?"

"She is not joking. I know all your objections, but that's the way you should do."

The Stranger looked at the Bird helplessly.

"Do you realize what sort of place it is?"

"No," she answered simply.

"I can explain. The tunnel is mined. Nobody knows where the mines are, we don't have the detector. We have a lamp, but I'm not sure if we will be permitted to use it. Anyway, there is little hope for the lamp. Mines are of on and off type. You press the detonator, and blast."

"You talk my ears off," the Bird said gently. "The mine of the off type is it kind of dangerous too?"

He smiled.

"The mine blows when you step off it. You hear the click and you can't move, because it will explode. Aren't you scared?" looking at the girl's happy face he wanted to laugh, he scarcely kept from laughing.

"All of my life I was scared and felt bad. And now, I'm not scared and I feel good. I am different now. I'm happy. I will go with you."

The Stranger looked at the Hermit.

"We will meet in the Town," the old man said confidently.

"How will I go through the tunnel? What am I to orient to? What feelings?" now the Stranger was worried only about the girl, risking her life recklessly.

"Listen to the Voice, only the Voice and don't be afraid," the Hermit answered. "The God is with you."

"Think again, please," the Stranger stared at the girl, but she shook her head.

"I will go with this woman," he said to the elder.

"There is nothing said in the prophecy about the woman," the elder said perplexedly: he looked as if this proposal took him by surprise.

"But this doesn't mean she cannot be near the man," the Stranger insisted.

"Good," the elder gave in rather quickly. "We will pray for both of you."

"Remember about the promise: you will lay down arms, if I go through the tunnel."

"We are the keepers of the tunnel. If there is nothing to keep, we will need no guns. By the way, you don't need the lamp, because you'll find a good lantern inside. Sorry for having checked the contents of your bag."

The Stranger pulled the lamp out of the bag, threw it aside and offered hand to the elder man who took it with both palms and shook passionately…

A chill crept from the tunnel stones. The darkness deepened. They made a few steps forward. The Stranger said to the girl quietly:

"You must do everything as I do. If I say, lift your leg and step over, you do what I say. If I say crawl, you must crawl. And don't even try to bicker."

What a strange place this tunnel is: the walls and the ceiling are perfectly surfaced, as if they were handmade. The air must be delivered via the special ventilating ducts. The ceiling is really high, about three meters; the width of the passage is one and half meters. Why did the ancients take so many pains for such a pointless exercise? It would have been enough to make the ceiling man's height. No vertical shaft at all. What did the workers orient to? They worked without the light, dug almost ten kilometers in the hard rock. Judging by the height and the width of the tunnel, only two people could work simultaneously. How many years did it take, if using the primitive technology they could dig in the rock about five centimeters per day? A job for several generations, even if they dug the tunnel from the both sides simultaneously. Another enigma...

The Stranger thought about it and felt his fear was leaving him gradually. Soon he saw something on the ground. He approached and wanted to pick it up, but heard the voice stinging like a lash: "No!" This thing smelled death.

The Stranger noticed the changes in him. It seemed that the Source of Information had opened for him and he could get the answers to all questions. "Such a shame," he thought, "it's a great chance to learn the secrets I've been trying to discover all my life, but now only one question of greatest importance for me is survival". He subdued the surge of anger.

"How long should we walk forward?" the Stranger asked in his mind. He made twelve steps serenely and steady, there appeared confidence in the invisible guide. He stopped, listened to his senses. "Jump", he asked and claimed at the same time and he heard the answer: "Yes". The Bird kept back, holding him by the jacket.

"We must jump as far as possible," the Stranger said. "I jump first, you follow me. Jump right from this spot."

"Ok."

The heart of the Stranger gave a thump: he felt her fear. He took a deep breath, got down and jumped. The Bird rushed after him without hesitation. She landed straight on him. The Stranger sat down on his knee but managed to base himself upon hand. The girl held his back with her arms and cuddled behind.

"May I have hold of you?" she faltered.

"Sure," the Stranger said, turned to her and thought, "She thinks I'm a saint".

"I'm ready to embrace you forever," she whispered.

"We have to go," he said quietly.

"One more minute," the girl asked, embracing him even stronger. "You must be thinking I was a prostitute?"

"It's not what I'm thinking about now," the Stranger resented. "You were born anew, you were forgiven. Don't turn back to your past. Walk the road of the truth, have hope and belief."

"I earned money by trapping the clients," the girl didn't let him go. "I didn't sleep with them, Bumblebee and his guys dealt with the dupes then, but they never killed or crippled anyone."

"Dupes? It's better to be cheated, than a cheater," the Stranger answered with a snarl. "No time to relax, danger is ahead."

He kept going forward slowly. "Don't think, don't think about anything. Throw all thoughts out, clear your mind for the Voice," he talked to himself and asked, "what am I to do? How long do we have to keep going?" But there was no answer. The Stranger sat on the ground. It seemed to him that he had lost the signal tuned into the Source of Knowledge.

"Is something wrong?" the girl asked.

"Nothing. I need to sit a little," he answered a bit crossly.

The Stranger started to lose his nerve as he hadn't got any answer to his questions. The fear was coming back slowly.

"You don't know how to go on further, do you?" the Bird asked serenely.

"No, I don't," he answered harshly.

"Do you believe it's better to sit down and do nothing?"

"Yes. It's better to do nothing than to make a mistake."

"They say, only he, who does nothing never errs."

"In this very case, if we err we will definitely do nothing anymore."

"How long are we going to sit?"

"Until I feel it's time to stand up. I'm tired; I need to sleep a little. Perhaps, this is why it's difficult to hear. Don't bother me."

He closed his eyes, snuggled against the wall, it was not smooth: peaks, grains, asperities…

The Stranger's sleep was short and nervous; he talked to somebody in a dream. Someone explained him how he should go.

When he woke up, he could not remember anything. He opened his eyes and looked at the girl.

"Why did you go with me?"

"I don't know. I wanted to be with you," the Bird answered fondling his hand.

"It's not a perfect place for dating," he said somberly.

"Why? It's quiet here and nobody bothers," the girl squeezed his palm with her hands.

"We should go," the Stranger gasped. He wanted to hear the Voice but not her hot thrilling breath.

After a while, he felt fear again, even more, he was terrified. They cannot go further.

There were a lot of voices inside his head, but they were his convoluted thinking, fears, illusions, and he could not hear the Voice. "If we can't go forward, we can go backward," he felt better, after this thought had come.

"Let's go back, near the walls. I'll take the left, you take the right. We need to touch the stones," the Stranger said to the girl. It seemed to him that the insanity was overwhelming, but he remembered that heard this very phrase in his tumultuous dream. "If you discover anything, tell me right away."

They went backward, touching the walls of the tunnel; in a few minutes, the Bird cried:

"Come here! Here's some cavity."

"Step aside, please, let me see."

The Stranger didn't feel anything dangerous; he stretched his arm, found something inside the cavity and pulled it out.

"Do you have a lighter?"

The Bird delved in the pockets and took out the lighter. The thing they found was a lantern, with a plastic bag attached and two batteries inside.

"Good girl. You've found it," the Stranger turned the lantern on, a ray of bright blue light flashed.

"Will the lantern help us?" she asked happily.

"I believe it is the only thing that can help us."

They walked for about half an hour. The Stranger inspected the floor of the tunnel. He saw the taut wire, warned the Bird and after twenty more steps he found another one strained unusually high, they had to crawl under it. It repeated three times: every twenty steps he found the traps. He noticed this regularity and started to count the steps. Suddenly the light went off. The Stranger clicked the switch a few times and put the lantern inside the bag.

"Will we find the next wire in the twenty steps? Or is it a trap? You get over the system, make the next twenty steps but the taut wire is located in ten or thirty steps: broken rhythm."

The Stranger sat down again, held the Bird and felt that she was shivering.

"Are you fine?" he asked, cuddling her.

"How are we to go on without the light?" she asked scarcely keeping back tears.

"If you want to cry, just cry. The tears will wash away fear, pain and hurt. The torch helped us: thanks to its light, we cheated death several times. And we noticed the relevance: there is taut wire every twenty steps. There is a good chance that it is the same all the way."

"Let's burn the lighter after the next twenty steps, there's not much gas in it, but it can last for a while," the Bird proposed.

"It won't help us; the lantern light was blue for a reason. I think it's done on purpose to see the wire."

"What are we to do?"

"I don't know yet. It's difficult for me to tune in."

"How are we to go on?"

"Let's sit with eyes closed for a while. Let's take some rest. The help will come."

Chapter 35. Time of the disguised

The Soldier ran swinging his arms and punching the air. He despised and hated himself and didn't try to hold back tears. He hadn't been crying so bitterly since childhood. "How could I? Why? Yes, there's death. I faced it lots of times. Why my courage left me? Why did I panic? I don't know." The Soldier subsided into a walk and humped himself to calm down. He was going back to the Seer and didn't want him to see his state.

The Seer was sitting in the shadow of the off roadster, smoking and pouring sand through his fingers. The Soldier approached him slowly, lighted up a cigarette with a shivering hand and said serenely,

"I betrayed him. I didn't go with him into the death tunnel."

"The test created by the rebels to recognize the prophet? I heard about that tunnel. You are not go through it or are you a challenger too?" the Seer smiled ironically. "You would definitely fall into a trap. Both of you would die."

"So, don't you think I am betrayer and coward?" the Soldier asked and for the first time looked into the abyss of the Seer's eyes.

"No. You'd made the right decision when you trusted your feelings. There's no need to be upset about that," the Seer reverted eyes.

"Do you mean when we believe our feelings we believe the God and that's why it is right to follow what we feel?"

"I'm not sure. I try not to go that deep. Feelings are the attributes of the soul. However I'm talking about the cultivated soul that knows what is better for the human being. You can call it the intuition. Still there's another option and I don't like it at all: we are under control and do everything by the will of someone else. We are in the grasp of demons, elements that control our feelings, create these or those situations. The world of magic. If you ever meet the Medium, maybe she will tell you about it."

"And you... What do you believe in?"

"I think we are controlled by the very structure of the soul. The truth is often balancing between the different concepts, even the contradictory ones."

"Will the Stranger forgive me?" the Soldier didn't feel like philosophizing.

"He will, of course. He can realize the best case scenario," the Seer gave him a countenance.

"Thanks. You really helped me. Tell me please, will the Stranger go through the tunnel?"

"It's not that easy. I'm trying to find out the traps disposal to help him. But a strange thing is that I don't feel anything," the Seer answered sullenly.

"What do you mean? Have you lost your ability? Are you tired?"

The Seer sneered and threw the stub away.

"Restricted area. Every time when trying to enter the tunnel in my mind I bump into the wall I cannot pass through. I have no idea who was able to set up such a powerful protective field. Anyway, the Stranger doesn't need my help. I see him in the City, it means, he will escape the traps." the Seer analyzed his senses. "Someone is helping him. Someone was able to go into the restricted area. By the way, what do you know about the tunnel?"

"A lot of rumors. The warriors of the desert can keep the secrets. As far as I know there are no our informers among them. There was a talk that the tunnel was mined by the Pyrotechnist, a famous specialist in explosives. As if he saw an angel in his sleep and he revealed him the ancient hidden tunnel and ordered to make a testing area for the prophet candidates. Then the same angel showed him what traps are to be installed. Soon the Pyrotechnist died and his grave became the sacred place."

"Sounds insane, but rebels-like. I don't understand why the Stranger decided to participate in this gamble. But I believe he had no choice. He was forced to undergo that stupid test. How did they treat him?"

"They made an agreement: he goes through the tunnel and the warriors go to some peacemaker, the Hermit."

"What for?" the Seer started to pace up and down nervously. "Who is the Hermit?"

"I don't know," the Soldier shrugged. "He must be one of those who left the world and lives in the desert."

"Perhaps," the Seer thought to himself for a moment and shook his head as if throwing off some illusion. "The Stranger is not a rebel. Suppose he will go through the tunnel, then what? Will the wolves turn into sheep?" the Seer seemed to talk to himself. "Then all of them will die. The ideology and the organization will be broken, and the money flow will stop. Maybe, when the Stranger shows them the miracle, they will name him as the prophet. All religious communities need a prophet, mage, authority: it raises the status of the community, making the ideology stronger."

"The Stranger won't go with them. There was enmity in the air. You are right: they forced him to go to the tunnel," the Soldier stopped talking, and then continued with anger. "They are dangerous fanatics. Sometimes I doubted, I thought: we should not shoot them, they are devoted to their idea, and they don't touch the civilians. The warriors of the desert say about themselves: only we are righteous, only we are the true servants of the God, holy remnants, and all the rest are unworthy to occupy the land, they are to be removed like fruitless trees. Avengers and justice fighters! And under that slogan they killed their political opponents and took money for murders. But now I know for sure, we should have killed more of them. One must not come to an agreement with beasts of prey."

The Seer kept silent. While the Soldier was talking, he felt something, compressed like a spring and jerked.

"The Stranger will pass... They will meet him with knives near the exit... Hurry..."

Large beads of sweat rolled down his face, breathing heavily he sat and asked for water with weak voice.

The Soldier scurried, found the bottle, opened it, slopped some water and passed to the Seer. The latter satisfied the thirst and said,

"We have to drive to the City, find the exit from the tunnel and neutralize those who want to harm the Stranger. I need to conserve power. You will drive," the Seer said while making himself comfortable on the backseat of the car.

"We'll get to the nearest station, take a train and, I guess, we'll be in the City in about four hours," the Soldier was happy: he was back in rotation.

"We'll make it. Don't drive too fast," the Seer asked in a tired and a bit irritated voice.

The head of the security service received the report of the Soldier's disappearance and immediately instructed to find him, bringing in the auxiliary resources. All the attempts appeared to be idle; they had not found the Soldier. The informatory in the Seer's house reported that the owner escaped in hurry at night, but the observation patrol saw only the tall beautiful woman leaving the residence in the morning. It was the famous Medium, by hearsay she was the ex-lover of the Seer. The Chief decided: if the Seer left the house in hurry, he got the scent of danger. And if he is going to leave the country, that's even better: less trouble. That sort of people is always unpredictable and dangerous. It's bad that the Soldier had disappeared, but, perhaps, he is busy with the Seer. The Chief turned down the request of the authorized operatives to look after the woman of the Seer; he decided that she was of no interest for the case.

The Seer made himself up in the car: he attached long beard, put on the cap, and hid his eyes behind the black glasses. After he settled in the coupe, he pulled chocolate and juice out of the bag. He ate with the Soldier, then closed his eyes, twisted his nose as if smelling something and said dwelling on the words:

"The friend of ours is in this train."

"Ours?" the Soldier asked. "The Medium?"

"Yes. Wait…" the Seer stretched, the coach numbers floated in his mind on the high speed, he marked the ninth, this figure pulsed as if screaming: "It's me!"

"She is in the ninth coach, stands in the passage. Bring her here."

"What if she doesn't want to?"

The Seer looked at him in surprise.

In the ninth coach the Soldier saw the familiar slim figure and tried to come up as quiet as possible. The woman turned quickly and threw a hard eye on him, but she could not resist smiling when she recognized the Soldier.

"Believe it or not, I'm glad to see you. Is your friend here?"

"I'd say, it is your friend here," the Soldier answered smiling too. "He wants to see you."

"I see," the Medium said with disappointment. "The Stranger would come to me himself. After all, the old mole decided to go out into the world."

"Are you going to change?"

"Sure, wait here. But I would let the Stranger in," the woman said coquettishly.

"And I have left him," the Soldier turned to the window.

"Has something happened to him?" there was alarm in her voice. "I am anxious about him, but he's alive, I can see it," the Medium said, she turned the Soldier back and looked into his eyes.

"He is alive. Change the dress. I'm waiting."

Entering the coupe the Medium felt abashed but looked closely and sneered,

"So you become a clown too? The disguised are all around!"

"It's time now. Time to hide behind the masks. The hard time."

"I understand. Sorry. Where's the Stranger?"

"He is in the death tunnel. Tries to go through it."

"Is he going to become the prophet of the desert warriors?" the woman was puzzled.

"Everything is much more complicated. Do you know where the exit from the tunnel is?"

"I guess. It's somewhere on the outskirts of the City, bit the exit is watched over too. Is this tunnel really so difficult to go through?"

"If I was physically able I would probably go through. Perhaps one more person, except me, is also able to, but as far as I know, he left the world for the desert. Retired," the Seer said thoughtfully. The image of the person who discovered his ability appeared in his mind and he remembered the words of the Soldier. "The Hermit, the Hermit... The Stranger knows him. It's a small world," the Seer said waggling, suddenly he shuddered, "I will meet him soon. He must be really old now, yet I'm not young as well."

"I've heard about the Hermit," the Medium interrupted. "As far as I know he doesn't leave the desert."

"The Hermit will leave the desert and head to the City. It means something really important is going on. We need to sort it out, until it's too late," the Seer was nervous. "There's no direction. All questions I asked were wrong. There was no visualization, I didn't hear the voices. It's hard to work now," he complained.

"I can try to tune in, but I also need the standing point," the Medium proposed. "It's difficult to do in the train. Let's go to my place, we'll have some rest and try to see. I will look into my crystal ball and maybe I will see something."

"You should go home and we are to meet the Stranger," the Seer shook his head.

"There will be people who meet the Stranger," the Medium disagreed. "If he goes through the tunnel he will become the prophet of the desert warriors."

The Seer smiled ironically, but said nothing. He knew the world better.

"Can someone, except you, see the future inside your crystal ball?" the Soldier asked the woman.

"When I was a little girl I believed that everyone was able to, just look into the crystal ball and that's all. But now even I can rarely see anything," the Medium answered with a sigh.

Chapter 36. The Voice

The voice sounded familiar.

"Is that you?" the Stranger asked and envisioned the Hermit's seamed face, with running and very bright eyes.

"Do not be afraid of anything. I'll help you."

"How should I go?" the Stranger asked.

"In forty paces there is a gap."

The Stranger took the Bird by her arm and started counting steps aloud.

In thirty eight steps they stopped. The Stranger lied down and crawled forward, knuckling the floor. The sound changed, and he guessed that it was a stretched cloth. Having founded the point where the cloth disguised as the floor relief was attached, the Stranger overburned the cords and pulled the cloth vigorously, it was attached by one side only. Then, he lied down the floor again to light the gap. A stone thrown down plumped. By the length of the cloth, he could define the gap's length: about three meters long.

"What's next?" the girl asked.

"Leap," the Stranger tried to seem as calm as possible,

"But I cannot make such a long jump. Maybe, I'd rather make it down, and then you'll pull me out?"

"There is a deep pit down. I think, this is a fatal trap, you cannot make it down, we'll jump it over."

"Jump alone, I'll stay here. Go," the Bird uttered sadly.

The Stranger stroked her hair.

"Once upon a time, I was in the army, and my commander used to say: the most important thing is to preserve the staff, and let things happen as they will. The man was absolutely right, though there were few who understood him. We will over jump, be sure. But you'll have to jump without your shoes."

"Do you believe that I'll be able to leap it over?" the girl asked in a hollow tone.

"No, I don't," and taking a pause he added, "I'm sure."

"Who jumps first?"

"I'll have to. I will spot for you," the Stranger said cheerfully.

"You will snatch me, will you?" she was still guarding composure.

"Provided, that you won't make a complaint against me about sexual harassment later," he tried to joke.

"It is what I'm dreaming about!" the girl huddled up to him.

"I'll kiss you on the other side," the Stranger felt abashed.

"Jump now," the Bird thrust him forward.

He took off her sandals to put them into the bag. Then, he burned paper near the gap edge to mark the line. Thrown the bag over and leapt over the pit easily: he used to clear obstacles no match for this one.

"Step back a few meters! Take a run! Go ahead!"

The Stranger moved to the edge of the gap and turned sidewise, his knees half-bent. The Bird was falling short of just some centimeters. He felt this, opened out his arms, caught the girl up, and swung right around. Feeling that he is falling, he threw the girl rather far from the gap, and flailed his arms to keep balance. One leg slipped down, but the Stranger managed to carry weight onto the other leg and jump far away. His heart was beating heavily, his knees trembling. The Bird jumped up to him and burst into tears, hugging him tightly.

"There, there… don't overdramatize," whispered the Stranger taking the girl to breast. "That was not the last obstacle. Let's go."

"You promised something," the Bird wept out. He bent over to kiss her on the lips.

"I love you," the girl said softly. "I like to be with you."

"We have to go," the Stranger took her by the shoulders.

They were following the tunnel corridors for a long time. The Stranger did not feel danger, yet his inner tension was developing, and when reaching the climax, replaced by indifference and apathy. "You mustn't relax. You ought to set yourself up for struggle, be ready for fighting, be cautious and concentrated." The Stranger vigorously went off, the girl staggering heavily behind exhausted. Suddenly, he stopped squinting into the dark.

"Don't you see anything?" he asked his companion.

"Where?" she tossed head looking around.

"Ahead."

"Nothing. What have you noticed?"

"Nothing special," he tried to listen to his feelings: uncomfortably, yet not too anxiously to make a stop.

In a few meters, they saw some contours. The Stranger moved the girl behind his back and started slowly for the silhouettes. He had come across cave drawings and ancient scriptures not once, but, as far as he knew, there was no picture in the tunnel; however, archeologists had no time to investigate it thoroughly.

"What is there?" the Bird whispered not daring to look from behind the Stranger's back.

"Perhaps, a phantom."

"Excuse me?"

"Pictures drawn to put the wind up the tourists," the Stranger was trying to speak in jest, as he decided that the danger has passed.

"They have performed a mission. I'm scared," the Bird was speaking in a level voice.

Coming closer, the Stranger heard: "It is not a phantom." He stopped dead. The girl bumped against him.

"What's up?" she asked.

"Do not come up, do not touch them and, the best of all, do not breathe when passing by."

"It is stalky," he thought. "First, you are frightened of a fluorescent picture, but when the fright is defeated, you think it blank to fall into a trap invented with a view to human curiosity…What's next? The Voice warns me, but I'm not sure it will do it always, that I'm armored. I am just an instrument…"

"What are you thinking about?" the Bird asked, breaking his thoughts.

"About life," the Stranger was short-spoken.

"You have ransomed me. Where was the gem coming from? As judged by your getup, you are not a rich man, only your boots are solid."

"Never judge by appearance. Moreover, if wealth does not serve good purposes, it is a trap more fearful than trip wires and mines."

"But why? After all, money is needed to live, and it gives a lot of comfort."

"I mean treating money not as a means to purchase goods but as an idol. It is awful when people believe in money as in God who can rescue them from troubles. It is awful when a rich man boasts his wealth and holds in scorn those poorer. Who can see the deprived suffering and starving but does not help them. It is awful when excess money provokes nice people to get pleasures that kill both mind and body. You know this better than I: that was the weak point you used to call dupes on. Sometimes, I can hear what people think… The greatest dream that seizes even the rich ones is to have money as much as possible. Mankind lives according to the formula: money can buy everything."

"All dream of money?" the Bird smiled ironically.

"Not all, but most of them. Some dream of fame, popularity, or power. Romantic girls dream of love. Then again, those sick dream of health, not of wealth."

"But could you redeem me without money?" the girl resented.

"Money is a neutral thing, it's up to a person how to earn and spend it."

"I see," saddened his companion. "For family life money is vital."

"Well, you hitch your wagon to a star," the Stranger burst laughing. "When the time comes, money will help nobody."

He felt a distance appearing between them.

"I had three gems, and I gave the last one. I have no savings, but can earn crust and shelter. God never left me alone," he went on stubbornly.

"And what had you done before? Did you have a family?" the girl inquired.

"I did have a family," the Stranger responded dryly. "Now, I am alone."

He cleared his throat, smiled and sang:

I'm free as a bird in the sky.
I'm free in waking life.
I'm free, I forgot what fear means.
I'm free like savage wind…

Chapter 37. The City

The Hermit knew about another secret tunnel leading to the City. He was the only one who knew – nobody else. He reproached himself that he had not time to share the discovery with the Stranger. There was a chance to avoid collision with the warriors of desert so as not to play their game. They turned their distorted and absurd interpretations of prophecies about the Messenger into fact. They cannot see the evident, for their hearts hardened. They cannot hear with their ears, for they do not want to hear the voice of the Truth. Their eyes are closed, for the light of the Truth hurt them.

The old man remembered that once, in the early morning, while gathering healing herbs, he found some clay grout hardened into stone of apparently artificial origin. By knocking the walls with a cane, he could hear a hollow sound. He immediately returned to his hermitage for tools, and went full tears back. He moiled the clay brick masonry to reveal a very tight breach, switched on a lantern and started moving along the gloomy tunnel corridors. Though having a difficulty in breathing, the sturdy weathered old man was going on and on, dragging the heavy moil.

In about four hours, he hit a wall, broke it easily to find himself on the skirts of the City.

Now, the Hermit decided to make use of the secret pass. It was likely the very same ancient tunnel cut through the mountain by order of the kings for besiege. But who cut the tunnel his friend is now moving along, and when?

The old man entered the tunnel, put his palm against the wall, and feeling cold and wet stone, closed his eyes to see... The paved narrow street lit with night lanterns was meeting a lonely tired wayfarer dressed in an old, old as could be, dark sweater and jeans worn to the thread in some places. His nut-brown hair is cut short. As judged by his step, a youth. The old man tried to look in his face, but made little of the feature, and, most essential, he failed to see his eyes. That made the Hermit very sad, and he lied down the wet uneven floor. The vision froze hard.

"Why?" the old man whispered.

The silhouette once frozen up came alive again; the young man gave a weeny nod, and said in a low but mighty voice, "Follow me." The old man opened his eyes, struggled to feet slowly and bent his neck to pass under the very low ceiling. He went giddy, his eyes shaded with pain, blood hammering in temples, but, having recovered his breath, the traveler moved on. It seemed to him that he got the reason for his friend's hurrying to the City.

The Hermit believed that the Stranger would escape all traps without his help. The Hermit only had to pray for the Stranger and pass him the old man's capacities at least for some hours. In an hour of wandering in the tunnel, the Hermit weakened, feeling his vitality leaving him, yet not disappearing but going to the Stranger. A meeting is reserved for his friend, to which, maybe, the old hermit who had left the earthly world for lonesome places has been also invited. But now the Hermit was returning back. He answered the trumpet-call of ancient prophecies penetrating the world. He was walking in anticipation of the greatest meeting that was promised by the greatest man.

Coming to the City, the Medium explained the Soldier and the Seer, how to reach the tunnel, and got home. Strained and concentrated, the Seer was keeping silence all the time. The Soldier, to the contrary, was in good spirits. He seemed not to feel any danger, resembling a battle hound ready to jump down throat of an enemy. The Seer hoped to solve the problems without blood on the floor, so, skewing at the Soldier, he tried to harness his willpower.

The Seer knew: the desert warriors are unfriendly to any aliens, especially to him whom they considered to be the evil force, because he derisively compared himself to ancient prophets, disrespectful both to the order, and to any religious authorities. The warriors of desert and adherents of militarized religious orders wished to destroy him and, despite being prohibited from leaving the City and the vicinities, tried to perform the act of revenge. The Seer felt danger well in advance and could prevent it, but he was bored to death with the necessity to hide and wait for attempt, so he offered apologizes in public and refused from mocking and rude statements addressed to the believers who could use not only a word, but even explosives as an argument.

The adherents have their passports stamped with a red mark testifying to their being in a militarized religious order or to their disloyalty to the system. And that stamp in the certificate forbade them to leave the City. Some people accused of disloyalty were brought here against the will, but the majority was rushing to the City ready and willingly. Here, they felt comfortable, for they could afford to perform their rituals, not exposed to mockery and insinuations, wear their uniform, and, ultimately, they had no risk of encountering worldly population so as not to be subject of its alien influence.

The City was overcrowded with prophets, magicians, fortune-tellers, healers, hypnotists, and mere miracle mongers, divided into enclaves represented by numerous ethnic groups, religious communities and militant orders.

Almost any district had community defense volunteer squads generally comprised of former military men with fighting experience. The soldiers of fortune were granted with the right to bear arms certified by a special document. In the City, there also were located government army patrols that seldom interfered with the conflicts between the competing religious orders, but preferred to take a detached view. The policemen avoided visiting some quarters as they might be attacked by young aggressive adherents.

The citizens took up arms in secrecy. The government was losing the reins of power.

The Soldier saw the City turned into a new arena for soldiers of fortune, mercenaries, feeling their significance and importance here, though they were the reserve officers who went through the war and defended the country at the expense of their life. But after the victory, the motherland did not recognize them, forced them out, and threw into the embrace of religious orders.

Tense and combative atmosphere of the City was necessary for the Soldier's lungs. But above all, he was eager to prove the Stranger that he was not afraid of death and ready to fight with any available methods: shooting, blasting, breaking arms and legs of those getting in the way.

The Seer, in turn, felt uncomfortable, especially because of his mate, with his hands bloodstained. Danger flies to such people like a fly to dung, and, is sure to befall those besides.

On the skirts of the City, the taxi driver refused to keep on driving. Getting out of the car, the Seer carefully examined the place.

"There must be steps over this hill, these're abrupt, some of them missing, and it will be difficult to climb them, but you will help me. When we descend, we'll see the cave, three armed warriors of deserts at the entrance waiting for the Stranger, and not with flowers. I'll try to neutralize them, but you must interfere only if the situation is beyond control."

The Soldier nodded dutifully, his eyes glistened: this time he will fight for the sake of the Truth, no less a person than the Seer being his mate.

Chapter 38. Slap in the face

They were walking on, having lost track of time. The Stranger was hardly dragging himself, giddy with fatigue. He sat down leaning against cool and smooth, as if polished, wall.

"Is there is anything wrong?" the girl asked stroking his shoulder.

"No. I'm just dead beat... But I think we've passed all traps and soon leave the mortal shadow for the light of the day."

He got a flask out of the bag and gave it to the Bird; she sipped and returned the flack back. Having quenched his thirst, the Stranger stood up to go ahead. The rhymes recurred to him:

Walk along the Road of Frustrations

Captured and delighted, once again,
With my mind filled up with expectations,
With my heart anticipating pain.

Such an anxious and uneasy question,
Voice from darkness whispering anew.
You have not completed earthly journey,
Is the road chosen laid for you?

Maybe, it is dark that stares round,
Maybe, it is still that screams with pain,
Where can the lost soul be found?
Just an eyewink - and your hair's gray.

While the Road of Dreamy Inspirations,
Where wind is furious and fresh,
Leads me in the way of transformations
To the world of broken dreams and crash.

Having covered some miles without meeting with any trap, they bumped up against an iron door. The Stranger flicked the lighter to see a coded lock with twelve buttons. He failed to batter down the door with his shoulder. The key is needed. Now, he has only to enter the code to step out into the fresh air. But how? Hit the combination of twelve digits? Impossible. Appeal for logic? Most likely, the good warrior of desert entered the digit code blindly, at random; and even if the Medium succeeded in raising his ghost from the nether world, he would have nothing to say.

The Stranger closed his eyes, concentrated, some digits, some code combinations, flashed through the mind. He has no right to mistake: there is an explosive device installed actuated by a wrong code entering.

"I don't know the right digit combination," the Stranger said.

"Don't you hear anything?" the Bird asked.

Suddenly, some noise was heard from behind the door, somebody called out:

"You there! How have you managed the tunnel? I told to our brother. You have impressed him a lot. He thinks you to be the prophet."

"I haven't opened the door yet!" the Stranger cried out back. "Maybe, you will supply a clue?"

"Maybe. The talk will tell."

"What do you mean?" the Stranger felt uneasy, a snaky fear probing his heart again.

"I do not know how you were able to escape the traps. However, they were not installed by me, and, maybe, there is no one. If exploded, we would know that for sure, and now… The secret died with the Pyrotechnist. But what if demons help you? I was reported what you were talking about! Do you really believe that our Order is not created by God, and we are mere pretenders, or we'll agree on the price?"

"I just said that the way your Order chose was not the best one to be used by God; it is your right, though. Let us go out, and we will tell nobody about the tunnel."

"A woman was together with you. Is she alive?"

"Yes. She is my companion."

"You may step out, but she must stay in the tunnel. This is a travesty of the prophecy. Blasphemy! She desecrated the sacred prophecy!" the warrior of desert cried out.

The Stranger bit his lip, struck with range, and fisted the wall.

"It is you who are a blasphemer! Because of you and those like you, God is abused. Who gave you a right to state that your interpretation of prophecies is true? Who?" the Stranger raised the voice. "Your money? Your guns? Did the agreement with the government, which recognized your religious rights, make you God's servants? Did you speak to Him? Did you hear His voice? Do you have His Spirit? No! You are the pretenders! And you will be dissipated except you repent. Then again, you cannot repent!"

The warriors of desert looked at one another in fear and moved back, but the commander of the guard gritted the teeth, drew a knife, and screeched out:

"I will open the door to slash your wrists! Hash key, zero, three, eight, six, star key! I'm waiting for you!"

Wild with anger, the Stranger stretched his finger to enter the code, but, all of a sudden, he could hear a shriek: "No!" The head was is if squeezed with a rim.

"Give me a slap," the Stranger asked slowly while trying to catch breath. "Do it."

He had not to reason her twice, for her nerves were stretched thin, and she hit him backhand.

"Slap again!"

She gave him another slap.

"I didn't know you like it," the Bird said near enough to tears.

The Stranger burst laughing. Having a good laugh and wiping tears, he explained:

"The slap has beaten my range out, which nearly killed us. Given a wrong code, I was on the verge of getting into a child trap. Never mind, we are alive, which means we have not lost. Let's wait."

Chapter 39. The Code

They were slowly going down the cracked stairs leading to the tunnel through the ruins of the ancient watchtower. The Soldier held the limping Seer by the hand and examined the surroundings carefully.

"There's an observation post up the tower, and there are sun glints on the glass of the optic sight. Dilettantes. However we can't get to the tunnel inconspicuously."

"Any ideas?" the Seer asked. However, what ideas can liquidation specialist have?

"We can sneak to the tower from the sunny side. We are lucky that the sun is bright today; they won't see me, after it as the occasion demands."

"There is no need to," the Seer said with some irritation. "I shall try to knock them down for a while. Deep sleep is for good."

The Seer possessed the ability of controlling men without seeing their eyes. He sat, closed his eyes: a ruined fortress appeared in front of him, he saw the repaired stars, the asphalted roof, the observation post and the two bearded men. One of them sat under the sunshade and pored over a book. The second one walked around the roof perimeter and sometimes looked into binocular. The Seer saw the mobile phones and portable radio set, two automatic rifles, some magazines full of rounds and two closed tin boxes. He looked inside of them in his mind. One box contained small white boxes with large figures '5.56' and small figures '32', there were round grenades in the second one.

The Seer discerned the eyes of the book lover, ordered: "Sleep!" and added more impulsively, "Sleep! Sleep!" as if finishing off the boxer who reeled with knockdown with two punches. The second guarding was a hard nut, he was not easy to hypnotize. Besides, he was busy with watching the objects through the binocular. The Seer decided to use this. He concentrated totally. The Soldier who had seen a lot in his life felt uncomfortable, he felt the desire to close his eyes tight and turn back but the curiosity got the best. The eyes of the Seer became bloodshot, the pupils expanded, he was completely pale, his forehead being covered with small beads of sweat, his hands shivered and he panted as if he had difficulty in breathing.

The Seer sent the guardian the image of the smooth sea. The warrior was amazed; he put the binocular down, peered: there was definitely the sea instead of the mountains and desert. He reached for the water can. "I got him", the Seer thought contentedly.

"You drink wine, it is heady and intoxicating. You feel good, you feel asleep, you need some rest. You are by the seaside, you are relaxed. Everyone is sleeping now. It's time to sleep. Sleep, sleep, sleep."

The observer swayed and lied down.

"That's it," the Seer said in a tired voice. "They are asleep, but we have no time. Go up the tower, be careful, take aim at the guardians of the tunnel but don't shoot. Do you understand? Don't shoot. I'm going to rescue the Stranger. He is here. Don't let us down."

The Soldier ran to the tower, near the entrance he slowed down, his heart sank. He looked closer and saw the trip wire. He stepped over it carefully. And felt better. Staying as close to the wall as possible he climbed up to the roof. He saw the sound asleep observers and shook his head admiringly, then collected the weapon and tied their hands behind. He took the automatic rifle, checked it, put the round into the chamber, switched the safety lock into the single-shot position and aimed the weapon at the guardians. He pointed to the different parts of their bodies. And suddenly stopped himself. "It's like an illness, time to do away with this. I'm over!"

Trying to throw away the thought of pain, the toddling Seer went down the stairs and came in view of guardians. He summed up the situation at a glance: "One is enraged, the others are puzzled. The Stranger's work, he can do it. I should deal with the nervous one, but first I have to control pain." The Seer imagined the leg before the injury, fixed the recollection. The pain subdued. He felt inspiration: it was time to show these boys who the Seer was.

He picked up the broken twig, raised his hand and made eye contact with the hysterical captain. The Keeper was astonished: he saw a very tall man with glowing eyes, in light clothes belted with glistening sash, there was electric sparkling sword in his hand.

The captain reeled and fell on his knees. He looked at the heavenly creature with veneration and tears in his eyes, unable to utter a word. Two others heard the command: "lie down in the dust of the ground," fell down and put dust on heads.

The Soldier looked at the Seer: a small man, with a twig in the stretched hand, at the prone-armed man in front of him and hardly resisted from laughing aloud at this comic picture.

"Open the door!" the Seer ordered to the kneeler.

The captain, still under illusion, reeling as if he was in dream came to the door and pulled the big iron door-handle. It didn't open.

"There is a code," the Stranger shouted, he recognized the voice of the Seer.

The Seer glared at the warrior of the desert and realized that he didn't know the code.

"How are you, Stranger?"

"Fine, thanks. Is the Soldier with you?"

"Yes. He keeps a bead on me," the Seer waved his hand to Soldier's side.

"Are you scared?"

"No more than you," the Seer snapped jollily.

"Will you help me with the code?"

"Can't the one that helped you to come to the door do this?"

"He will do it through you."

"I can leave now."

"I wouldn't do this. You are kept covered by the Soldier," the Stranger played up to him.

"Ok. Let's not waste the time. What lock is there?"

"Ten figures, a star and a hash key," the Stranger answered. "Wrong dial means explosion. By the way, I am not alone, here is a young girl with me, try not to kill us.

"Don't worry." The Seer humped himself. Figures flashed in front of his eyes, some of them thumped in his brain. "Listen!" he shouted suddenly. "Star, zero, one, three, seven, two, one, hash key."

The Stranger entered the figures without hesitations, having hidden the girl behind his back. The door clanked loudly and got stiff. The Seer grabbed the door-handle, dug his heels into the ground and opened the door. The Stranger stepped out from the darkness blinking in the sunlight. The girl fell down on the ground and burst into tears. She embraced the earth, stroked the grass and cried.

"The prophecy has become true with your help, Stranger," the Seer said shaking his hand.

"And with yours too. Give the Prince his entrance and the exit to his Messenger. You opened the exit. Congratulations, you are the Messenger," the Stranger said smiling.

"And you must be the Prince?" the Seer stared at the Stranger trying to read his thoughts.

"As much as you are his Messenger. We played by the rules of the desert warriors, that's it."

"Good. I see you are fine."

The Seer shook his hand again. The Stranger helped girl up and wiped her tears.

"It's not over yet," he smiled dully.

The Soldier looked up in the sky and cried. The mobile phones of the desert warriors rang on and on. One of the observers woke up, saw the unfamiliar man with a gun, shook his head as if throwing away the illusion. He jumped up on his feet, but with his hands tied behind, he could not keep the balance and fell down.

The Soldier said in authoritative voice,

"If you jump up again, I will lay you down forever. How soon will your people be here?"

The warrior of the desert kept silent trying to gather wits.

"They'll be here in a half an hour," he replied.

"I see. It means we have about fifteen minutes. At most."

He waved his hand to the Stranger, pointed on the wristwatch and crossed his throat with the finger.

"We have to leave," the Seer said. "The warriors of the desert will come soon. I'm not able to hinder all of them."

"Sit on my back, I'll give a ride," the Stranger proposed. The Seer started to walk upstairs hanging on the Stranger's arm and mumbling something.

A small posse hurried to the tunnel.

"Go up to the Soldier," the Seer told the girl. "Tell him not to shoot. There are not much of them. You both stay there until I call. We will deal with it without shooting."

The girl looked at the Stranger, he nodded. But when she moved, his heart sank: she should not go there.

"Wait. I'll go myself. I'll be right back.

The Soldier saw the Stranger, smiled but suddenly became pale. He rushed downstairs but his instinct 'never leave an enemy behind' made him go back. The Soldier jumped and punched the observer with the club.

"Stop, Stranger!" he screamed. "Don't go!"

The Seer realized what is going on and having summoned the rest of his power gave a sign: "Stop. Trip wire. Entrance."

The Stranger didn't hear the Soldier screaming. On his way to the embrasure of the fortress he suddenly stopped, looked down, whispered something and stepped over the trip wire of the mine. The Soldier ran up to him, his face contorted with terror, carefully took the stretched hand, held his friend and whispered,

"I'm sorry, I'm so sorry. I'll never leave you again."

The Stranger told him with a smile:

"If you'd gone with us, we all would have been dead. You saved me with your decision. That was God's will."

"Is it true?" he asked looking into the Stranger's face with doubt.

"It is. The Seer has a message for you: don't shoot."

"Ok. Is the Seer going to put on a show?"

"I'm not sure. He is tired and whacked to the wide. I'll talk to him myself."

"It's dangerous, Stranger," the Soldier said, but looked at his friend and added, "it's difficult to become accustomed to all your tricks. I do not have enough faith."

"It's easier to rely on weapon, but it's not better."

"I got it. I won't shoot. I'll admire the ruins from above," he whiffed and returned to the roof.

Nothing had changed: one of the observers was sleeping, the second one lied unconscious. The Soldier brought him round. The warrior of the desert vomited: it was concussion of brain. He hardly resisted crying of pain and fear. The Soldier brought water, let him drink and wiped with some cloth.

"Don't be hurt. You'd better rejoice, your prophecy has become true. My friend, his name is Stranger, went through the death tunnel and your elders wanted to kill him for that."

"Why did they want to kill him?" the observer asked jerkily trying to overcome the pain.

"Because he is unlike you," the Soldier answered clicking the safety lock of the automatic rifle.

"One can't be killed for this."

"Not half he can be," the Soldier smiled ironically.

The captain prayed devoutly and thanked God for the vision sent.

"Forgive my blindness, the God of the sky and the earth, the sea and the desert. I was up to no good against Your slave and you sent the heavenly messenger in the shining of Your glory to save him. Forgive our infidelity, mighty God. I shall wash away my guilt. If you want, take my life. If you want me to serve you, I am your slave. I shall find the Stranger and beg for forgiveness. I shall serve him and I shall persuade the brothers to bow him."

The keepers woke up of the hypnotic stupor, kneeled and echoed the captain, stretching arms to the sky and exclaiming after his every phrase, "Let it be!"

"How do you feel?" the Stranger asked the Seer. "Can you go?"

"I can go, but I can't run," the Seer said smiling.

"They will catch us. Maybe we should let our friend open fire. I'm sure he will shoot all of them."

"No. I'll go out to them and talk. And you should leave."

The Seer stopped for a moment listening to something.

"Go. You'll be surprised, Stranger."

"I'm hard to surprise."

The Seer opened the wallet and gave him the piece of paper with address.

"Take it. She is waiting for you."

The Stranger nodded and turned to the girl.

"You will go with the Seer. He needs help. And I am not alone," the Stranger pointed up. The Bird thought that he spoke about the Soldier.

"Let's go, baby. Don't worry about him," the Seer said.

The Stranger went down to the tunnel again. Three guardians were praying. Five warriors of the desert went in the combat formation: two foremen, two sidemen and one rear man. The Soldier saw the grenade attached to the belt of one the warriors. He aimed at it:

"If I hit it, two or three of them will be killed by the explosion, I can shoot the others, I have to do this now but they asked not to shoot."

The Stranger assuaged his doubts. He spread his arms demonstrating that he was weaponless and moved towards the five guests.

"Who are you?" the kneed captain called.

The Stranger turned.

"I'm nobody. A slave of the God living."

"Are you the Stranger?" the captain asked gingerly.

"It's me."

"Forgive me, Prince. We haven't recognized you. Forgive us. We did as our fathers did."

The Stranger remembered the words of the Seer. "Yes, you're right. I'm surprised. You're a sly one! I'm not ready for this development. I got out of the tunnel and the traps are still here."

"Kneel up, please. I am blood and flesh. I am not the Prince. I am just a man as you are."

The captain got to his feet. Five warriors came closer looking at the Stranger.

"This man passed through the Tunnel of Death, and I sinned against him. I wanted to kill the holy man, but a heavenly messenger appeared, three meters tall, in shining power and glory, with the sward like lightning in his hands and opened the door. Today the ancient prophesy has become true, brothers. It's a big day. The liberation of the City starts from here and after all the whole world will become free from the dark powers," his voice sounded solemnly.

The Stranger groaned in his mind. "Nice situation. If only they knew that the miraculous messenger was one meter sixty centimeters tall and his name was the Seer, they would kill me in a blink of an eye. How did he get the sword? It seems in the same way as three meters size."

"Have you seen the heavenly messenger too?" one of the warriors asked the other keepers of the door.

"We haven't seen him but we've heard his voice and fear hung upon us, after it we remember nothing."

"Here, brothers, I was the only one to see the vision," the captain said proudly. "And now we all place ourselves under orders of this man."

The prospect of being the head of the terrorist organization surprised the Stranger even more.

"Good," he answered serenely. "Now I should go. And your task is to guard the exit and not let anyone into the tunnel. I shall find you. But promise that you will keep the secret. My time hasn't come yet."

Without saying a word they bowed unto him. The Stranger quickly walked away.

The Soldier put gags in the observers' mouths, tied them so that they were not able to move and went down to him stealthily.

"Let's move out of here until they came to. Throw the weapon," the Stranger said imitating the Soldier's intonations.

Friends left the ruins, headed to the nearest neighborhood, stopped the taxi and drove to address written on the card.

Chapter 40. Divine reed pipe

The Chief of the security service received a hot report: somebody has passed the test of the warriors of desert. That meant that the events got out of control. The riots that had such a trump card are certain to violate the peace treaty. Disturbances will arise, while his agency aims at crushing opposition and acts of protest in the egg. Description of a man who passed through the tunnel made him shudder, and in a few minutes, another message came, the one from a personal agent, very close to the warriors of desert. The message contained just a single word. The Chief lost control completely. However, there was nobody to blame, he overlooked the affair despite the Seer's warning. People kind and fair are everywhere, they are sure to report his incompetence.

The Chief fussed over how to solve the situation without loss. To present the matter as a planned operation, with the Stranger being a well-placed agent, who had a mission to destroy a dangerous religious order? Then the question arises, how could he pass through the Tunnel of death? There are some versions: There is no, and never has been, death in the tunnel. He did not pass through it at all. The Stranger is a hypnotist none the worse than the Seer, he made them think that he entered the tunnel and went out. The versions are raw, they will fail a thorough test, yet the commission is unlikely to be formed to investigate the affair. Now, it is important to keep a wary eye on what is happening in the City, to contact the Stranger, and then, maybe, everything is to turn up trumps. The Chief immediately made all necessary arrangements.

The Stranger was regarding with curiosity the streets of the City out of the window of the taxi. He has not set foot on its pavements and squares for many years. The lines recurred to him:

> And clouds are floating above the City,
> Covering the sky-blue color,
> And above the town there's a yellow smoke,
> The City is two thousand years old,
> Lived through under the light of the star
> Called Sun...
> And there's a war over two thousand years,
> A war without special causes.
> A war the work of the youth,
> A medicine against wrinkles...
> And we know that it has always been like this,
> That we like more the destiny
> Who's living according to other rules
> And who's doomed to die young.
> He doesn't remember the word "yes" and the word "no",
> He doesn't remember neither the deeds, nor the names.
> And able to reach the stars,
> Not reckoning that this is a dream,
> And falling, scorched by the star called Sun...

A waft of the Wind appeared, then, the words were speaking of something important. The Stranger asked the driver to stop the car.

"We were right to get out here, it would be silly to take the wraps off the address," the Soldier approved.

"Do you understand that I am not associated with the ancient prophecies?" the Stranger asked.

"You have passed the Tunnel of Death! Only the Man of God was able to do that."

"I know two people who can feel traps, and there are many not familiar to me! If a man has time reserved to live and die, nothing will happen to him before. You know this better. However, one must not tempt fate or play with death. First, you never know your fate, and second, you violate the law of value of life when put your life in the line. Yes, I have passed the Tunnel of Death, but I was supported. God hindered me from falling down. Perhaps, I am to do something more important."

"Whatever the case, only the chosen one could pass the Tunnel. As for me, I wouldn't be able to pass, though I checked my abilities with a revolver bullet. Do not be surprised, I'll tell you. A six-shooter, with one bullet in the cylinder, rotate several times not to know where it is. Then I put the revolver to the chin, call for silence and feel... If all is well, I move the trigger. If not, shoot the gun in the air. I was young and silly then, wanted to hit fancy of the friends and women, and needed money, of course."

"Never mistaken?" the Stranger smiled.

"As you can see. And you know what? Your deed will affect everybody, especially, the warriors of desert," the Soldier uttered confidently.

"This is what I'm afraid most of all. People like miracles. An especial kind of entertainment they are willing to have every day. I am not the Seer, who can impress on a man that he is eating watermelon instead of onion, and I cannot catch one's imagination. My power does not belong to me; I speak and do not on my behalf."

"And what about the Seer? Wasn't it God who gifted him?"

"I don't know. However, I feel it is something different, some other spirit. He has suffered sleepwalking since childhood, could warn of disasters, hear thoughts, find lost things, and control both his own will and the will of others. The Seer can manage his power, but I cannot. It is hard to imagine that God can help to find an object hidden by a spectator for a laugh of the audience. And whether one could question it?"

"Well then, who helps him?"

"Every person has some or other inborn abilities, some people improve their skills, some other laze away or they merely don't know how to develop them. This is like training a body. One waters building up physique for years. Another inherits the power, if you prefer, genetically, so he has not to turn himself inside out, and some other resort to doping, which gives immediate result and bad consequences. However, eventually, without training, abilities will tarnish."

"I see…" the Soldier nodded. "We are in the City at last. It seems to me that not three days passed but a lifetime. Do you know, what's next?"

"I haven't the slightest idea. I'd like to rest a little, take a shower and nap."

"We will come soon. The Seer is waiting for us."

"The Bird is waiting for me."

"What a bird?"

"The girl we took along with us. I have called her the Bird."

"Like a song about a bird," the Soldier gave a wink.

"A bird is so anxious to fly!
That bird has a mother with wings,
That bird has a father with wings,
But it cannot fly as if had no mind,
It cannot fly, nothing more…"

"Not exactly:
A needless person in the street
Was seeking love obstinately.
I left the matter for the end,
I told myself again:
Nothing to fight for,
Nothing to share,
This is the thing
Useless be angry
Over there
I am a bird…"

"Why does this song reflect the essence?" the Soldier laughed. "Remember something:

The fire stank not far away,
A crane was falling down soft,
The stars were spiting, the liftman
Found out the truth…

The roofs could see sunset afar,
The walls remembered awful war,
But I am happy, I am glad,
That someone happy…"

"The fire stank," the Soldier took thought. "The Seer also paid attention to some fire."

"That's a given. Rhymes like dreams: sometimes worthless, but can be prophetic. Information can be transferred in many ways, including rhymes. Poets, the people with delicate psyche, can catch heavenly signals to translate them into words. A wise man said: "I understood that poets create poetry not through wisdom, but through especial spirit and inspiration: they, like prophets, utter beautiful things not seeing the point".

"Tell me, why do gifted poets, so called divine reed pipes, not only poets, but also some other dowered people die young?"

"Precious wine can be poured both in a golden cup and in a plastic glass. The glass is throwaway, while the cup is too expensive to discard."

"How to define, who is made of gold and who is plastic?"

"By behavior. The plastic glass raises a big smoke," the Stranger smiled. "A carrier of important information takes great risks if his lifestyle is not worthy of revelations. To whom more is committed, from him more is required. The chosen ones always bear risks: they are between a rock and a hard place. God is merciful, while people are not in the least."

"I wonder where you are. How will the servants of God take your doubtful company?"

"People consolidate in front of common disaster."

"What disaster? What are you talking about? All disasters come from people, or you mean a natural disaster?"

"The wave will cover everybody, do not stay on the shore at this moment," the Stranger explained.

"So, what if a righteous servant of God is also on the shore at the moment, then the wave will not cover the beach, won't it?"

"Maybe, but the righteous people know what will happen, and alert the others. All the same, who listens to them? After all, both now and always, the righteous were wandering about deserts and hills, caves and chasms, suffering from scorching sun and heavy downpour, instead of sitting under the tent on the beach sipping a shake and staring at girls in bikini."

"Do you know at least one righteous man?"

"The Hermit. To tell the truth, I do not encourage monkhood. A lamp should not be covered with an opaque cap, it is also must not be lit up under the bed. After all, it is designed to give light to much everyone's delight. When not exposed to ordeal, one cannot define whether he is righteous. Human essence can be revealed only in emergency. In the desert, dangerous situations are more than enough, but we cannot choose between bad and the worst-case scenario, so, it is not what I mean exactly. Everyone has a weak point. And everyone can be thrown dirt at. The most important thing is to get out clean, realize the weak point, and never fall down any more. We gave a chance to the Bird, time will tell whether she makes use of it or not."

"Did you fall down often?" the Soldier recollected his dossier.

"Things happened, but I fell into more often."

"Got into a mess?"

"To the point."

"So, what is reserved for us?"

"Don't know. To my certain knowledge, everything will pan out differently from what we figure. It is possible to see the future, but this is just a reflection of some or other deeds, thoughts and dreams of ours. As for me, I am interested in making choice, the right choice."

The Medium was standing on the balcony. Hardly had she seen the familiar images when she ran out towards them, gave a nod to the Soldier and embraced the Stranger.

"Pleased to see you."

"May I have a wash and rest a little?"

"Sure, but the bath is occupied by the girl the Seer has brought. The bath is rather large though, there's room for both," the Medium looked at him crafty.

"I will wait."

The woman shrugged her shoulders. The Seer was standing by the open window smoking.

"Anything's happened?" the Stranger asked.

"Disaster hovers over the City. This place has reached rock bottom. A single sparkle will make everything flame up," the Seer said under his breath.

"It is not too late to leave the City, or, even, the country. Take our friends and leave," the Stranger suggested.

"I will not go," the Soldier said firmly. "I am with you. And now to the end."

"Let's clear up the situation to decide on whether to go or not," the mistress was excited. The Seer's sinister pale face inspired her with fear.

"He would stay even if he foreknew that he would be killed. This man does not decide for himself. The only thing you right on is that we must get ready," the Seer said.

"You had better go, indeed. I can show you something to make you see that the place is getting too hot to stay here. You have helped me to reach the City, but now you must run away!"

"Later. Rest a little. You have a headache."

The Stranger smiled.

The Seer came up to him and touched the aching point.

"No. The problem is not here…" he put his palm to the Stranger's neck. "Lie on you back."

The Stranger lied obediently. The Seer put one hand on the top of the head, the other to the chin. The Soldier toughened (with such a movement neck bones can be broken easily) and moved towards the Seer in a threatening way, but the latter just curled lips.

"Relax the head. Exhale!" the Seer shouted simultaneously pressing the head and chin, and gave a sudden twiddle to the side, then to the other way round. A loud click was heard.

"The block is removed. Get up slowly, then sit for a minute, and go to the bathroom. It is vacant now," the Seer pointed at the staircase to the second floor.

"Thank you. It became easier now," the Stranger thanked, made a few steps, and wavered. The Soldier ran up to him to look into his eyes.

"I am all right," the Stranger gave him a wink while walking upstairs.

The Bird dressed in a snow-white bathrobe hung on his neck raining kisses upon him. He embraced her continently.

"Ask a towel for me."

He went to the bathroom and opened the tap. Water was relieving nervous stress. In the meanwhile, the Bird found the mistress.

"Okay. I'll bring him the bathrobe," the Medium responded.

"I'll bring it myself," the Bird was persistent. The Medium peered into the girl's face.

"A poor thing, she fell in love with him."

"They passed the Tunnel of death together," the Seer interfered, angered. "Give her what she asked."

Chapter 41. A sense of trouble

The Hermit was looking for a narrow paved street with lanterns. He was walking sprightly, peering with curiosity into the people passing by, examining the sides of houses, shop windows, billboards and curses on the fences:

"Woe and suffering to the City of blood." A bustle was distracting the Hermit, though his heart was deceitfully pinching when he treaded along the places familiar to him since childhood. Exhausted, the man sat down onto the steps leading to the ruins of the ancient palace, somewhere two thousand years ago glaring with gorgeous ornamentation.

The City is dishallowed, faces of the bypasses wearing the print of fatality. The Hermit examined the ruined place, and some visions flashed before his eyes: the City overcast, clouds getting bloodshot. His body was shuddered with apprehension. Suddenly, the Hermit sprang to his feet; it seemed to him that he forgot what the fear is. His heart was beating desperately. "They begin to appear, it will be easy to see them soon, and nobody can resist them, they are intruding on consciousness to capture the minds. God, have mercy!" the Hermit pleaded. "Give me piece, I am begging You! Is it possible that I will not get protection? You are everything for me." The Hermit looked up to the sky: "Father of the Sky and the Earth, tell me, what I need to do? How to act? Give me the answer." Unexpectedly, he could hear unmistakably clear: He who came from outside cannot be a helping hand to one who is inside. Find the friend.

The Hermit was trying to make sense of the phrase heard: "I must find a man from my vision. I am here because of him. Did the Stranger get the reason for his striving here? The City cannot be helped out, and the Stranger cannot help it, either. The great turned against this place. Justly, they have a right. They came to cleanse the City of wickedness. Only he who went through the gate of horror and death is the only one who can rescue people from the on-coming horror and death. Whether does the man from the vision look like the Prince? I could not see his face, and I know that he is young, but great, great... I need to find the Stranger to tell him everything."

The old man began slowly moving the palm sideways, felt a slight tingle in the fingers: that meant that the direction was right. Invisible needles were sticking worse, so he was approaching the target. Sometimes, having lost the sense, he had to stop, return back, and seek again; he found and rushed forward, over hedge and ditch.

The Stranger was lying in the bath, dreaming. The door opened softly, the Bird came in, put the underwear and towel on the marble stool.

"Thank you," he muttered, with his eyes closed. The girl took off the bathrobe, walked up the steps to the bath, and sat down besides looking at him hot-eyed. Her stare effused desire, her lips slightly swelled, nude plastic body trembling.

"I love you and want you very much," she whispered.

"It is not time to love," the Stranger said guiltily. "Sorry."

She came nearer to kiss him on the lips. The wave of desire overwhelmed him. His heart leapt furiously, fire seized him, but he recovered himself, grasped the girl by the shoulders and brushed her aside.

The girl rose slowly and graciously, tossed on the bathrobe and went out, softly closing the door. Smiled. The Stranger snorted out and burst laughing. Dried hurriedly with the towel, got dressed and took the stairs down to the parlor to join his mates. There, he drank some tea, snatched dry fruit and nuts, and asked for a bed. The Medium took him to the bedroom.

Concentrated, the Seer was looking out of the window, drinking coffee and smoking almost all the time.

"You smoke like a chimney," the Medium noticed. "Have some pity for yourself."

"I will not die of cancer of lungs, and I am safe from heart attack," the Seer responded with slight irritation.

She lifted her hands in dismay.

"Why are you so nervous? You believe disaster is in store for the City?" the Medium asked.

"I do not know yet, what is in store for the City. I cannot get my questions answered."

"A wrong question?"

"Maybe. But why do not I ask the right one? This is another question," it was as if the Seer was talking to himself.

"Fear? Are you afraid?"

The Seer smiled ironically.

"Look into your magic ball to see a horror film."

He scorned any magic expedients.

"Stop arguing. The Stranger will rest and tell you. He seems to know many things," the Soldier broke upon.

"The Stranger does not confide us. Not one of us," the Seer said.

"Why?" the Soldier asked.

"He hides his thoughts, overlaps others," the Seer answered gloomily.

"He rightly does. To read somebody's thoughts is mauvais ton," the Medium was growing impatient.

"Stop it!" the Seer raised his voice. "You have no idea of what is happening. The Stranger also knows little. Really, want to know? Well, then. The City is on the verge of annihilation. I saw corpses in the streets and houses; they have no time to bury the dead, so throw them down into the chasm and burn. Who is guilty?"

"The Stranger?" the Medium glared.

"He is just a link in a long chain," the Seer uttered in an unexpectedly calm tone. "All believers hallowed by the prophets are waiting for disaster for the prophecies come true. They expect calamities so that to add to their strength: something like you were told but you did not listen, so gather the harvest of His rage for your sins. The only thing is that they do not understand that everything will start with them."

"Why?"

"They are guilty of distortion, moreover, deliberate distortion. The system of destruction, first, will seek for those getting at the Knowledge too closely," the Seer explained.

"What system?" the Soldier looked at him attentively.

"This is a part of global system of response. The law of cause and effect relationships," the Seer syllabified.

"How to survive?"

"Run right off, if only weather and circumstances permit," the Seer looked at his hurt leg.

"Is there anybody to stop the calamity that is to come?" the Medium inquired.

"I know whom you are thinking about. You think about him all the time... He can just accelerate the process."

"Does it depend on him? Do you really believe that one man is able to influence global processes?"

"Generally, a team is behind the loner. If you cannot see it, this does not mean it does not exist. Calamities were prevented seldom or never, and this was for a while. Owing to requests, preaches, penance, or chosen ones, the mechanism of annihilation would freeze, but if consciousness and lifestyle did not change, it was triggered again, completely and entirely. Crowd will not accept the Stranger. It likes those who point at enemies and promise redemption, who do not hesitate to shed blood of foes and favor friends."

The Seer lighted another cigarette, but taking a whiff, he ground it out and closed his eyes wearily. The Soldier went to the bathroom, the Medium to the kitchen to cook dinner. The Seer forbade ordering meal in a restaurant. Yet another phobia.

Chapter 42. A Meeting

A meeting of the elders of the desert warriors was held in an ancient catacomb. Many centuries ago, here, saints and martyrs were buried. The commander who guarded the entry to the tunnel was called to the extemporary rostrum.

"Brothers," he began. "Yesterday morning we encountered a man who attempted to open the mouth of the tunnel. We explained the terms to him. He seemed to us to be a deserving candidate. His name is the Stranger, but he also made it a condition: if he passed the tunnel through, we must accept the Hermit's way."

"Go on, brother. The Hermit is a holly man, although he cannot accept active actions against extirpation of injustice."

"The Stranger was waiting for help, so we allowed him time. His friend came, looked into the tunnel, but took fright and declined blankly to take the test. Later, the Hermit himself appeared, together with a girl. He talked to the Stranger face to face, and then the Stranger and the girl entered the tunnel."

"A woman came into the tunnel? What a shame!" disturbed voices thrilled.

"I am guilty, brothers," the narrator kept his head down humbly. "I do not know how the thing happened. It was as if in a fog. I supposed they could not pass the tunnel. Anyway, if the woman agreed to martyrdom for the sake of love, the deed were well deserved, it would be credited for her in the Kingdom come. However, if you believe me guilty, I will not find excuses and receive any punishment, up to interdiction."

"Calm down, brother. It is not time for punishment," the chair of the meeting assured him. "We ask to speak the leader of the guard watching over the exit."

A man of forty mounted the rostrum.

"Brothers," he started speaking solemnly. "I happened to become a witness of a miracle. I was informed about the candidate who challenged the Providence. We were waiting the brave heart at the exit; he passed the tunnel but could not open the door with coded lock. I did not know the cypher and said digits at random, decided to test him. He did not believe me and set waiting. Then, a miracle happened. I saw a messenger of heaven in sparkling clothes and heard a thunderous voice: 'Open the door'. I lost strength and fell down. When coming around, I started praying and saw the Stranger. He ordered that I would not take him great or tell about him."

"Are you sure that you saw the messenger of heaven?" the chair asked doubtingly.

"Yes. I am. Moreover, I am sure that the Stranger left the tunnel by opening the lock."

"Then, answer three questions. Why your fellows did not see him? Why the messenger ordered to open the door? Couldn't the angel know that the code was unknown to you? What has happened on the roof of the observation point? I was talking to two sentinels. One of them is useless to talk to, but the other one told me a lot. They fell asleep at watch. Someone got to the roof and tied the warriors. One of them woke from a stupor to receive a blow on the head with a butt, and he is sure that was not an angel who hit him, but an experienced army man."

"I know not all about God's mighty works," the guardian responded. "I do not know why I was honored with a vision of the God's messenger, while my comrades just could hear his voice. I do not know, maybe the divine order 'open the door' was given not to me but to the angel. Brothers, I do not know what happened on the roof. After all, I was not present there."

Heated discussion began. No version suggested could link all facts together. Failing to reach a common ground, the elders decided to keep silent.

The Chief of the security service received the detailed report from his agent about the reason of the eventual meeting. The head of the special service revised the Seer's file and had every confidence that the man had extraordinary mesmeric abilities. "He could both a monster and a messenger of heaven. It would be fine to give the cue to the warriors of desert who took appearance of the angel of light, they will find the Seer to embowel him and find the truth. However, what benefit can it bring? Wouldn't it be great if the Soldier eliminates the Seer to put an end to the competitive special service? A political row of scale is inevitable, even if the office is not closed up, it will be reorganized, renamed, all staff and the entire system replaced. Nevertheless, the Seer and the Soldier play the same game. The Stranger has passed the tunnel. Now, he may reckon upon fame. Let's wait until he appears."

Chapter 43. The Mediator

The Seer was right. The Stranger did not confide any of his companions. How can one place confidence in a person who is not devoted to God with all his heart; who hasn't found their demons and defeated them having kicked them away from the soul, but is concerned with vanity. Under certain conditions the demons will find that person themselves.

The Stranger woke up but he was not eager to join his friends. "Through the weak spots, unreason and flaws the Cover can use my teammates to disserve my mission. The Soldier is looking for the miracles and wishes to be a participant of the great events. The Medium is an easily carried away person; she is attracted by all unusual things. The Seer feels instinctively that he should not do any harm to me, but, perhaps, he wants to influence me by being

near? I can trust the Hermit only. The worst that can happen, he will just step aside in case he disagrees."

The Door opened slightly and he smiled to the Medium entering the room. The woman brought flavorful coffee and pancakes with honey, but the Stranger shifted gaze to her troubled countenance.

"You should leave the City as soon as possible."

"Are you going to stay? Could it be not so bad in fact?" the woman looked at him hopefully.

"I can do nothing to change the situation. What does the Seer say?"

"He sees the calamity on the streets of the City."

The woman left the room, closed the door quietly, leaned her forehead to the cool wall and cried silently.

The Stranger went downstairs to the living room. The Soldier slept on the leather sofa, the Seer sat in the chair and stared at the Stranger with a heart-searching look.

"Are you worried?"

"You should leave the City."

"It's not us you worry about. You don't know why you are here."

"I shall find out."

"What if you are here to kill? They can order you to…"

"I shall not do this. One doesn't give such orders to good people and I don't want to become an evil one."

"There is a lethal weapon inside of you. Do you know how to control it? Do you know how to constrain it?"

"I know, Seer."

"How?"

"I must not fight with people."

"You must not fight with people?" the Seer asked. "Will you hide the sword that pulls out of the scabbard by itself as soon as it feels prey or danger? Will you escape to the desert? Or do you fondly believe that your gift can be used against the human flaws only?"

The Stranger didn't answer. He knew what the Seer was talking about and it worried him.

"I shall go for a walk. I need fresh air."

"I'm with you," the Soldier said in a sleepy voice.

"Don't. Sleep. I shall not go far."

"Why have you attacked him?" the Medium flung her arms up. "He's gone through so many things in these few days. He takes it personally, as all of us."

"Stop it. There is danger in the air. I feel as we are trapped."

The Medium jumped into clothes and ran out. The crowd of people listened to the preacher on the street:

"Woe unto the city of Mages, woe unto the city of False Prophets, woe unto the city of Violence and wickedness.

Woe unto those living under the skies. Moaning is all over the Earth. They shall not drink wine and shall not sing songs.

A guest shall not enter the house and shall hear no fiancé's voice and no happy bride's whoop.

There shall be no joy, for tears are on the faces and there's no comforter.

The arrows of the calamity are aimed on the City. The walls are shaking like the boat on the waves.

The nets of wickedness are spread and everyone is a prey and the lot of wrath is upon those left and outpourings of fury on those hiding. The bounds of death are around and there's no escape.

And rivers of fire shall flow burning every fruitful tree and fruitless tree.

And the corners of the City shall shake and all those inside shall be stupefied with fear.

And the eternal foundations shall tremble, and the war of the Greats shall start, and there was no war alike from the beginning of time.

God!" the preacher exclaimed. "Be a wall for me and protect me from the disasters and storms."

He stopped, fixed his eyes on a woman who approached the long-haired man and pointed the finger on her:

"The daughter of evil! I know you! Your pride will be your downfall. Your divination is bringing trouble. When you foretell future, you take the choice off people and give them the false hope that they can be saved without God and that they can escape death without the truth of God. You trap the souls with your strong nets, with the nets of the archenemy."

The Medium became pale, the crowd surrounded her. It seemed they were on the verge of attacking her.

The Stranger was filling with the Wind. The Power emerged quickly in the City. He came up to the preacher.

"Do you see who I am?" the Stranger asked in an altered voice.

"Who are you?" the preacher suddenly shrank, astonishment mixed with fear appeared in his glance.

"I am the Stranger. Listen to me. This woman is wandering in the dark, as well as other sons and daughters of men. We are stumbling upon each other like blind kittens while vainly trying to find the escape. But how can we find it? We just interfere with each other and spend the precious time on pointless conflicts. You are right, there is a calamity approaching, the grief is coming for every creature. By immolating the reprobates you will not save yourselves. By immolating the good you will make the calamity closer and close the way to salvation. This woman is helping me. It is not for you to blame her."

The preacher exclaimed,

"This is the true messenger! I am glad to welcome you, the man of God."

The Stranger got breath. He was reeling a little.

"I shall take her home and come back," he promised.

"They are unfair to me," the woman trembled. "I am not the daughter of the evil. Everyone has their own way. I saw the mistakes of people, I corrected them, I took off the generational curses. I helped, I didn't harm. That prophet is a fanatic, he knows nothing. I should really leave the City otherwise they will kill me."

"Everyone should leave," the Stranger agreed.

The Soldier approached. He was a bit strained but walked with light step.

"I felt worry, asked the Seer and he said, 'They will deal with it themselves'. How's that? Without me?"

"It's OK, Soldier," the Medium calmed him down.

"Who hurt you?"

"Nobody. It's just dangerous to leave the house."

"See her safely home. I have to come back," the Stranger told him.

"How did it happen that the preacher took me to be the messenger of the God with no doubts," he was plagued with this thought.

The preacher rushed to the Stranger hardly had he seen him.

"I know who you are. I am the Mediator, the prophet and the preacher of the community 'Power of Light'."

"And I am nobody," the Stranger smiled. "I do not belong to any community, order or party. I serve God in spirit and do not depend on the people's rules. Your multiple communities are just clubs. You give magnificent names to common and undeserving things and by doing this you abuse the power of Light. Still you can be useful. People with broken souls need help like people with broken hands need plaster cast, but don't forget that it hinder movements. It's a temporary measure but you wear it forever."

"Aren't all people have broken souls? When sheep tramp the field and there is no shepherd with the gun, lash and dogs, the wolves will eat them!"

"Your shepherds take off the fell of their sheep and make kebab of them. It's enough talking about it. How did you know about me?"

"A vision. A man in white clothes appeared and said, "A man of God has come to the City, soon you shall see him"."

"Is it all?" the Stranger asked.

"Is it not enough?" the prophet was surprised. "I want to introduce you to brothers. The spiritual center of the community is situated not far from here."

"Are you sure it was about me?"

"Of course. I can interpret the visions."

"Have you seen that man in reality?"

"No. I was between the dreaming and awakening, in this state the visions are as real and bright as in reality but it's not so dangerous."

"Why did you fly upon the woman? We could have been killed because of your words. How can one hold the vengeful crowd?"

"I didn't want her being punished. I see you don't know what is going on. Everyone is in fear and despair. The prophets are talking about the calamity; they go to the streets and preach for contrition. Maybe God shall have mercy on us and protect us. And now, you are here. I believe you can help, God have given you the power to expel the Exterminators."

"What Exterminators?" the Stranger grew wary.

"The ancient prophesies of the Alien people invasion become true: "The strong unmerciful people shall appear on the earth and all the inhabitants of the universe shall moan and thrill with horror. They shall go through the walls and climb upon the roofs. Their very appearance shall make everyone lose heart and bend knees and no one shall confront them for everyone shall be corroded with fear and despair."

"That's right," the Stranger confirmed. "The prophecy is to become true. 'For he shall hack his sword on their heads: those running shall not escape, those seeking salvation shall not be saved.' Is it possible to avoid the trouble?"

The Mediator shook his head:

"We need to fight for there is another progression of events. The Exterminators are the echo of our crimes. We need to look for the seeds of our disease. We have to find and to exterminate it."

"Do you know what is to be found?"

"The ancients knew. We are studying their recipes."

"The ancients knew how to prevent the disease, they were able to avoid it, but when it emerged it was too late. I was glad to meet you, but I should go now," the Stranger stretched his arm.

"We shall look forward to see you." The Mediator put a booklet with the community's address into his palm.

Chapter 44. The Immunity

Near the house, the Stranger met the Soldier.

"What's new?"

"I've been invited to the headquarters of the 'Power of the Light'."

"I will come with you."

"I haven't decided yet should I go at all. How is the Medium? She changed, didn't she?"

"Yes. She is a sort of freaky. She could hardly keep from crying. As soon as she entered the house, she ran without a word and locked herself in the room."

"What about the Seer?"

"He just smiled. Well, just as usually."

"He risks a lot. There is no order that doesn't wish to destroy him."

"Why has he come here?"

The Soldier kept silent.

The door was opened; the Seer was watching the local news and smiling strangely.

"Has something happened?" asked the Stranger.

"The City is announced to be a closed zone. We are trapped."

"What's the reason?" inquired the Soldier; he wanted to smile as well.

"It's said that a group of terrorists got into the City with a dangerous weapon. There are victims. It's not recommended to go out into the street," the Seer explained.

"What's there in reality?" the Stranger became alerted.

"That is a lie. But there are victims. But you know what that is."

"Can you help find the Hermit? I think he is in town."

"Why do you avoid answering? You care about no one just as those fanatics? Are you happy that the ancient prophecies have come true?"

"OK. Our evil world will be destroyed and there will come a just world instead. But who will survive? Who will have the honor of entering the new world? A few thousands? The rest will burn? And you don't care much? And who is the enemy of the mankind? Someone like me or someone like you?" pushed the Seer.

"I serve God," the Stranger raised his voice. "And everything, you talked about, just are the consequences of ignoring the rules.

Can one do evil deeds and prosper? Shed blood and enjoy the gifts? Haven't we been warned that the mankind will pay for the evil deeds? Haven't been pleaded to turn away from the evil? And what happened? The messengers, the prophets and the Prince had been killed. He risked his life because he preached the path of truth during tyranny and lawlessness. He could destroy the enemies but he showed an example of love and mercy. I don't rejoice about disasters you know that, Seer. But our deeds and desires have ruined the immunity, and now we are powerless in front of the Exterminators. How can we restore the immunity?"

The Seer came up to the window.

"This is a long and very difficult process. The level of ozone, the immunity of the planet, is easier to restore than to get rid of the vice. We are not as bad as it looks like. The humankind survives. A baby is fed with milk, then is given soft food and only after it grows up, he or she is fed with hard food. For the stomach of a baby is not adjusted to the hard foods: he can't digest it, can't swallow, he will choke on it. You don't know the limits; you try to impose the world with rules that are difficult to understand. What you call the Cover is only a greenhouse for weak plants. Have you thought about why the Source let take more than is needed for today? Probably, it's to save for the future, to use it tomorrow, for the future generations? Yes, you are right, the nations and civilizations have vanished. The societies that broke the laws of ethics, stopped in their spiritual development. Destruction is reserved for us as well. Is it possible to stop the upcoming disaster? I don't know. If you put your fingers into the fire, you will get burned, but all that the mankind is doing is playing with the fire. And you are happy to put more wood into this fire."

"What do you advise us to do?" the voice of the Stranger slightly trembled. "Hide the truth? Hide our inner world? Run away into the desert or mountains? And let the hypocrites, liars and just blind people twist the path of the Lord! They teach lies. They mix truth and lies so subtly that it's impossible to distinguish one from the other.

Maybe, you don't care about the truth and the questions that are important to us don't bother you much. But who can we listen to? And whose interest shall we stand for God's or human's? The spirit's or the flash's? The prophets of this world take care of the body and the people of the knowledge take care of the soul."

"What is the soul?" queried the Seer.

"Ask the Medium. You trust her more."

The Seer looked in expectancy at the woman standing at the door.

"I saw the essences that have conscience and memory. You know that people have the desire to communicate with the dead relatives. The world of the dead is not less real than ours," the Medium suddenly kept silent.

"Well, how is it there?" asked the Seer without any sarcasm.

"It is depressing. It's dark there. Everyone is waiting for something, but they all know that it's something important, something they didn't want to know here," the woman's lips trembled. "I am sorry, I keep crying all the time."

"I think that you are mistaking. Our conscience is given mere images that it wants to accept. Well, I don't like talking about it.... What do you want to do?" he turned to the Stranger.

"I've been invited to the headquarters of the order 'Power of the Light'. The preacher of this community knows something," and the Stranger told about the meeting with the Mediator.

"I wouldn't advise you to go there. It's dangerous," warned the Seer.

"Is it dangerous for me or the Soldier?"

"It's dangerous for them."

"Why?"

"There will be a situation, when the Power will show itself and you won't be able to hold it back. I don't take pity on these fanatics, but you will not be able to calm yourself down, you will run away, like a Hermit, into the desert. Still, your gift will come useful for a special thing."

"Do you know what for?"

"The Hermit knows. Probably, he will explain it to you. And now you know," the Seer said affirmatively.

"You too. I am not the one who should be talking about one whole information field," smiled the Stranger.

"There words 'Alien people' are spinning in your mind. There are many creatures in our world, the ones we can see and the ones that we can't. They all fight for their lives, the lives of their descendants. That is a biological program. Surviving is connected with capturing the territory. It's quite natural to suppose that our resources attracted the interest of other forms of life. But I don't understand what will be changed in this? Does it matter if your house will be captured by cockroaches with spiders, ominous viruses-mutants, cancer cells or something else? Does it matter what to die from?"

"That is all so, Seer. But if these creatures will destroy the mankind and there will be no one, not just in the City, but in the whole world?"

"I don't believe in destroying the mankind. I do believe in the big shake-up, yes, but I can't believe in the total destruction," said the Seer with a push in his voice.

"The people have the weapon of mass destruction. Sooner or later, they will use it," objected the Stranger.

"This weapon is the factor that restrains it."

"You don't believe in the human's intellect, in their ability to control their emotions?"

"No, I don't. I don't know about those awful crimes against the mankind. I can see the mechanisms that regulate the historical processes."

"If we don't create the condition for a well-coordinated work of the mechanisms, if we don't fulfill the tasks, there is an error in the system of the Creation of the World. And then through the chosen ones God...or human saving instinct, depends on those who believe in what...will show what needs to be done in order to be saved. But the society is blinded, that's why they don't want to listen to the holder of the Word. Probably, the humankind is inclined to suicide? Or someone is trying to use his subtle game to prevent the mankind from finishing the task, that's why the error is getting worse."

"Why does the powerful intellect try to destroy the mankind? What for?" disagreed the Seer.

"It's not necessary to destroy it. This is a side effect. A man has something valuable: unique abilities and possibility to have eternal life," continued the Stranger.

"This isn't a new idea. I think that there is a program that aims to destroy the man. It needs to be found and erased. But this will bring to great consequences, the mankind is not ready to stay on this planet forever, that's why the Cover restrains our development. You say, people do not follow the rule, they destroy the protection. Let's suppose it is so, the lawless men will be punished, they are stupid. You can't demand much of them. But any mind that has the knowledge of the universal laws has to understand that he will be responsible for breaking the rules," the Seer used the Stranger's language.

"This all is so, that's why the Enemy plays subtle, without obvious interference. He uses his representatives in earthly guise. The Enemy creates situations, conceptions, false ideologies and religions: this is the Cover that doesn't let to get through to the Source."

"Do you believe in this system?" the Seer inquired.

"It's all much more complicated. Our conscience is not ready to fit all the difficulty of the system, but even a simple mind is able to influence on the process in a certain way. For example, the weapon that is inside me is tuned in by the influence of my primitive thoughts and emotions."

"Weapon... Will you fight..." the Seer stretched his thin lips in a smile.

"I don't know. Right now, I am trying to grasp the destination. Someone is leading us..." the Stranger stopped short.

"I like this phrase. So, who is leading us?"

The Stranger pondered over it: he has responded to this question long time ago for himself, but he couldn't say that was the messenger of the Prince.

"I will help you," said the Seer. "You think that you do not fulfill the mission. Than I have a few questions for you. How do you know who you work for? You have heard the Voice. So what? There are lots of Voices but not all of them are from the Lord. Have you met with the heavenly representative? No? Even if you did, how do you know who that is? You told about subtle game. Aren't you a part of this game? Have you been helped? Even I have done something for you. However, why did they help you? Do you have a weapon? Do you want to use it? I understand. But do you know its destination? Aren't you afraid that during your experiments you will ruin, break human lives?"

The Stranger kept silent. The words of the Seer puzzled him.

"If he is the darkness, then who is the light?" a loud voice came from the yard of the house, this voice made the Seer trembled with his whole body.

"The Hermit," the Stranger whispered and ran out to meet him. They hugged.

"I will not come up into this house," the Hermit said. "And you shouldn't stay there. The crowd wants to find those who are guilty and they are going to cleanse the City from the sinners. But that is not the most terrible thing..."

"Why do the people die?"

"The citizens believe that this is the punishment of God for their sins. The people are driven crazy. The fear gets into the soul and starts capturing it."

"So what shall I do?" asked the Stranger.

"Search and find the reason. Haven't you understood that already?" the old man grasped for some air.

"Speak distinctly, I plead you," the Stranger grabbed his shoulders.

A crowd armed with knives, bats and even weapons came from behind the corner. They were shouting angry tirades against those who are guilty in the coming disaster. The Medium was one of the first in the list.

"I will be back" the Stranger ran back into the house. "There is a mob here! We have to leave!"

The Soldier looked out of the window, his teeth greeting. The Medium was trembling. The Bird looked sides in astonishment. Only the Seer was calm. He came out into the street, saw the Hermit and made a guilt gesture with his hands:

"I am sorry, I didn't live up to your expectations."

"I loved you like a real son," uttered the old man. "Who did you serve? The world? Look at its face. This is the real face of the world," he pointed to the crowd of people.

"This is not my world, Hermit. Will you help?"

The Hermit kept quiet.

"Then do not interfere," The Seer was confident in his force and felt that he could govern the crowd.

"I am with you," said the Stranger. "I will not let the people dear to me be destroyed. Hermit, haven't you come here for my sake?"

"No. Leave. Find the reason why you are here. This," he pointed to the crowd, "isn't the reason. Come with me."

The Stranger shook his head. The Hermit looked at the sky and slowly walked away.

The crowd was coming closer. The Seer drew a net in his mind that seized the conscience of the enraged people, and unseen net seizing the crowd. The people were too stirred up, and the Seer decided not to put them to sleep. He impressed them with a vision of a great growing fire. The crowd shrank back and ran away with loud screams of horror.

Large sweat drops trickled down the Seer's forehead, but his face was shining with a smile of a proud winner. Still, his younger fellow didn't express any joy for some reason; more over it was vice versa. The Stranger was looking at one spot with a focused sullen look. The Seer came up to him.

"We won. Calm down," he said mildly.

"Go home. This is not your entrance," said the Stranger indistinctly, making a step forward. A strong Wind enveloped his whole body and pierced his head with sharp needles. The air became thick.

The Seer couldn't understand a thing, but after he looked closer, he saw something looking like a human's silhouette. He started tuning on this image when suddenly went pale, made one step back, gathered his strength, looked back again. Now he saw this silhouette more clearly. Fear. His breathe was squeezed, he became weak in his knees.

The Seer wheezed, staggered and collapsed oddly onto the foot path.

The Stranger didn't even give a look in his direction. He remembered the words of the Soldier: 'First put out the weapon emplacements. And then...'

The Wind grew stronger.

"Go away! You have no power over me! Go away!" roared the Stranger.

It seemed to him that his hair stood on his head and he will fly up into the air
any moment. He stretched his hands upfront, as if trying to hold some sort of pressure.

The Stranger felt surprise, coming from that disembodied essence.

"The Prince is alive. Be afraid and come around his friends!"

The Stranger set on the ground and cried without a sound. He didn't feel like a winner. Nobody fought against him, he understood that well enough. He had been watched, probably with certain surprise, though he wasn't touched for some reason.

The Bird came up to him and started kissing his wet face. The Soldier saw the Seer lying on the ground, picked him up and carried him into the house in his hands.

The Medium tried to bring the Seer back to his senses. The Stranger listened to his pulse, asked for a needle, burned it in the fire and abruptly pierced it between the fingers, and pulled it back. The Seer's eyelids batted, he screwed up his face with pain.

"It's all right, Seer. You have chased everyone. Now get some rest," the Stranger patted his hand.

The Seer tried to say something but he couldn't, he mumbled, a helpless tear went down his cheek. The Stranger drank some sweet tea and made a sign to the Soldier, they went out to talks.

"We can't stay here. The mobs can come back."

"I will find a weapon, get on the roof and shoot at some of them, the rest will run away."

"We can't do that. There will be a crossfire started. There are people around."

"Then let's leave. Let's ask to come into any house, stay there until it's all gone. The most important thing is to leave the women and the Seer in a safe place."

"OK. I will try to talk to my acquaintance; he invited me into the headquarters of the 'Power of the Light.' Tell them that I will be back soon."

Chapter 45. Power of Light

The headquarters of the 'Power of Light' was located in the lower part of the City. The entrance had been guarded by two people, with their guns ready to shoot. The Stranger was checked by a metal detector, after they didn't find anything suspicious, they let him go.

The respected members of the community were sitting in the front seats of the gathering hall. The Mediator was speaking from the rostrum:

"There are alien people walking on the hills of the desert,

The mere sight of them makes one lose heart, and his loins weaken.

Repent, before the darkness comes.

Our sins expose us, but stand up for us. Protect us in times of troubles.

Why do You torture us? Why there is no healing? We were expecting peace when horror came! The City, who will take pity on you?

Who will cry after you?"

The preacher looked up, with his eyes full of tears, and saw the Stranger.

"Brothers!" the Mediator raised his voice. "Look! A man of God came to us. His name is the Stranger," and he pointed to the man standing at some distance.

"The Stranger?" exclaimed someone from the front row. "Isn't it the Stranger who passed the Tunnel of death?"

Everyone got up from their places, wishing to see the man of God. He looked around at the neatly cut and dressed in expensive suits members of the community. He saw perplexity on their faces, because a poorly dressed, blue-eyed man with long hair faded in the sun and long wrinkles and a nice tan, a man of uncertain age appeared before their eyes.

The Stranger slowly walked to the rostrum:

"The prophecies come true: 'I will send the dwellers of the land timidity of heart, rustling of a withering leaf will chase them and they will stumble over one another and they will fall, although nobody is after them. And they will not stand against the Enemy'... But the biggest sorrow comes from us ourselves. The fear pushes us to search for the truth in somebody's fault but it's not there. I need your help, for my friends are in danger. I want to bring them here, under your protection."

"Bring anyone you wish," said the Mediator. "Just not the servants of the darkness, for this is a holy place. Their presence will desecrate it. The Medium is our enemy. People like her open the door to the Enemy and his servants."

"The Medium and the Seer helped me. God tells us to do good, and to forget evil. You can't bring a defenseless woman into the temple, but can bring a weapon? Each one of you has a gun under his jacket. If you believe that God has sent me, listen to His messenger. I have passed the test of the desert warriors, but they still searched to kill me. You are waiting for the one who will approve your path. If the Prince comes, you will not accept him either. You say that you are the servants of God? On what grounds? Maybe, due to your seniority or due to your own testimony? Spiritual gifts aren't proves of righteousness. In such a case the Seer is the most righteous of all the people."

A grumble rolled down the hall, angry shouts were heard.

"He was right," the Stranger remembered the warning. "I came here in vain."

"Brothers," shouted the Mediator. "Calm down, please. God wants peace, not a war. The witch will not enter our temple, but let's respond to the request of the man of God, let's send people to guard her house."

"No," said the elder firmly. "This man is of alien spirit, I can clearly see it, but let him leave in peace. We let you go. We forgive your pride and ignorance."

The Stranger was boiling with anger; he didn't need the forgiveness of impostors. He was filled with the Wind. The Stranger held the power, gasping air convulsively: "Just a few more seconds and the power will come out, and then something fatal will happen."

"Mediator! Come with me!" he shouted and ran out of the building. The preacher hardly caught up with him.

"I have one question for you," said the Stranger. "Do you remember what the heavenly messenger looked like?"

"He was dressed in light clothes, or of light-grey color. I don't remember exactly."

"Do you remember the cut of the dress?"

"No. No, I don't."

"Now eyes. Remember his eyes."

The Mediator weary sat on the ground. The Stranger confirmed his worst fears: what if the Enemy has pretended to be the heavenly messenger and the vision is false? Then all his revelations are a deception?

"I don't remember," moaned the Mediator. "What is going on? What is going on with all of us? Why is it all so scary? We predicted. We were waiting. And here is this day, on the threshold, knocking at the door, but nobody is ready to let it in. Fevered conscience prompted wild solutions. Can you help?" he looked at the Stranger in hope.

"I don't know. Nobody is listening to me. People will start killing each other in a short while."

"They are already killing. We are ready to seize each other's throats because of this fear. Why did you ask about the heavenly delegate?" the Mediator hung his head.

"Not everything that comes from heaven is from God."

"Don't say things like that. Who can we trust then?"

"I don't trust anyone but the Prince," said the Stranger.

"How do you recognize him?"

"I will… What have you decided? Are you coming with me?"

"No. I will go to ask people to repent. I will try to stop this slaughter. Maybe, God will give us mercy. You are my brother," the Mediator gave a reserved smile.

The Stranger shook his hand; a lump came to his throat. He was seized by a bad feeling.

"Hold on, brother!" shouted the Stranger to the Mediator who was walking away.

What a pity, that they have not met earlier. The Stranger couldn't understand how the Mediator maintained sensitive soul, being in an environment where they don't stand another opinion? What was he doing in a community that is not able to accept the truth, and disregards the regulations? Probably, he realized that the elders were mistaken, he preached under the protection of the order to have some access to the congregation?

Stranger didn't rush to judge people without finding the reason for their deeds.

Chapter 46. A Single-Shot Fire

The Soldier regretted that he did not take the automatic rifle off the desert warriors, but it was not difficult to find a gun in the City, especially in the times like these.

"Close the doors and the windows," he told to the hostess. "I'll go outside for a while."

"Do you want to leave us?" her eyes filled with tears.

"I'll be back, I promise, and the Stranger will be back soon too."

Young men were darting about like vultures, but they didn't try to touch him, probably they were looking for some easier prey. He saw men in the military uniform, came to them, named himself, and showed the dog tag built into the boot.

"Brothers, what's going on?"

"We don't know," the patroller answered. "The City went crazy. We don't interfere. We are watching."

"Why don't they bring troops into?"

"I don't know. They say there is a dangerous virus in the City, but nobody knows exactly what it is."

"Who has given the order to close the City? Security service?"

"No idea. But it was definitely not the security service. The cordon is made by border troops and police."

"I see," the Soldier drawled. "We're in deep shit, men, so many idiots are here! The gun is a necessity."

"We got a spare automatic rifle and a couple of magazines. Stay with us, it's safer."

"Thanks, guys, thanks a lot, but I should go."

The Soldier didn't expect that getting a gun would be so easy. Glad, he hurried home and from afar he saw the crowd gathering near the house.

With no hesitations, he switched the gun to his favorite mode: a single-shot fire.

"Get out of here! I'll fire for effect!" the Soldier shouted and flicked the switch loudly.

A young man pointed a gun at him but he didn't manage to aim. The rifle banged. The weapon may not be fixed, that's why the Soldier aimed to the body but not to the head. The bullet hit the boy's belly, passed clear and nicked somebody else. The young man dropped the gun, sat slowly with his hands pressed to the bleeding wound. He moaned with pain and fear and whispered, "Help, help."

"Go!" the Soldier shouted once again. "Now!" and he gave another shoot, this time in the air.

The crowd dispersed quickly, having left the bleeding man on the ground. The Soldier took his gun, pulled out the charger, racked the slide, the bullet didn't came out.

"Idiot!" he whiffed.

He entered to the entrance hall, went upstairs quickly and knocked on the door.

"It's me, don't be afraid!"

The hostess opened without even looking at him. The Soldier entered, saw that everyone was safe and sound, and calmed down.

"How's our patient?"

"He has not recovered consciousness, it looks like catalepsy," the Medium answered.

"Looks like what?"

"He's asleep. In a deep sleep. Was it you shooting?"

It seemed that Medium was able to cope with fears and emotions or she pulled together as if there were no vengeful crowd outside. She took care of the Seer and even found time to calm The

Bird who didn't understand what was going on and that scared her even more.

"Yes. I put one down. I would kill a dozen of beasts and covered the street with blood, the rest of jackals would not dare to come close to your house, but the Stranger will not like it. Where is he? It's dangerous outside," the Soldier growled. He saw the Bird's eyes and realized that he said too much. "Calm down, girl. You know the Stranger. Everything's going to be all right."

Chapter 47. New colors

The head of the security service handed over the administration to his successor. He destroyed the folder with the last case and felt the great relief. He knew what had happened to all who took part in the old litigation on the Stranger. The judge died of the sheer heart attack a couple of years ago. The policeman that pushed the Stranger died in the fire-fight. The court clerk was killed by her ex-lover. And the last in the list was the Prosecutor who committed suicide a weak ago.

The Chief was happy that he didn't manage to arrest the Stranger, though he was curious to see him and talk to him. But such an acute person as the Stranger could not even glance in his direction. A heavy load of doubtful and sometimes cruel decisions pressed on conscience of the new pensioner.

He decided to devote all his time to reading holy books and praying in order to find the peace of mind. He was glad with all his heart that he had chance to devote time to family and there was so much ahead.

"The life sparkled with new colors," he thought and suddenly felt a prick, a hit in his heart, he could not breathe, darkness spread in his eyes. "Too late," these dreadful words burnt in front of him. They burnt and faded.

Chapter 48. The Promise

The Stranger saw the bleeding young man near the house. He stopped beside him and examined the wound. The Bird ran out of the house, rushed towards him but the Stranger ignored her and ordered:

"Go back to the house and bring the medicine box!"

"He is one of the rioters," the girl flared up.

"The man is hurt, he needs help. Don't argue…"

The Soldier appeared, and passed him the medicines. Without a word, the Stranger started to debride a wound. Soon an old woman with two young men ran up. She bent over the wounded and burst in tears.

"He's alive, calm down," the Stranger assured her. "We have stopped the bleeding but he should be taken to the hospital."

"The hospitals don't take the wounded," one of the young men said. "We'll take our brother with us and take care of him at home. Thanks to you, he's alive. Thank you. Thank you very much!" and he shook the hands of the Stranger and his friend who avoid looking into the crying mother's eyes.

"You need to find antibiotics and a drip bulb. It's ok, he is a healthy young
man, he'll stay alive. The bullet went through, his vital organs are not damaged," the Stranger soothed.

Going upstairs he asked the Soldier:

"Where did you get a gun?"

"People kind and fair are everywhere," the Soldier answered serenely. "Protected friends. I did it my way."

The Stranger came to the Seer, felt his pulse, listened to the weak heartbeat and started to shake him immediately.

Seer's eyelid twitched.

"Don't sleep!" the Stranger shouted, slapped his cheek and dashed water in his face.

The Seer opened his eyes and mumbled,

"Head, my head…"

The Stranger put hands on the head of the Seer but jerked back as if he touched something extremely hot. Then he pulled together and again put his palms on the aching spot. He felt his hands got heavy. The Stranger released the tension and pressed his palms to the Seer's head again.

"Thank you. I feel better. You woke me up in time. I didn't sleep and I wasn't awake." The Seer listened to himself and muttered, "I feel nothing."

"You need to eat and have some rest. I and Soldier will take care of you," the Stranger shook his hand.

"I had no friends for many years. I'm glad I met you, especially in these dark days," the Seer was moved deeply.

"These are not last days. Here's tea and honey. Refresh yourself."

"Stranger, I know you want to leave," the Medium said. "Don't do this. There's death on the streets, we can barricade inside the flat. The Soldier has the automatic rifle, we'll hold out. I'm sure the government will send the troops to establish order. Please, I beg you, don't go out!"

"I have to find the Hermit. Don't worry about me. The Soldier will stay with you. We need to talk," he addressed to his friend.

The Soldier turned, pulled out a cigarette, sighed and looked at him expectantly.

"I have to leave," the Stranger started. "My heart will be easy if you stay here. These people are very important, they need to be protected but try not to kill anyone."

"No. I'm here to be with you. I don't think those people will come to this house again. I'll explain how to defend and leave the riffle," the Soldier smoked nervously.

"I need you here. Trust me."

Limping severely the Seer came to them.

"They won't go on rampage again," he said quietly, "but the Soldier shouldn't go, and you too."

The Bird ran to the Stranger and held him tight.

"Don't go," she whispered. He put her aside. His gestures became accurate, his face estranged, he exuded calm and confidence. The Bird sagged down on the floor.

"Promise that you'll be back! Promise!" she shouted.

"We'll see each other again," the Stranger said quietly.

The girl nodded happily. She trusted him. The Seer just sighed heavily.

Chapter 49. The Reason

The old lamps, houses made of stone, pavements with pebbles: the Hermit's vision has become alive. The street was empty. A grey cat tossed aside and hid behind the bushes. The old man startled, looked around and made his way on the pavement. Suddenly he felt somebody's look and quickly looked back: nobody was there. It seemed as if he got trapped, somebody made an ambush. He needs to leave this deserted street. He hurried away without looking back. There appeared a shadow in front of him, the Hermit slowed down straining his eyes. He came closer, then closer.

"Oh, that's you?" drawled the Hermit. "Let me go. You have no power over me. I am not under the protection of your cloak."

"I don't need you. Your life hangs by a hair, a wind blows and it breaks," he blew some air and smiled, showing an even row of white teeth. "I need another one."

"It's not you who should meet him," the old man looked at him in contempt.

"You are in a square and you can't get out of it. You can't help anyone even yourself. Warn the Stranger, tell him to leave. He isn't the one who should be fighting with me. You will stay here. It has to be like that," he said in a well-wishing voice.

After casting a glance at the windows, the Stranger realized that he will never come back to this house. "That's it, my time is up," a thought flashed across his mind. "It's weird, why there is no fear? Hermit, where are you? What do I need to understand?"

The Stranger was walking down the streets of the City, he was passing through the crowd and nobody touched him. There were gun shots constantly heard, the houses and the shops were on fire. The streets were filled with cries and shouts for help. The preachers tried to stop the slaughter but they made good targets of themselves for those who love to shoot, as they stood at the high places. Coming closer to the Kings' square, the Stranger heard a familiar loud voice.

"Repent, repent while it's still not late, change your clothes, cast off the old once and put on the new and clean once. It's close, it's coming. The horror that is hanging over the City. Let him come, our Saver, and our Enemy, the ancient opponent, who has covered the whole land with his cloak, will run away."

The Stranger was filled with the Wind at these words, his body became light, as if the laws of gravity disappeared, and he felt he could fly. "Let's fly," he said to himself firmly. The most important is not to doubt and not to be afraid. The most difficult thing is to pass the barrier of disbelief, but the Wind increased, got stronger, sweeping the last doubts away and he believed in the impossible. He took off, came up higher, but sudden doubts pulled him down.

"No. I can. It's not hard!" fiercely, desperately he told himself, as if pushing off the air, and flew up.

"Look, look!" shouted people around, pointing at the flying man. An old preacher, the elder of the order "Power of Light" recognized him.

"The prophecy has come true! A servant of the Enemy came, and his name is Stranger. He got the power from the darkness, and now he deceits the earth with false wonders. He is an opponent of the ancient truth and ancient traditions. This man has incurred the curse onto the City."

"It's the Stranger! He is the servant of God!" shouted the desert warriors. "He passed the death tunnel, he fulfilled the ancient prophecy. He is the promised forerunner of the Prince."

"He stood up for a witch! He is not from God!" insisted the preacher.

People underneath were shouting, arguing, somebody wanted to shoot at the Stranger, but he didn't pay any attention, stretched his right hand up front, took it aside, bowed himself a little bit side, held himself and it seemed that he swam in the air. It's important to hold balance: as soon as he lost it he fell into. The frozen and charmed crowd was left aside.

After getting rather high, the Stranger got suddenly scared of the height; the fear seized his trust and his muscles. He started to fall down. The earth seemed to get closer very fast. "No!" he shouted. "It's not hard!" He was able to stop the fall a few meters away from the earth after he remembered how he swam in the air. After that, he decided not to get too high and instead fly a little bit over the three–story houses. If you are not afraid of the altitude, you won't fall.

He landed softly on one of the most ancient streets of the City. He walked around as if in a fog, and found himself near the ruins of a fortress, made of uncultivated stones. This tower was the first barrier on the way of intruders coming from the north in ancient times.

The Stranger set on the stones, looked at his body, listen to his pulse and... realized his weakness. "Any miracle will be interpreted wrongly. They honor the power and the fear. Who am I here for? They didn't fit in the Prince and they will not understand me. There will come another one who will show this land wonders. How do we distinguish them? Only by his deeds, the true messenger of the Lord reveals a lie and hypocrisy; he tends to justice, helps, cures...

What if the disease has been neglected? Doesn't the surgeon cut dried with gangrene limbs for the sake of saving the rest of the body? Doesn't the Man of Law destroy those who give trouble, in order to stop the wave of violence that threatens to burn the whole country? Who will judge him? Only the one who hasn't seen a cruel and merciless rebellion.

Will a kind teacher throw a careless pupil out of the class even if he messes up the lesson to the prejudice of the other pupils? To the contrary, the laws of the World System, the laws of nature aren't like these: get rid of everything that is weak and not useful, and leave what is strong and promising. No, this is a trap for us, representatives of another world. We cannot destroy weak, we have to help them and care for them. What if it's too late, and there is no time to drag the one who is behind? Those, who were able to reach it, will get a ticket for the train, but those, who could not, will stay on the platform."

"Hermit," called the Stranger loud. "Why did you come into the City?"

The Stranger was sitting and talking to himself without paying any attention to the people coming close to him: three women and two men.

"Why are you here?" asked a short woman with blond hair.

"I am looking for the Hermit," calmly responded the Stranger.

"He isn't here. Have you come here for his sake? I can see the light of God in you."

"Who are you?"

"We came to the Prince," said the woman tenderly.

"Is the Prince here?" The Stranger quickly rose to his feet.

"He is in the City."

"Where? How can I find him?"

"We don't know. We are waiting for a sign."

"How did you understand that the Prince is here?"

"We've been called," explained the woman.

"Do you know the reason?" asked the Stranger.

"No. But we know it anyway. We are waiting for the Prince every day. The signs of his arrival come true."

"Misfortune befell the City," reminded the Stranger. "Do you know how to stop the disaster?"

"We can't," said a man. "We aren't here for this. You also shouldn't try, you can't help them anymore. The City is doomed.

It's a sign. If the people don't understand and turn away from their sins," the disaster will come to the whole world.

"Is the Prince going to come secretly? Only for chosen ones? May be he came to save the City?"

"It's the beginning of the end here now. The Prince is present in the beginning and in the end. He came to judge," said the woman confidently.

The Stranger didn't like these words. He didn't want to be an observer. "If I find the Prince, he will stop the disaster."

"It's safe here. They won't come here. This place is closed for them. Stay with us," offered the blond haired woman.

"I didn't come to the City to search for a safe place."

The Stranger slowly dragged himself away. "Is the Seer right and the chosen ones don't care for the fate of the people? The most important thing is for the justice to triumph and the prophecies to be fulfilled. And the suffering is a fair payment for the sins. They aren't trying to stop the disaster, for they know that all the attempts are in vain? But to be indifferent and not to participate? What if there still is a chance, a slight chance?"

The City was filled with rumors. The old preacher who insulted the Stranger was cruelly beaten. The warriors of the desert have announced coming of a prophet and they were sure to take a leading position among a large number of religious communities. People kept passing away. A horror grimace froze on the faces of miserable and they fell onto the ground in agony. People were afraid to come close to them, fearing that they are affected by a deadly virus, that's why a special team in waterproof suits gathered corps and burned them behind the city gates. The Stranger tried not to think about his friends and he only asked God to protect them from the disaster.

The news about the Prince arrival has astonished him. "Why does he need to be present at the City's destroy?" he asked himself. "Something is not right here. I have to find the Hermit." The Stranger shouted: "I need you!"

"Where do I search for the Prince? Will he preach in the squares? Is he hiding in deserted places or in the ruins? Maybe he is waiting till somebody comes to him? Or he will knock on the door himself?" The Stranger listened to his feelings, and his heart was filled with joy: "The Prince is really here." He turned around hearing some noise and saw the Hermit. The old man was hardly holding on.

"I am so happy to see you!" the Stranger exclaimed. "I see that you are very tired. Here you can have some rest."

"Did you understand the reason?"

"I've been explained."

"You have to find him."

"Do you think we are here for this? He came for our sake?"

"Listen to this prophecy! I wrote it twenty years ago, but I keep forgetting to share it with you. Looks like it's time.

February is in the air, the winter has come down to the land,
It promises us no hope.
The plague is no longer in the air but
Some alive are still in the land,
We will live and death is not around.
Let's endure, the lonely two will say
The two lonely remnants of great cities.
But how can we endure, for the power belongs to those,
Who lived, who died and those who have gone.
While those who are alive,
They wish for the death to come,
But it will not come for a long while,
The debts bring it to another shelter..."

The old man held his heart, the Stranger reached to the Hermit in concern, but he only breathed and continued:

"Hey you! Soaked in mud
You draw shame in wantonness.
You won't find His favor,
The servants of insanity and evil.
Give me Your wonderful Wind from Heaven,
Give me understanding of where from the rings of bell
in my heart was   given.
For this lunar month
Is already giving vine to drink, giving vine to drink.
I've never seen you,
The One who is sitting at the throne up high,
But I know that at this holiday
A young messenger will come and speak of the dream.
He will say:

"Your sword is in the field,
Your enemy is standing
And he is as high as a thousand of deaths.
Take your bag and rush to the road
And take everything you need for kids.
All the pearls, gold wrap up in wool,
And you go to cut somebody's hands-legs,
Knock down the bridges, get ready for death."
Here I am forging a cruel king,
Whose step is like thunder,
Whose look a sea reduces to ashes,
A cold wind from the mountains hides in his nostrils,
Sorrow and distress are in his feet.
I will give him success
I will bring each prophet in by lips,
Will bless his path not easy.
He will take his heart out from calculation.
For the sake of those plants of mortuary,
Where the people will bend their knees,
I will wipe sweat off his face,
But I will not let him fall asleep."

"I don't want to kill," whizzed the Stranger. "And my Prince didn't kill. I don't want to become the sword. I will not cut down legs and arms. This is not about me. I know that for sure."

"Calm down," said the Hermit in a weak voice. "Nobody is making you kill. You are a human but don't prevent the power from coming out."

"Who is this cruel king?"

"I don't know. He is standing at the threshold already... I have met the ancient evil but I haven't met the Prince. He came in modest clothes...You will be able to... He is very...."

The old man shook front, his face became light-yellow, he gasped for air and fell on his side.

"What's wrong with you?" the Stranger grabbed his shoulders. "Hermit, what's wrong with you?"

The agony lasted just a few seconds. Accidentally he broke the fragile ribs of the old man while doing artificial heart massage, but all his attempts were in vain. A painful grimace on the Hermit's face smoothed out, and there appeared a light, childish smile behind the old man's beard.

The Stranger was standing on his knees, looking at the sky and praying. A woman came up to him and sadly asked:

"The Hermit?"

He nodded, raised to his feet; he grasped for air, seemed like the world has come down on him and squeezed him with the ruins.

"Burry him, please," he asked and went away. The woman caught up with him. She gave him a strong hug.

"You are our brother. Don't leave."

"Why is it all like that? Do you know the answers?"

"I am here not to find the answers but to meet the Prince. He will come here, remember the prophecy: And he will be standing on the ruins and he will come to the grave of the Righteous, of whom the world is not worthy.

"The Righteous, is it the Hermit? Will you burry him in the ruins?"

The woman smiled.

"See, it's all easy."

The Stranger shook his head.

"Now you have everything coming together. You are happy that the prophecies come true, and I have a friend who had died, the earth has lost a righteous. You say that it has to be this way. You are mistaking. The prophecy is only foretelling the future, it depends on our deeds. However, there are secrets that will not be opened even to the best of the best…"

"We don't do brain-twisters. We simply believe," said the woman in disappointed voice.

"I won't destroy your faith," he said. "If you are right, I will be happy for you."

Chapter 50. The Enemy

People were talking about the miracles of the Stranger, only a small part of which happened in reality. The Stranger smiled: if he criticizes, the crowd will stone him. He looked at a body in blood. The face was disfigured and in blood bruises, an opened mouth showed debris of teeth, but his clothes looked familiar. He came closer, recognized. He stood near the dead man for a while and remembered his bright, sad eyes.

THE ENEMY

"Who did that?" shouted Stranger.

"This man is from the community 'Power of Light', and they blemish the great prophet," he got the answer.

"It's the Mediator, he is the only one who knew about the Stranger's arrival and he accepted him like a friend. And you killed him! Why did you take his life away? Whom did you make a service to? The Prince? He doesn't know about you. The Lord? God doesn't need such workers. You are a shame for Him," the Stranger didn't belong to himself any more, words came off his lips and stroke right into the hearts of the people. They fell on the ground with screams for forgiveness, offering prayers. "I could eradicate you, weed the land out from people like you, but I am not going to become like you. Breathe, the air is poisoned anyway. You shout that you are the servants of God praying daily. Once a week you gather together, sing sweet songs and you think that you labor for Him, you are expecting a reward. Your reward is reserved for you: they are moth and worms."

The Stranger took a lot of effort to get back to himself. He looked at the land staring at something. Not everyone was on his knees, not everyone repented. One young man recovered from the shock, caused by the Stranger's words, he took a stone and threw it into the Stranger. The pebble got into the window, a few pieces of glass fell on the Stranger's head. Blood splashed on his shirt. The folks were frozen. Everyone was looking at him, but he only smiled.

"The Prophesy! The Prophesy!" shouted someone from the crowd. "Remember his clothes stained in blood, caused by an unrighteous, and he is laughing. His face is in blood and he is smiling!"

The people ran up to him:

"Who are you? What is your name?"

"I was just passing by," he said in a quiet voice.

"What shall we do? What shall we do?" people turned to him from every side.

"Don't kill anymore and don't let anyone kill," responded the Stranger. "Go to your homes, pray and wait. May be God will have mercy on you."

"Do you know the Stranger? How can we find him?"

"I know another Stranger."

"Is there another Stranger?"

"You have twisted his image, you ascribed him the words that he didn't say and the actions he didn't do."

"Can you find him?"

"What for?"

"People are dying in the City and we don't know why. We believe that he can help."

Crying women and scared children were looking at him with hope. The Stranger didn't know how to help, the antidote should be in each one of them, but how can you find it? What if to take away the reason of the deadly disease? He thought about the Prince again...

A few men came up to him, one of them carried water.

"Not all of the people among us are insane or killers. People are scared, most of them have weak knees and they have hanged their hands. The Courier came up the steps and started to preach that our faith will not save us during the disaster. He accused us of spiritual blindness, deceitful lips and hypocrisy. He said that the Stranger called him a brother. People couldn't stand this and some young people attacked him. We were not able to stop the slaughter. The Courier didn't deserve to die. Lots of people get killed nowadays. People are insane, we are not even trying to bring them back to reason, but the authorities aren't respected, the power and weapon are in honor. Believe us, we pray daily, we do the ancient rituals and sacraments, we honor the holy books with all our hearts, we preach and gather sacrifices, we help priests and everyone who is in need. Aren't we working for God? Aren't we the workers in His field?"

The Stranger thanked for the water and said:

"A master of the estate sent a servant to dig around his garden; he went further on into the pure field and started sowing poppy seeds. That servant came to his master at the end of the day and said, 'Be happy for I've sowed poppy seed in the field behind the garden.'

The Master was in rage, he shouted: 'You are insane! My son sowed best wheat in that place. Go away, you have no place in my house, you have ruined the labor of my son'."

The Stranger raised his voice and continued:

"I saw how you honor the holy books with kisses. Tell me, does the wisdom come into those who kiss stones, copper and wood?"

Someone from the crowd shouted: "Idolatry!"

"OK," agreed the Stranger. "How about those who kiss paper, skin and velvet? What are the holly books in reality? They are the God's plan. Is this what you believe? Which of you will say that he has touched the thought of the Lord with his lips? Who holds His will in his hands? If an apprentice kisses drawing of a carpenter in respect, whom will he please by such service? But if accomplishing the work exactly following the drawing, he will be praised. You are perfecting yourself in silliness and expect favor from wisdom?

'The need had come for a fool so that he came to get an advice of a wise man, how to put obedience into his son. The wise man responded: 'Obedience is put in by the whip through the back when the whip doesn't get off it.' Since the wise man had great respect, the fool did exactly what had been told. And his son walked with a whip tied to his back, not knowing what it was for.

Coming to the wise man again, the fool said: 'The whip doesn't help my son.' Then the wise man advised: Stubbornness is straightened by the knowledge of wise books. Tie him to the books so that his forehead and his hand wouldn't get up or down without them.' And the fool has tied a pile of books through the forehead to his son's hand. The young man wasn't able to keep his balance and fell down under the books' burden. Of course, you are priests," continued the Stranger. "You can't be compared with sinners, the servants of their own passions, but you've taken the responsibilities that nobody gave you. You blemish the plan of the Lord by your action. You give empty hope to people's souls, promising them a ticket to the country of the Eternity. You have set up organizations, parties, and orders; you have built square buildings. God doesn't live in the buildings of certain shape, but in the hearts. Your system is a delusion, a trap for the best and the worthy ones. You help some people but you destroy the others."

The Stranger was ready to leave when he noticed a lonely figure. Someone was standing aside of the square, away from the crowd and nobody came close to him. The Stranger was seized by a strong feeling of worry. He felt power and horror coming from this person.

"The Enemy," he whispered with pale lips. "I will not be afraid. I have the Power on my shoulders, the Wind in my palms, while my fists are ready for a fight." The Stranger was filled with the Wind. He felt hoops on his head, squeezing his temples. His shoulders were filled with strength and his palms were pouring out power. The Stranger decided that it was time to look into the eyes of the Enemy, and he slowly approached him.

"I know you. You are the Enemy," he said loudly and distinctly.

"I am the Prince," said the man with eyes of a snake.

"You are the ruler of this world. But you have no power over me because I am not of this world."

"I have the power. I am the only one to chase the Exterminators out. Go away or you'll die. Your time is up without even starting."

The Stranger was ready to fight till death, but he asked and heard a loud familiar Voice: "Retreat." The tension, caused by the foreboding of the fight started reducing.

"I am leaving," said the Stranger as indifferently as he could.

The Enemy didn't respond but his eyes of a snake looked happily and mockingly at him.

Before leaving, the Stranger cast a look on the square.

"Why did I retreat? Why haven't I tried? Blindly trusted the Voice and didn't fulfill my mission? Still, it was the same Voice that saved me in the tunnel, though the Seer helped me as well. Has the word 'Prince' deluded those who are chosen? For he calls himself Prince, but only of this world. The Enemy will chase the Exterminators away and receive the power? He will free the people from horror. And everyone will give him honor. But the Hermit couldn't have been mistaken. It means there is still a hope. I need to search."

Chapter 51. The Friend

The Seer drank some tea, the pain and weakness slowly abated. His impatient mind requested explanation of the reasons for this horror that stroke the City.

"Alien creatures. Either they came from a different world or they are a result of our fears and prejudices. It doesn't matter which one they are. They destroy the City by their presence. Is there an escape from them? The Stranger? Is his power able to drive the Exterminators out? Probably... What's next? The Stranger will not accept the power given by the released crowd. He will not judge and punish, but this system doesn't allow any merciful rulers. Only fear is able to hold the crowd from their thirst for blood. What did the Hermit come for? To fight? No. To preach? It's too late. To meet with the Stranger? He met with him, so what?" the Seer reached out for a cigarette, but quickly drew his hand back. "The Hermit's eyes glittered; he was searching for someone for he wanted to tell the Stranger something important. He was so much in a hurry that refused to help his friend?"

"What's going on with you?" the Medium asked, looking at the paled Seer. "You need to rest and not to ponder over anything."

He closed his eyes and nodded.

"It's not necessary for me to be here. I will go to look for the Stranger," announced the Soldier.

"You promised to stay with us," the Medium reminded.

"You are not under any threat. They will not come here again." Having felt the look of the Soldier, the Seer opened his eyes and said slowly, as if dividing by syllables:

"There is death in the streets. You shouldn't go."

"I've been walking under death for many years. These are side effects of the profession. If I feel something, I will leave."

"If you feel something you will not have enough time to leave."

The Soldier stood up, straightened his shoulders, took his rifle and winked at the woman.

"It doesn't matter, since none of you can shoot. Close the door behind me."

He went to the square, hoping to find the Stranger there. He came closer to a small group of people who were violently discussing texts from holy books.

"Listen, what is written here about this time: 'There is fear on the faces of the land dwellers, for who will not be afraid this day? The day of sorrow and suffering has come. The people will receive according to their deeds. And there will be robbers and nobody will be able to oppose them.' And here, in a different place it says: 'He will come and the Lord's glory will become his shield, and the sword of faith will be in his hand to strike those who are strong.' Look, brothers: the Exterminators are the strong; it means that there will come someone who strikes them."

"Could be," said another one. "Let's suppose that the Exterminators will come to the City, but who is he who will drive them away?"

"Have you heard about the Stranger?" somebody asked. The Soldier started when he heard a familiar name.

"Of course. Many of us have seen him ascend over the ground and fly away."

"Excuse me," broke the Soldier into the conversation. "Has the Stranger flown up? Are you sure about it?"

"Yes. Many people said so..."

"Where is he now?"

"We don't know. We don't even know his face really."

"I know him. I have his photo," and the Soldier had been handed a picture, confiscated from safety agents.

"This one doesn't look like him. He has a beard up to his chest."

Tensed silence hung in the air.

"The Stranger has cut his beard..." the Soldier felt danger.

"Why?" he was interrupted. "To disguise himself?"

"Exactly..." responded the Soldier and stopped short.

"Will the Stranger disguise himself? Hide himself? Be afraid? Who are you to insult the great prophet?"

The Soldier didn't expect that these obedient and disposed people could turn into angry beasts in just a few seconds.

"The Stranger is my friend, we came into the City together," said the Soldier as calm as possible, but only curses and swearing came down on him. He jumped aside, jerked the bolt.

"Stand still! Another step and I will shoot!" shouted the Soldier, but it was too late. He became weak in his knees, his palms covered with sticky sweat. He pulled himself together with great effort.

The crowd froze. The Soldier has already looked out for a place to retreat, but suddenly a short frail man showed up from nowhere.

He stretched his hand up front, looking right into the eyes of the Soldier and started speaking:

"You are a son of death, slander and liar. I know the Stranger, and you don't. I honor the Prince and you don't. You threaten with your weapon, but the real weapon isn't made by man. You want to kill us, but you will die instead. I don't kill, your sins kill you."

The Soldier unclasped his hands; the rifle fell on the pavement with a loud crash. Cold inhuman eyes were looking at him, the eyes that take life. He heard ringing, as if anvil started working in his mind. His heart beat fast but uneven. The Soldier felt with the rest of his conscience that he needs to wake up, come to himself, and throw off the nets. His heart began to wave like an autumn leaf in the strong, gusty wind. And he stopped hearing it. Everything around him span and mixed. Seized with deadly horror, he screamed, but nobody heard his scream, only the Stranger felt his heart squeezed by a bad foreboding. The Soldier fell down, hit his head over the stones and a small stain of blood flew out onto the pavement. The crowd with terror and excitement looked at the man who struck the slander with the power of his lips.

"I didn't kill him, but his sins," the man repeated in velvet voice and everybody around him started smiling. "He is a big sinner. Brothers, I am no one, but God works through me, I can direct sins of the person against him. And I have the news for the citizens of the City. The unseen Exterminators, spirits from the nethermost are bonded with the sons of men that opened them the door into our world. We have to find the betrayers. I ask you don't kill them, for God is merciful. It's easy to recognize them: they are aliens, they don't have the stamp. Of course, not all of the citizens have a connection with the Exterminators, but we will be able to distinguish them. Well, devout citizens, find them all and bring them to me. Meeting is at the King's square."

Right then small units were arranged and sent out to search for aliens. The savior had been named as the Friend of the people.

The local television kept repeating shots of the victory of the frail man's spiritual power over a big guy with a rifle. The Medium wept stormily. The Seer almost pierced the screen with his eyes. The appeal of the Friend to the citizens on TV has astounded him.

"Who is he?" the Medium asked. "What a terrifying look he has. What is he doing?"

"He is looking for someone," the Seer walked around the room nervously. "He is also searching, but I am too weak and I can't penetrate this secret."

"Just a bit longer, and you will become like before," the woman supported him.

"Who are you, the Friend of the people? They look at him in such an ecstasy! Like an obedient dog looking at its master," spoke the Seer through clenched teeth.

"Do you think he is looking for the Stranger?"

"I didn't say that... The Stranger rushed into the City. The power pulled him, it wanted to fight. This is the only weapon to fight against the Exterminators. Looks like they created obstacles on the path of the Stranger. Unfortunately, even through me. Probably, the Friend had been leading him from the very beginning, so that the Stranger would drive the exterminators away and would free place for him. Have you heard about the Friend before?"

"I have never heard about him, although he is much stronger than we are."

"One can kill with hypnoses, especially after your opponent falls down on the stones," the Seer was irritated. "Nothing unusual. Unless he used energy, power. It didn't look like hypnoses from a detached view. It looked like God's punishment in the eyes of the believers. Oh, the Soldier didn't listen to me," sighed the Seer heavily.

"What will the Stranger do now?" asked the Bird.

"This is a good question," responded the Seer. "I think that he won't pass it by like that. They are all searching for somebody. But who is he?"

Chapter 52. The Moon

He was sitting at the grave of the Hermit, upbraiding himself for the weakness. "Why have I retreated? Got scared of death? I don't think so. I wasn't ready to kill a man, but is the Enemy a human? I doubted my power, and the weak can't win, that's why the Voice told me to retreat. Did he save me?"

The Stranger came up to a lonely woman standing aside, the one who had called him brother before.

"What's your name?"

THE MOON

"Moon," responded the woman and smiled, showing a row of white teeth.

"Does everyone who comes here hear the Voice?"

"There are other sheep that we need to bring…"

"How will you recognize the Prince?"

"What kinds of slaves don't know their master in face?"

"The prophesies say that he will come in power and glory. Won't he?" the Stranger gave a light smile.

"He will come now for those who are chosen. He will warn and prepare them. The terms don't depend on the time but on the circumstances."

"A dozen of those who are called… that's not too much," the Stranger looked around, pointing with his eyes to the people sitting around the fire.

"There isn't ever too much of our own people. But have they all come? They are on their way. Somebody comes every time. We believe that the Prince will come here as well."

"I hope so, because the Enemy has come into the City. He called himself the Prince," said the Stranger gloomily.

"The Enemy? Here? Are you not mistaking?" blue eyes of the woman narrowed with unbelief.

"I talked with him. Do you remember?

And when the water recedes,
The shore will show up and open the Hero!
The shore will show up and open the Enemy.
And again, there will be two of them left."

"We need to find the Hero, before the Enemy finds us, for he can destroy the chosen once as the prophesy says."
"Don't worry. He is nothing before the Prince:

Here the Enemy is again before me,
A subtle, ancient spectacular.
He has left traces when I came back home.
But he, the one who gave me the path – the Lord
of heaven and the earth.
A star drops its life to a star,
And he calculates his murder.
His shining black cloak
Has plunged the forest into rigor roughly.
But he is nothing before me,
Shameful timorous in the middle of the circle…

The Enemy will come here before the Prince. He is always one step ahead. You have to leave. You can't keep all the eggs in one basket," warned the Stranger.
"The Enemy will be stopped, but we have to hurry. The Divine Voice hasn't called us here to destroy."
"If it only was divine…" the Stranger mumbled.
"Find the Prince. They will not leave the ruins," the Moon has looked at her friends, with faces shining with joy, in fear and even despair.
"You, visionaries! Show us where to search for him?"
"The Prince is a secret. There are hints in the prophecies, but they can be understood by those who are destined. You are one of them, but you have too many doubts."
"The one who doesn't doubt doesn't search," responded the Stranger.
"Let's not argue," said the woman meekly. "Do you remember the ancient image of the Prince?"

"We know what the Prince looked like, but is he still the same now?"

"His image has come to our days so that we would be able to recognize him. God has a reason for everything."

"We don't know in which body he will come. The Prince can come in a different guise, let's say because he doesn't want to be recognized. Are you looking with the eyes of your flash and not the eyes of your heart? I even suppose that the Prince can be a different personality."

"How is a different personality?" amazed the Moon.

"Why not to suppose that God will send another man who will act in one spirit with the Prince?"

"It's hard for me to believe this. The Prince is one and he is the only one who has the power."

"Does he need power?"

"Dreaming up is not forbidden," the woman smiled leniently.

"Why dreaming up? Hasn't the Prince said: "I will leave you but there will come a time and I will send a Comforter, who will witness the truth just like you?"

"The Comforter is not the Spirit? This is not about a man."

"The Spirit acts through chosen ones. He needs a carrier."

The Moon wrinkled, nodded, but a lenient smile disappeared from her face.

"Hasn't he said: The Prince is the only leader."

"The Prince isn't a name, but a destination, a title. Not many people called him this name when he was alive, and now everyone is calling him this name. I have a friend, his name is Soldier, but there are many people with such name…"

The Stranger started and turned pale.

"Has anything happened? Give me the hand that he shook with you," asked the Moon and covered his palm with hers.

"He has been killed. The body of your friend is in the square," she said quietly.

"Who did that?" asked the Stranger indistinctly.

"The Enemy."

The Stranger stood up, straightened himself.

"I have to go."

"Stay. It's late. Night is coming. This is not our time."

"My time is always."

"Be careful. May God help you!"

She gave him a strong hug, setting her little nose against his chest. The Stranger gazed into her eyes, they seemed so dear at that moment that his heart was squeezed with tenderness and he hurried to the square to take the body of the Soldier whom he had brought into this town to die.

Chapter 53. The Prince

The Stranger has remembered the prophetical text of the manuscript that supposedly had been written a few years before the life of the Prince. "A man of perfect age. Two braids on his head, on the right and on the left side. His beard is thick, touched by white frost, the look from his deep eye-pits pierces deep into hearts, his bronze forehead is low but wide. The shoulders of a smith, but his back is round from our sins, his fingers are long and a ring of inheritance covers his finger."

He meditated, "The signs suit the image of the Prince. Looks like the author saw him and that's why he gave such a detailed description. But it's not wise to rely on these signs now. It's not too hard to grow long hair and beard. Besides, there are lots of people with long fingers and wide foreheads. I need to reject all the stereotypes, even the most authoritative once. God's plan doesn't fit any theories, conceptions or interpretations of men. Dogmas limit thoughts, preventing their development... The Hermit met with the ancient evil, the Enemy, the servant of the Adversary, who has made it his goal to harm any truth that leads even the chosen once astray.

The Seer is sure that the ancient have come up with some sort of mythical image in order to shift from the Creator any responsibility for injustice of the world. The world had been perfect but there came the Enemy and he spoiled everything.

Haven't the ancient said: 'Choose good, and you will live. Choose evil, and you will die.' Will liver be able to bear too much alcohol? Don't drugs ruin brain? We incur trouble ourselves by our irresponsible acts, but it's not that simple. Since there is someone who gave us the laws of life, then there should be someone who doesn't want us to follow them.

No matter where you are,
No matter what you do,

There is a war between the Earth and the Heaven!

THE PRINCE

No, Seer, the coverlet is not a greenhouse for weak plants, the Enemy needs it to help him govern people and not to let them get to the new level.

The creatures, which I met in the desert, aren't people. They are visible and tangible; they left footprints on the sand, three meters high, just exactly to fit in the tunnel. Probably, they are those whom the ancient called gods, demons, while the prophets called them the

Alien people. 'There are gods on earth and in heaven, but we have one God, the Lord.' I don't know if we need to take gods into consideration, but ignoring them isn't wise. Is our coexistence independently from each other possible? Only when there are no mutual interests involved. Looks like they got interested in us and our resources. It means that, sooner or later, we will face them. If we don't get the Protection, they will simply erase us from the surface of the earth.

The Exterminators of the City are invisible to an ordinary man but the once who can feel their presence will die. They didn't touch me. They are incomparably stronger than I am, they have authority. Didn't they expect to see this power in a human? Has the presence of the Wind stopped them? The Alien despised, the Enemy was afraid, while they, who are stronger than all of them together, were surprised, searched and stepped away with respect. Why? They thought I was of their blood," it dawned upon the Stranger. "They came to repair a malfunction in the mechanism, and I got in their way, becoming a pawn in the subtle game of the Enemy," moaned the Stranger.

Near the Kings' square armed people, dressed in camouflage were checking the documents. The Stranger tried to pass unnoticed, but he was called.

"Your identification!"

"I forgot my documents at home."

"It's good that you didn't run, otherwise we would have shot you," grinned the patrol. "We will go to your home; it's not far, is it?"

"Who are you looking for?"

"We are looking for strangers, who have no registration in the City."

"What for?" the Stranger was surprised.

"Directions of the Friend of the people."

"Who is he, the Friend of the people?"

"Don't you know what happened in the square? Someone attacked the brothers, but there came God's chosen man and killed the villain with the power of his lips."

"Have you checked his documents? It seems to me that he is also a stranger!" the Stranger didn't try to hide sarcasm.

"How dare you!" the patrol gripped his weapon.

"Fools! You are being deceived. What has he done? Killed?" shouted the Stranger and the Wind broke outside. "If he was God's messenger, he wouldn't have killed, but brought people to repentance. 'Evil comes from an evil.' All you can do is to kill. How difficult it is for the Heaven to look at your crimes! I tell you: the Friend is an Enemy."

The patrol stood frozen. The Stranger realized that he has less and less love left, just a little bit longer and he will pass the thin border and he will pass the sentence. He became silent, controlled himself and went away speeding up. He was sure that they wouldn't shoot at his back.

"Am I able to stop the Enemy without destroying him? Can I punish the evil? Who can do that? How can I destroy the evil without destroying the body where the good lives as well? If I can't do that, why do I start? Has the Prince killed? No… I don't want to behave like his closest disciple who has punished a weak woman only because he wasn't able to control the Power. But if I don't stop the Enemy, how many more will he get out of his way? The Enemy has killed the Hermit, my best real friend. He killed the Soldier, a man who trusted and helped me. He will destroy the chosen once and the sweet, kind Moon. I can't let this happen."

His memory suggested the lines:

Please understand, I am not crying,
I have to get back to the fight.
Oh, Heaven, my tender land from far away,
I am dying, a young voice.
I am weeping, knelt down.
My blooded brother
is laying down at my feet like a raven,
While he, the subtle enemy is happy.
Look, the whole crowd rejoices,
The whole world rejoices – we aren't here.
The tables are laid – the wives are weeping,
The grand dinner is brought in.
But there is darkness in the sky, rake with your hand,
Throw into the fire, burn it down,
And cast these ashes to the sky,
And everything around will moan and whine.
And somebody's neck, some ten

And the wood squeaks with their weight.

The Stranger searched for the body of his friend in the square, but without success. He's been recognized. Some people touched his clothes with respect and kissed their fingers.

"Where is your savior?" asked the Stranger.

"The Friend of the people will come soon. Look, how many strangers we've caught."

"Although I was born here, I spend almost all of my life in a different place. I am also a stranger," said the Stranger.

He stepped over the barrier, and stood next to the confused people, looked at each one of them. May be somebody from the chosen people had been caught here, they could come into the trap called by the Voice but it doesn't look so, they are all scared. Though his attention was drawn to a young guy, who was sitting on the pavement, he was wearing a gray sweater, jeans, and comfortable high shoes. The Stranger felt confusion. His heart started beating fast. He looked at the young man. Short haircut, open wide forehead, brown hair, hairless round face, eyes, deeply set? The Stranger didn't notice his eye color, it was too dark, besides, the young man didn't look at anyone. He motionlessly stared at the pebbles of the pavement. The Stranger turned giddy with a sudden suggestion. "No. This can't be true!" He was shivering when he came up to the young man. It was hard to make each step. The Stranger took a seat next to him and asked with excitement,

"Who are you?"

The young man looked at him. The eyes of the young man were of deep light-gray color, but the Stranger hasn't seen such look in anyone who lives on earth. His eyes were shedding kindness and power at the same time, mercy and authority, an impossible combination. He understood who was in front of him. The young man took his hand and gave it a strong squeeze. The Stranger was absolutely happy. The path, he was walking, filled with hope, searches, falls, pain, disappointment and faith has brought him to this meeting.

"Did you come to show yourself to the world?"

The young man didn't respond, only smiled with his eyes. The Stranger understood with his heart: "This world doesn't need me."

"Why are you here?"

"For your sake, for their sake and for my sake."

"The Enemy is searching for you. He uses ordinary people to render lawlessness."

"There are no ordinary people. Everyone can become great, but you are all in captivity. The war has been going on from ancient times. His time hasn't come yet, my time hasn't come yet, but your time is always. There still is kindness and love in this world, there are you and people like you. You are not lonely. You are seen, you are known. Don't be afraid. There is a long way ahead of you and a great Meeting. I know you have got lots of questions, but the answers are all here. I will come to the ruins in my time. I need to leave right now. Give me some service."

The Stranger was surprised. The Prince has the power to command: he says a word and everyone will fall with their faces down. Why doesn't he use his authority?

He came up to the guards and said,

"We are leaving. When the Friend comes, tell him that the Stranger said Hi."

The guard tarried, but the Stranger looked into this eyes.

"Didn't you understand who is in front of you?"

The guard has nodded with obedience. They walked almost through the whole square, but an authoritative call has made the Stranger grow cold. He looked at the young man and saw him smiling encouragingly.

"Let the man go!" ordered the Stranger.

The Enemy was coming close fast, he looked fixedly at the young man, who calmly, slowly kept walking away from the square, carelessly keeping his hands in his pockets.

"Arrest him! It's he who has brought the trouble!" ordered the Friend, pointing to the young man.

"It's a lie!" shouted the Stranger. "This is the Enemy in front of you. Go away! You are the biggest trouble. Go away! Our souls are not yours! You have killed the Hermit! You have exceeded your authority! It's not in your power to kill him. The righteous blood chases you away!"

"No. His blood is not enough, but there are a lot of sins. I haven't killed him, he died himself. We don't kill the righteous, we have them for this," the Enemy pointed to the frozen crowd. "I have spared you, but now I don't need you anymore. Are you ready to die? This world is mine, just one flick between the fingers, and you will be torn. I know each one of you. I have let you come up to the ancient ruins, but as soon as there will be an even number, I will destroy everyone."

"I doubt it," grinned the Stranger. "This is not your world. You haven't created it. You haven't created life. Sooner or later, the coverlet will be torn down and everybody will see the truth. The people will learn about their destination."

"Your truth ruins the earth."

"You are lying! We are the protection of this earth. Go away!"

The Stranger looked around, searched for the young man with his eyes, but hasn't found him. The Enemy nervously looking into the crowd, mumbled:

"I will find him. I will find him anyway."

"Who are you raising your hand at? Who is the Prince and who are you?"

"He is merely an ordinary human with blood and flash. He hasn't dressed himself in the clothes of gods yet."

"Is this why you search to kill him?"

"I want to reach an agreement."

"He will not sit down with you at the bargaining table. What can the light and the darkness have in common?"

"People. We are here for your sake."

"Stop it. I don't want to kill but I will do it without any hesitation if I have to protect him."

"Is this a challenge?"

"You are talking too much," wheezed the Stranger and openly looked into the Enemy's unblinking eyes.

He felt right away how invisible grips squeeze him; it was difficult for him to breathe. His heart trembled, it seemed like it is going to jump out of his chest. It stopped for a second, but started again. He felt the beats with his whole body. Forcing his way through the veil of horror, the Stranger remembered the words of the Prince, remembered his calm, tender but powerful look. The Wind covered the Stranger with a strong wave. His head was spinning, his knees became weak, but he came closer to the Enemy, grabbed his hands. "The Wind is on me! God's power is with me," he was repeating and felt how the chains that were holding him lost their strength. "I held the Prince by his hand. He gave me hope. This is the end for you, Enemy". The Wind has completely seized his conscience. He started saying something without understanding the words. The time has thickened, and the Stranger has brought all of his strength down on the Enemy.

"I will be back," said the Enemy in cut speech. "I will be back, and I will not be alone. Wait…"

Deathly pallor came out on his face. The Enemy stepped back, staggered and collapsed onto the stone slabs.

The Stranger sat onto the pavement, embraced his head with his hands: it was bursting with pain, but he was happy anyway…

The Seer looked at the women.

"He has died. Take courage," he said and cried bitterly. The Medium embraced her throat, sobbed violently. The Bird shook her head:

"I don't believe it. He promised."

Epilogue
(three days later)

The Stranger opened his eyes and found himself in a room with a white ceiling. He tried to get up and a young girl ran up to him.

"Sweet face, but she has suffered a lot."

"Well, how are you? Totally awake?" she asked.

"Who are you?" he could hardly untangle his dried lips.

"What's going on with you? I am your friend," the girl looked in astonishment into his eyes.

"Why am I here?"

"Don't you remember anything?" it seemed to her that now he will smile and they together will laugh at this silly joke.

He tried to remember, but a sudden attack of headache made him refuse this idea.

A short man showed up in the room, he was laming in one leg a little bit.

"Why haven't you died?" one couldn't say by his tone whether he was happy or disappointed.

"Will he get better?" asked the girl.

"He has a short memory loss. Amnesia. May be that's right. What will he do with such memories? Do you want to stay with him? You will have to make the acquaintance again."

"That's OK. I love him."

"I will help you. You will never experience a need. The girl happily fell on the neck of her benefactor."

"There is a beautiful girl in the hall, she is crying. Is she my friend too?" inquired the patient.

A tall woman has peeped into the room; she smiled through tears and waved with her hand at him.

"Hi, Stranger. I am so happy that you are alive."

"What has happened to me?"

"It's all over," she assured him. "Isn't it, Seer?"

"I don't know, I don't know. It seems to me that everything has only started. What do you think, Stranger?" the Seer looked fixedly at him, with screwed up eyes.

The patient has raised himself half from his bed and felt something like a mild wind touching his head. He smiled:

"Yes. Everything has only started."

Contents